The cancer of time is eating us away.

HENRY MILLER, *Tropic of Cancer*

1

When inclement weather rolls inland from the Atlantic, Dartmoor's seductive, pastel panorama can be drained of its charm within minutes. And punish anyone ill-prepared for its fury.

But now clouds were scudding from the west - nothing dramatic - nothing threatening. On the contrary, the strengthening wind on her back was comforting Gina as she cycled away from Princetown with her three friends. The start of the ride had been hard to get up to the highest point on this side of the moor, but now, payback. Mostly downhill at pace, heading due east on a smooth two lane blacktop. Perfect for this, the third leg of Gina's charity rides.

Craig was the first to notice the impending threat when he sat up and swung round on his saddle to check where the others were behind him. His casual expression changed the moment he noticed a wall of ominously dark, rain-laden cloud arriving from the west.

"Shit. That's not good." He gestured to the others who turned to see the gunmetal grey backdrop to the road just travelled.

"Jeez! Where the hell did that come from?" Gina asked no-one in particular. They pulled over to let Craig and Safia take lightweight waterproofs from their backpacks and wriggle into them.

"They did forecast showers," Safia declared. Dizzy stared at her for a moment then checked the threatening storm clouds and smirked.

Three lycra-sprayed riders passed the group at speed, evidently attempting to outrun the storm. At that moment the first flash of sheet lightning drew Gina's attention to see more striplight starter flashes in the inky cloud mass. Then came a low resonant rumble of thunder.

"Come on guys, let's go," Gina urged with a last glance at the cloud bank that was already engulfing Princetown and hiding the giant radio mast that had provided a marker on their approach. Their next planned stop was due to be at the village of Widecombe. Gina reasoned to herself that if the weather beat them, they could get their driver in the support van to meet them there, but now they needed to sprint. The atmosphere was changing as quickly as distant rumbles were getting louder. Were they all counting the seconds between the lightning and the claps of thunder? Gina assumed so. If she calculated that it was catching them, the others must do too but she was ahead now and only briefly glanced back to check that they were still together.

This was all I needed to wash out what was left of a mega fiasco. I guess we'd only got about three miles down the road when the mother of all storms caught up with us. It was like, all around us so fast - unbelievable. It literally engulfed us. Bloody scary. We could smell it like damp dust in the moments before the downpour hit us.

WACK-WACK-WACK. First the advance party of large droplets then a turbo-powered deluge. WHOOSH. The sudden ferocity slowed the group to a standstill on a long exposed incline.

"Ahhh – I've gotta stop!" Safia shouted over the noise of the rain hitting the tarmac and driving them sideways towards the verge.

The others dropped their bikes onto the grass and scrambled to a gateway in a granite stone wall, but Gina dragged her bike to hold it for some protection as she crouched with the others. She managed to pull a waterproof jacket from her backpack then attempted to tie the sleeves over the bicycle frame to create some protection, but the wind ripped the flimsy nylon from her grasp and propelled it away down the road.

"Well this's screwed everything," she shouted over the wind. "As if it wasn't bad enough. Shit it!"

Safia summoned a more optimistic response.

"It can stop as fast as it starts here."

"What, this shower you mean?" Dizzy grimaced.

6

They stared into the monochrome distance that vanished in cloud a few hundred metres away.

"Where are we?" Safia shouted as she noticed Craig pulling his phone from a pocket.

"Here." He pointed to the screen, enlarging the map. "It must be mostly downhill into that Dartmeet place there in a valley. It may have some better shelter….. What d'you think?"

"Give it a bit of time," Gina shouted above the noise of the trees being ripped by the gale above them. "There's a chance it will calm down and we can get to Widecombe at least."

Craig's phone rang as she spoke. The name 'MATT' appeared on the screen. Craig could barely hear:

"Hi Matt …… Yeah, right in it ….. Not much – a wall but it's better than nothing ………. Okay …..... Between Princetown and somewhere called Dart – something ….. Yeah, that's right …. Matt? Matt?" The reception had cut the call dead as….

CRASH !

The thunder followed the lightning by a spit second. And again.

CRASH ! – CABOOM !!

The lightning hit the wall just feet from where the group crouched. In the same instant, Gina's bike flew into the air, accompanying the explosion of granite shrapnel. Shards of rock propelled in every direction, carrying Gina's bicycle frame that bounced along the grass verge, twisting and gyrating until its momentum expired.

Instinctively, three of the group had dived away and now lay tingling with the after effects of the lightning in the sodden ground. But Gina was motionless beside the wall, still crouching in a foetal ball.

Safia stared for the duration of an intake of breath, then screamed – a piercing scream, dulled only by the howling wind. It continued until her air was exhausted. Dizzy and Craig scrambled back to Gina. They panicked. What to do? What had hit her? A rock? The lightning? Her clothes were smoking... or was it steam?

"Kiss of life. You have to for electric shocks," Craig bellowed against the storm.

"Did the lightnin' hit her?" Dizzy shouted back.

"I don't know. It hit the bike. She was holding it. Out the way."

Craig checked her quickly as he adjusted her limp body. "Call Matt. Make sure he's coming. Get him here fast."

Craig was trying not to fumble but the wet, the emotion and the wind made it difficult to control himself and his breathing. Dizzy was transfixed. Craig realised and bellowed:

"Dizzy – Now!"

But Dizzy was distracted by car headlights approaching through the downpour. He ran into the road, arms waving, before realising that the Land Rover was already lolloping onto the verge towards them. Dizzy rushed to the driver's window as the door was opening. A Barbour-clad woman stepped out and past Dizzy, seemingly aware that she was needed by Craig and Gina.

The rain had slowed a little as the lady crouched beside Craig who was pounding Gina's chest. She took Gina's wrist to check her pulse.

"What happened? Did she fall off?"

"No, we think she was hit by lightning."

The lady turned Gina's hands to reveal her palms that were raw pink as if the skin had been singed or removed. The woman said nothing, but her air of calm control was reassuring to the others. Still Gina lay motionless as another deluge of rain drove down the road towards them, carrying more leaves and debris to pound into the group.

Craig blew once more into Gina's lungs then sat up to press her chest. Gina's eyes flickered and opened briefly.

"Let's get her out of here," the woman announced. "She needs to get dry and warm. My house is close."

Craig hovered as he considered their situation. Dizzy noticed.

"You should go with the girls. I'll wait for Matt. I'll call you later."

"Right..." Craig was trying to think logically but could only manage: "... Err, right...."

The group carried Gina to the car through another cascading downpour then pushed her limp frame onto the back seat of the Land Rover. Safia slid in beside her as Craig ran to the front. The doors slammed and the woman bounced the four-track back onto the road. Craig began to relax in wet discomfort.

"Thank you for this. You're very kind."

"I couldn't leave your friend half-conscious out in this."
The woman was forthright, almost abrupt.

"Right." Craig was more cautious now, but asked: "You
seem to know what you're doing - with Gina I mean - are you a
nurse?"

"Was, once. Retired now." And that was that. She made it
sound final. Craig watched the rivers of water fighting the
wipers with only the whine of the Land Rover engine and noises
of the storm to keep them company.

You know what? I still can't believe the marathon's a bad idea. Yes, it started like, a late night brain wave but it looked good the next morning – and still does. Okay, I know there's nothing original about a sponsored bike ride to raise money for charity, but the five hundred miles over ten events idea was brilliant. Basically, that's how it works – or supposed to. Ten, fifty mile rides during the summer – each across a different national park. That's mega isn't it? Each one attracting a fresh supply of local riders that all have to sign up to raise a minimum of £25 for Watersource. That's my charity – my employer, if you like, except I'm the only full-time employee. We help provide packaged water purifying systems for villages in Africa using a new divining and extraction system - right now we're working in Kenya.

Yes I'm passionate - perhaps like, a bit too much at times, but I'm not apologising for that. It's fucking criminal that shit governments aren't doing it themselves but they aren't so we're doing our tiny little bit to help make a difference. Basically, about a billion cases of diarrhoea every year and like, two million deaths from dirty water happen in Africa. And most of them are children – that's fucking shameful. So Watersource is doing its tiny little bit to help fight the problem. That's why I need the money, but we're a small voice with no big PR machine to raise our profile or to drum up interest. I did what I could with my website and social media, but basically, the local media at each location was useless. The first ride on Brecon Beacons only got twenty-eight riders – well, twenty-eight signed up and literally half have paid their £25 sponsor money so far, but on the day there must have been another fifty or more riders that just attached themselves for a Sunday ride around the

Brecon Beacons. Bollocks. I admit I literally didn't see that coming.

For this one on Dartmoor, we had thirty-nine sponsors signed up on our website. Thirty-nine. Shit-it. If we get all their sponsor money that's less than £1,000 and after our costs........I don't want to think about it. So that's why I was riding with a bunch of friends who I dragged in to make up the numbers, bless 'em.

2

Gina slipped into the day from a dream in which she was riding a monocycle through a densely overgrown forest. It was interrupted by a click somewhere in the room and a clock-radio came to life with its red neon numbers showing the time as 07:05.

Female voice: *".....Gordon Flynn reporting there.........Last night's extra-ordinary Lottery result of all seven consecutive numbers has resulted in the largest number of winning tickets in the history of the UK Lottery. The latest estimate is that there are nine winning tickets each sharing the £6.2 million jackpot. But as Professor Si Peters of UK Statistics Authority points out, the odds were no different to any other draw.*

'The odds of any combination of six numbers is always the same – almost 14 million to 1 – even longer when you think that last night all seven numbers from 1 to 7 came up – that's unbelievable. Basically, the chances of this combination happening ever again is billions to one, so it's probably time for all last night's winners to change their numbers.'...."

Tap-tap.
Gina's attention turned to the door. She spoke cautiously.
"Hello. Come in."

The door opened slowly. An elderly lady entered with a tea cup and saucer in her hand.

"Good morning. How are you?"

"Okay," Gina replied slowly. "Sorry, who are you? Where am I?"

The woman considered the question as she placed the tea on a side table then switched off the radio.

"My name is Hilary Flik. This is my home. I brought you off the moor yesterday. You were in an accident. You may have been struck by lightning."

Gina looked so puzzled by the suggestion that Ms Flik added:

"You were on a charity bicycle ride - do you remember that?"

Gina had been vaguely aware of the bandages on her hands. She brought them up to her face to make out what appeared to be white gloves in the dim light of the room.

"The lightning hit my hands?" She was incredulous at the thought.

"Your friends think your bicycle was hit. You were probably holding it in the storm. You don't remember any of that?"

It was coming back to Gina when Safia arrived in the doorway.

"Hi hun – how are you?

"Saff – hi babe. I'm okay," Gina responded without any certainty.

"How are your hands now?" Ms Flik asked as Gina was mentally checking herself over.

"I think they're probably okay. Can I take the bandages off?"

"Yes, let me. They should get some air. Let's check them."

Ms Flik unpinned the bandages on Gina's right hand. As it was revealed, they could all see that the palm was raw as if the skin had been peeled away from parts of it. The left hand looked almost the same.

"You'll live."

Safia was shocked by the abruptly dismissive summary, but Ms Flik appeared not to notice the reaction and added:

"My work here is done - you should go home via a hospital when you feel up to it. I suggest you go to the A and E department in Exeter - that's the nearest with cover on a Sunday. It's on your way back."

Craig appeared in the doorway looking only half awake.

"Morning Gee."

"Hi Craig. Who else is here?"

"Just us. Matt and Dizzy are at the B+B – they'll pick us up whenever you're ready, if I can get a mobile signal. You look better than last night. You okay?"

"Yeah, sort of."

Ms Flik turned away from Gina.

"You'll have to forgive the sparse breakfast - I wasn't expecting guests. The shower is in the next room. Water should be hot enough soon," she announced whilst ushering Craig and Safia out of the bedroom ahead of her.

3

The journey back to London was crucial.

Too right it was. The black dog was on my back when we set off from the hospital in Exeter. Everything looked like shit. The banter in the car and blue skies of the drive down were all gone. Now even the weather was shitty grey and wet.

Basically, without being confined in the truck for all that time on the road, it might have taken me too long to work out what to do next. But, listening to the constant tyre noise and the jangling of the half-empty horse box that we used to transport all the kit, had like, a calming effect. And the pain-killers must have helped. Anyway, basically, I started to think about the next outing to the Peak District in two weeks and how I was going to cope if my hands aren't healed. Then I started to think like: Why though? What will we do it for? Pride? Yeah, basically that's it. No other reason cos they're just not profitable. And replacing all the stuff that was scattered across Dartmoor, that will literally cost more than we're gonna make from the next one. Bollocks to it. Time to admit it's time for early doors.

Watching the countryside passing by as the south-west eventually became the south-east was like therapy. Things started to look so obvious. And I have the perfect excuse - being struck by lightning. Who's gonna question that?

Gina broke one of the long silences in the car with her announcement when they were on the M4 motorway somewhere near Swindon. No-one was surprised but everyone in the car knew that the reason was entirely financial and that meant Gina would be beating herself up until she found another method of raising cash for her beloved obsession.

By the time we got home I had the plan worked out – well, almost. And it was a good one. And if I got it right, I might even get some publicity that could get some more donations. I even had the press release wording. The headline would be like: 'Charity prospects dashed in a flash...' or something like that with a play on the flash of lightning. And I'll get Dizzy to photograph me with my bandages and the trashed bike.
Ah yes, Dizzy. He'll be glad to get off his work placement. I'll write him a good reference for his probation officer - he'll be fine with that.

But Gina was wrong. As the week progressed she became aware that Dizzy was reverting to the character who had arrived in her little flat a few weeks earlier. In the interim, he had loosened up and blossomed by comparison with the tetchy introvert who found it difficult to make eye-contact less than two months ago.

It was Friday afternoon. Gina was surprised by her reaction to Dizzy's impending departure as she handed him an envelope with a written reference and a can of lager with a ribbon tied around it in a bow. She nervously made a clumsy speech that she hoped didn't sound like one and found herself saying that he will always be welcome to drop in and keep in touch.

Dizzy stared at her for a moment then looked away.

"Yeah, whatever." Then he turned to leave.

"Hey!" Gina snapped. "Don't you dare *whatever* me!"

Dizzy froze. But Gina wasn't finished.

"That was the Dizzy that arrived here, not the Dizzy I know. Don't you dare shrink back into that old shell when we both know that's not the real you. Fuck it Dizzy, I mean it. I'm hating you

17

leaving because you're a real... I dunno ...a real help. No, that's not right. Basically, you're the best help and best company I could have hoped for. You've been my prop and if I forgot to tell you, well I'm telling you now. So when I get another project sorted, I want you to come back (if you're not like, in a real job) and that's basically because you're the best person I could hope for - no question. Or would be if you lose that chip off your shoulder. . . Right? . . . I mean it. Seriously. Come here."

But Dizzy was transfixed by her rebuke. Gina grabbed him in a hug that he slowly returned. They had never been that close and Gina now smelled the musty aroma from Dizzy's coat that immediately reminded her of the worst of her friends' student accommodation. It evoked an instant impression of his home life. They pulled apart.

"Thanks Gee. I'll be in touch, I promise." Then he thought for a moment before tentatively adding: "You know, you're great too."

Gina broke a smile.

"Yeah, whatever."

4

I was in a restaurant a few years ago. I dunno – six, maybe seven – it's not important when, but it wasn't last week. Anyway, I'd like, just paid the bill after lunch and turned to the door out into a very bright day outside where we'd left our bikes, but there was like, a full length floor-to-ceiling glass panel between me and the entrance. I literally didn't see it so I banged into it with a real smack. Not particularly hard but it made a lot of noise and the staff all rushed to help me. Probably worried I'd sue them because there wasn't anything to mark it out. I didn't hurt myself – more embarrassed than hurt. A few minutes later I was outside laughing about it with my friends as we rode off on our bikes, none the worse. End of.
So why did I just dream about it? I haven't thought about it from then until just now. And the dream was exactly as it happened…. except it was like, in slow motion. Strange. I'm starting to remember my dreams. I never used to remember my dreams, but I do now. Odd.

It was Sunday morning after a late Saturday night in a local pub – a great antidote for black dogs, Gina reasoned. She had piled into bed after midnight with a warm glow but no voice, after raucous karaoke and a few too many ciders. She remembered leaving someone called Griff, who had walked her home from the pub, on her doorstep after his clumsy suggestions about spending the night with her. It brought a smile to her face as she recalled their daft banter before she slipped through her front door, alone.

Gina glanced at her bedside clock showing 08.58 then reached out to click on the radio to an anonymous music station before pulling the duvet aside to slip away to the bathroom. She loved Sunday mornings in her flat. It was her time to indulge herself in its cosy and comforting embrace. It was frugally furnished but every item of furniture was hand-picked with loving care. More seventies retro than twenty-first century chic.

Gina returned to her bed with her iPad and a mug of tea. One of her weekend indulgencies had long been to sit in bed clearing her personal emails and sifting through her on-line private life with a cup of Earl Grey within easy reach. The news was on the radio as she plumped up a second pillow and climbed back under the duvet. Luxury.

".............Last night's extra-ordinary Lottery result of all seven consecutive numbers has resulted in the largest number of winning tickets in the history of the UK Lottery. The latest estimate is that there are nine winning tickets sharing the £6.2 million jackpot. But as Professor Si Peters of the UK Statistics Authority points out, the odds were no different to any other draw.

'The odds of any combination of six numbers is always the same – almost 14 million to 1 – even longer when you think that last night all seven numbers from 1 to 7 came up – that's unbelievable. Basically, the chances of this combination happening ever again is billions to one, so it's probably time for all last night's winners to change their numbers.'...."

Gina smiled when she realised why the news item was familiar.

So I assumed the radio station was playing an old report. Well you would wouldn't you? It made me smile. I love it when things go wrong on live radio and TV – don't we all?

20

*Then I literally didn't think another thing about it......
Until.......*

".........Last night's extra-ordinary Lottery result of all seven consecutive numbers being drawn, has resulted in the largest number of winners of a single main lottery game in the history of the UK Lottery. Nine winning tickets will share the £6.2 million jackpot as Janet Wallace reports."

Gina was making a sandwich for lunch when the report started on the one o'clock news bulletin. Now she stared ahead at the kitchen wall.

"The odds for the UK Lottery draw last night were no different to those of any other – just under 14 million to 1 as Professor Si Peters of the UK Statistics Authority explained to me................"

My mind was totally befuddled. Literally, I couldn't have been more dumbstruck if I'd been one of those winners. I was listening to a report about news that I'd heard a week earlier. I was reliving the morning in Ms Flik's house on Dartmoor. It was the identical report, basically. How can that be? I had definitely heard it last Sunday morning..... didn't I? Or was that like, another dream?

She came to her senses abruptly, placed the butter knife on the countertop and walked robotically through to get her iPad from her sofa bed that was still filling her sitting room. A few taps and she was looking at the BBC News page on the screen. There was no mistake. The numbers were drawn last night, not last week.

Gina sat on her bed without moving for several minutes; reliving everything on Dartmoor, or the bits that she could recall. There were gaps. Were they significant? Who can she ask? What would she ask? Did anyone else hear the original news item? No, she was alone before the others came into her room first thing in the morning. But she had heard it; of that she had no doubt. She was trying to recall everything in second-by-second detail.

Not the easiest process given my state of mind last Sunday morning. Now, the more I thought through all the bits I could remember, literally the more frightening it was. Yes 'frightening', that's right. Odd, I should have been excited and I was for a moment. I knew the lottery numbers like, a week before they were drawn, of course that's exciting – or would have been if I'd realised, but why – how – why me? Shit. That's seriously scary.

My mind kept going to Hilary Flik. No idea why she would know anything except I was in her house when I heard the news. Basically, the more I thought, the more confused I got. Literally there were more questions than answers.

5

Gina didn't sleep well that night but thought it best to get into her normal Monday routine. Up at eight-o'clock; breakfast; pack up her sofa-bed; shower; then into her office (that was supposed to be the bedroom) by nine. She still had money to raise and a living to make; still lots to clear up from the three bike marathons before she had shut down her project; sponsors to chase for payment and the press release to punt. Plus a big hole in her finances to plug with a new source of income as yet unidentified; a problem that she hadn't expected, but was very real since her marathon dream had died on Dartmoor. It had been worrying her over recent weeks as she realised that her bright idea was not going to be the Eldorado that she had hoped, but the result of that failure had become a serious concern.

Oh shit!

Immediately Ms Flik came back into her thoughts, she remembered that she had never sent the flowers as she had planned.

I felt really bad about that - about forgetting something so important. So stupid. But I was very ill when I last saw her so I'm sure she'll understand.

Gina found the note that she had made of the house name as they drove away, but where was it located? She would need a village name or a road number for the delivery of some flowers. She was annoyed at herself for a moment for not making a better effort to get the address.

Matt'll know. I just need a road number.

She texted Matt for help then went back to her tasks. Gina was so absorbed that she didn't hear Donald Trump arriving in her office until he proclaimed loudly:

"We gotta drain the swamp!"

Gina spun around to see the US President's face staring around her door. She screamed as she jumped away, falling from her seat. The president instantly ripped his face off to reveal Dizzy's. He was almost as shocked as Gina.

"I'm really sorry, Gee. I thought you would have heard me come in. I didn't mean to scare you - I'm sorry."

"Fucking hell Dizzy...What the hell...?" Gina fought to hold back her tears. That shocked Dizzy; he had no idea what to do. He couldn't imagine Gina crying about anything, let alone a silly practical joke.

"Hey, come on Gee. I've brought your keys back. I forgot to give 'em to you on Friday. Shit Gee, I'm really sorry; I didn't mean to frighten you. This was hanging on the railings outside." He waved the mask aimlessly. "Shall I make some tea? Earl Grey?" He turned away leaving Gina to compose herself.

They sat on her sofa. Gina sipping tea and Dizzy occasionally glugging water from a plastic bottle. Gina felt the need to explain her over-reaction that she blamed on stress. Dizzy felt the need to apologise for letting himself in too quietly and scaring her.

"Yeah, bloody stupid." Then she smiled. "No, not your fault, Diz. The truth is...." Gina thought for a moment about how much to tell him. "...I didn't sleep much last night. Basically I'm really tired and I don't think I'm better yet. I keep having like, weird dreams that I never have normally. And something else weird has happened...."

I wasn't intending to talk about my premonition of the Lottery results, but it sort of came out.

Dizzy stared, disbelieving, as Gina related her story. A long silence followed before Dizzy spoke slowly, as if to a child.

"Gee, you know that can't happen. You know you've imagined it?"

Gina hadn't expected that reaction. She was shocked. He didn't believe her...but why would he? Why would anyone? It's nonsense, unbelievable nonsense. For the first time since yesterday lunchtime, Gina questioned that she had heard the original news report last Sunday morning in Devon. That's the bit that hadn't occurred to her until now. No-one else heard it; and she was in shock from the accident at the time. She needed to think that through.

As soon as Dizzy left the flat, he pulled his phone from his pocket to make a call.

"Hi Saffy....Yeah....Fine thanks..... I've just come from Gee's apartment....... Hey stop it....... No, don't be daft, nothing like that - I just dropped her spare keys off, but she's not good....... Not really worried - well, a bit. Are you gonna see her soon?........ I think maybe that'd be good because she's...well, like a bit messed up still.... Yeah, she could be in her apartment for days on her own, so that'd be good ..... Yeah ..... Thanks, see ya."

Gina returned to her desk with a cup of fresh tea to find a reply from Matt on her phone. He had left the road number and a brief description of the location of the house. A few minutes of on-line searching led Gina to a flower shop in a local town that offered a delivery service. A lady with a Devonian accent was very helpful with advice about a seasonal bouquet and understood the vagueness of the delivery address.

"I know where the house must be so you just give me the house name and I'm sure it'll be fine, dear."

Gina read the house name from her hand-written note:

"Coombridge." Then she spelled it out.

"Coombridge - okay...With two 'o's, just like the horse?"

"Sorry? Did you just say house, or horse?"

25

"Horse. You don't follow the horses?"

"No."

What is she talking about?

"They will be there sometime this afternoon. Is that all right with you?"

"Of course, thank you very much."

She paid with a credit card after wincing at the cost then hung up with a sense of relief that it was arranged and she could tick that off her list. She went back to chasing money.

Dizzy was aimless. He had no plans for the day after dropping the keys off with Gina. Now, without purpose or schedule, he decided to walk home via Camden Market where he could probably find someone to blag a cup of coffee to kill some time. But he didn't see anyone he knew. That surprised him, but as he leant on the railings overlooking the canal, watching a pair of mallard ducks urgently searching for food, he started to think about....well, lots of things. About what he would be doing now on a weekday morning if Gina's marathon project was still live. About how much he had enjoyed having a reason to get up and get out of his flat each morning. He had never met anyone like Gina. Her focus had impressed Dizzy within a few days of meeting her. She charged at her cause with blinkers against any distractions.

And Kenya. He couldn't place it on a map until a few weeks ago. The more he came to know about the villages where the clean water was a life-saving luxury, the more Dizzy assessed his life in London and how he took so much comfort for granted. He had found it so easy to be angry about the cards he had been dealt. About having no father; no money for essential trappings like clothes; the latest phone; holidays. That was his excuse for his thieving and eventually for the drug dealing that had resulted in a police record and probation. By his sixteenth birthday, Dizzy's destiny looked bleak.

But he had clean drinkable water at the turn of a tap and a bath or shower whenever he wanted. He had squandered his free education that Kenyans half his age might walk to for miles every day, just to sit under a tree for lessons that they considered as precious as the clean water.

He reflected on Gina's tirade and found it surprisingly reassuring. He wanted to believe that she was right. She had seen some potential for him in just a few weeks. If she had, he must. Easily thought, but not so easily achieved with so few positives in his favour. No job; no prospects of a job; no money or income; next-to-no qualifications.

The two ducks flew up from the canal and wheeled over Dizzy's head as he also turned away.

6

The phone rang somewhere under a pile of papers on Gina's makeshift desk. There was no name on the screen and she didn't recognise the number.

"Hello."

"Is that Ms Melina?"

"Yes, can I help?"

"Hi, my name is Guy Tozer. I'm a researcher on the *7 O'Clock Show*, the TV programme. Have you heard of it?"

"Yes, of course."

"Good. Well, we've seen your blog about getting hit by lightning when you were on a charity bike ride in Devon - is that right?

"Yeah."

"Gosh. Are you okay? Well of course you are, you're answering the phone – but we thought it would be a good story for our programme. Would you be interested in coming in to be interviewed?"

Gina was overwhelmed, but contained her excitement as she composed herself.

"Errr …yes, I suppose so. If you think it's that interesting."

"Yes we do. Have you still got the bike in the photo on your blog?"

"Yes."

"Can you bring it with you?"

"I suppose so."

"Cool. Are you available in the next week?"

"Er, yes, I suppose so." A thought then occurred to Gina. "Providing I can mention the name of my charity. Will that be okay?"

"Yes that's an important part of the storyline so that's probably cool…I've got it here….. Watersource. What's it do?"

"Basically, we supply clean water systems to villages in Africa using a new divining and pumping system, but the charity rides have had to stop because of the accident, so I will want to like, promote it if I'm on your programme."

"Let me check that it's okay and I'll come back to you. I should have an answer in the morning but I'll give you my direct line number in case you need to speak to me before that." He chirped out a number that Gina wrote down with a shaky hand. They said their goodbyes then Gina checked carefully that she had cut off the call before she yelped very loudly with excitement.

"Fuck it. Why couldn't I get that interest *before* we started?"

Her phone rang again. Another anonymous number appeared on her screen.

"Hello."

"Ms Melina?"

Gina recognised the Devonian accent.

"Yes, is that Betty's Blooms?"

"Yes, that's right. It's about your flower delivery…"

"Uh-huh. Is there a problem?"

"Er yes. T'iz a bit odd this but the driver has just come back because he says there's no house where you described. He did drive around quite a lot before he's come back. I'm sorry, dear, but I don't know what to do."

To be honest, I was annoyed. I thought something like, 'country bumpkins'. How many houses called 'Coombridge' can there be on a stretch of road less than a mile long?

"Well I don't know what you expect me to do from here. Look, I'll get you better directions and phone you back. I assume you're not going to charge for a second delivery."

"Not if it's our mistake of course, but we followed your directions exactly. He's very good, my driver. He's driven that road, ooooh, probably hundreds of times over the years. But you're okay - if you call me back with an exact address, I'll get them over there in the morning."

"Thank you. I do appreciate that."

That had been a distraction from the most exciting development I could possibly have hoped for. An interview on national TV. Oh yesssss! What are the viewing figures? Like millions for sure. Fan-bloody-tastic! I must tell everyone......er, no, better wait tll it's confirmed.

Gina was so excited that she couldn't stay seated. She stood up and walked around her small flat rehearsing her answers to imaginary questions to ensure she shoehorned Watersource into the interview. Maybe they would let her spell out the web address. What to wear? She should have her hands re-bandaged. And she should Tweet in advance to get all her supporters to watch it. She was lost in the details of her performance and everything she could think to capitalise from it.

I can tell my team though. Yeah, I must do that – they'd be gutted to find out that I hadn't told them first.

Hi All
I thought you'd like to know I've just been asked if I will be interveiwed on the 7 o Clock tv Show about the lightening strike on Dartmoor.   Should be next week and a great opertunity to get some publisity for more funds.
Love to you all,   G

30

No sooner had Gina sent the email to her inner circle of friends and family that included everyone who had been with her in Devon, than two replies dinged back into her inbox. Both were very impressed. A third arrived from Matt who also asked if the road number was okay for the flower delivery. Gina had forgotten about it again with the distraction from the 7 O'Clock Show.

She pulled up a map on her screen and tried to work out the location of Coombridge. She soon found the road and traced the route that she thought Matt had driven when they left the house, but she couldn't find any house located where she knew it to be with its drive next to a wood on the side of a valley. She had a vivid memory of the entrance to the drive from the main road. She had memorised that much as she left on Sunday morning and noted the house name on a wooden finger signpost.

You know that feeling when you're absolutely certain about something - sometimes for years, like it's just a fact of life - then you find out it was impossible to be as you recalled it? That was my reaction.

Gina 'drove' down the road with Google's Street View. For miles... then back. Then another route.... and another. She was getting nowhere. Not even the woodland was evident. She went hunting for that. The moor was quite denuded of trees in that area so she found three woods very quickly, even one with an adjacent driveway on the very road that Matt had noted. Her spirits lifted briefly until she realised that it just led to an overgrown ruin.

Gina rocked back in her seat. Too many co-incidences had happened too quickly. Why? Were they really co-incidences? What else could they be? A conspiracy perhaps? Is this what conspiracy-theorists get hooked on? Nothing made sense.

She walked into her sitting room and collapsed onto the sofa, staring at the ceiling before closing her eyes to think through her situation and her options.

It was dark when she woke. Gina took a moment to orientate. She lay with her eyes closed listening to the part of London that surrounded her flat. It was humming with a peaceful reassurance.

When she opened her eyes she was comforted by yellow streetlight percolating into the room. A pulsating red neon added to the atmosphere. She had needed the sleep and now she needed to wake slowly.

It was only after a few minutes that she realised she was not alone in the room. Her first reaction was cold fear. Her breathing almost stopped until her sense of smell reacted to a familiar aroma of White Charm eau de Cologne. A moment later:

"Don't be afraid, Georgina. Life's a gamble - you have to take some in life. Be brave."

The perfume; the voice; her full Christian name. Gina was alert and elated.

"Mummy?"

Nothing happened. Gina stared wide-eyed into the half-light.

"Don't go. I need you Mummy. What's happening? Please don't go."

The temperature in the flat changed abruptly from cool to humid. Gina knew that the moment had passed. She sensed that the spirit was gone. She was equally certain that it had been her mother; and that she had spoken to her. Of those facts there was absolutely no doubt in her mind as Gina quickly reran the last few minutes. That realisation was just too much. Gina broke down and sobbed uncontrollably. The pressure of the recent days released in a noisy outpouring in her yellow and red neon room. She made no effort to control herself, knowing that she had been holding in the pressure, alone. For a moment she had the very person with her who she needed to help her through this. Her mother had never made herself known to Gina since her death, so why now? Gina sobbed out her pent up angst then continued to lie on her sofa, sobbing and thinking. The longer she thought about it, the more convinced she became that there was good reason for her mother's visit now and that reason was linked to the activities of the last week – the lightning; the Lottery numbers; and the TV approach. Perhaps she should add Ms Flik and the difficulty in finding her house.

And why that message about taking gambles in life? And being brave. Why 'brave'? About what? Nothing came to mind that needed her bravery…..not yet.

Gina's parents had both died in the Asian Tsunami in 2004. They were on a holiday of a lifetime to celebrate a belated twenty-fifth wedding anniversary over the Christmas holiday because, for the first time ever, both Gina and her sister would be away from the family home for Christmas Day and New Year. Gina and her sister felt wholly responsible for their parents being in the eye of the disaster. They caught the earliest available flight to Vietnam but it was a pointless exercise. Pointless for her family, but the experience changed Gina's life. She had never travelled outside Europe, so to see such poverty in such devastation had an immediate and lasting impact on the sensitivities of a teenage British girl from the Home Counties, living a privileged upbringing. That was the start of Gina's mission to help those in need of the basics of life that she took for granted.

Gina reasoned that she should be alarmed or concerned or even frightened by the possible consequences of the events of the last ten days, but she wasn't and that surprised her. She was intrigued and puzzled, but not frightened. Her outburst of emotions a few minutes earlier had been essential and now, in the lee of that release, she felt a reassuring calmness as she lay on her sofa until she once again fell into a deep and peaceful sleep.

7

Gina quickly became obsessed with the location of Coombridge
when she returned to her computer at seven-o'clock next morning.
She searched every inch on the map showing the central and western
side of the moor. Nothing. So she changed direction to investigate
Hilary Flik, but again, the few avenues that came to mind each
terminated at a dead end. This was becoming too much for her to
bear. She wanted to archive Coombridge, Hilary Flik and Dartmoor
in a remote file somewhere away from her thoughts, but that proved
impossible, drawing her back to replay the incidents and images and
players in her drama. Had she not experienced the oddities of the
previous week, Gina would have convinced herself that her accident
had caused a temporary mental imbalance. Her memory could have
been to blame for misplacing Coombridge, but Hilary Flik was as
real as any of her friends who spent the night in the cottage. Now she
had vanished, along with her house .... hadn't she? Then there was
the Lottery. Gina sighed with exasperation. She sat deep in thought,
replaying all the events that she could recall since getting caught in
the storm. There were blanks, of course, but Ms Flik and
Coombridge played such a major part in the story that Gina
convinced herself that both were significant – somehow responsible
for the oddities that she had been experiencing since arriving in the
cottage. The phantom cottage with its phantom owner.

She had spent enough time at this on her own; it was time to involve
the others. Four friends had witnessed everything with her. They
could all compare notes, couldn't they? She thought about the
prospect for a few minutes – how she would do that; about what their
reactions would be; and the possible consequences. If she was right
and the house and Hilary Flik don't exist, what would they think – or

perhaps worse, what would they do? The more she considered the prospects, the more her instincts convinced her to keep this as her secret, at least for the moment.

Well I'd tried. I felt better that I'd tried all I could to locate then thank the lady who'd done so much for me, literally in my moment of need, but now I had to get on with other things. Better start by telling Betty what's happened ... basically she'll just have to give my flowers to someone deserving.

Gina made the call as soon as the shop opened and explained to Betty that she had drawn a blank on her investigations. She apologised for her previous abruptness but didn't want to provide an explanation and none was required. Betty was happy to send the flowers to the local nursing home which she suggested was a familiar process in similar circumstances. Gina wondered how often such odd circumstances could possibly arise.

Gina was about to hang up when, for no apparent reason, she thought to ask about the reference to a horse during their last conversation.

"Coombridge is famous in these parts," Betty explained. "It's a race horse trained just across in Somerset – it's been in the local news a lot because it's entered for the Gold Cup during Royal Ascot but a car hit it a few weeks back when it was exercising and it was badly injured. Well, I say *badly*, but obviously not so badly because it's got well enough to race ... next week, I think it is ... Whenever Royal Ascot is."

Gina was intrigued.

"How interesting ..... Thank you ..... Good bye."

Fucking right it's interesting. A race horse called Coombridge entered in a big race this week. 'Life's a gamble....' Oh my God....!

35

Gina reacted as if a light had just illuminated her future. Suddenly several random dots had been joined. She attacked her keyboard with invigorated energy, searching the name, *Coombridge*. There it was, on local TV News. Coombridge had been one of the favourites for the Ascot Gold Cup on 18th June but was now a questionable starter since its accident in March. The 18th was this coming Thursday. Gina was getting physically excited. She sensed her breathing speeding uncontrollably until she forced it back to normal with long, deep breaths.

Gina knew next-to-nothing about betting but a search of some bookmakers' names that came to her mind, quickly revealed that Coombridge was a rank outsider. 50-to-1 odds were consistent. Her heart sank. Hardly surprising, when, after some more checks, she realised the quality of the rest of the field for the Ascot Gold Cup. The favourite was a horse owned by the Queen with odds of 3-to-1, so it was only to be expected that some poor nag that was probably still recovering from injury was at the wrong end of the odds. It was a romantic story for the West Country news services, but entirely unrealistic for the hard-nosed racing world.

Even as I dug deeper into the research, my mother's words, 'life's a gamble, you have to take some - be brave' kept coming to me. It was literally the only thing in my life right now that linked 'gamble' with a need to be brave – to put money on a horse at 50-to-1 odds would be like, the bravest thing I've done for a long while - well, it would be if it was a lot of money that I bet. An amount I couldn't afford to lose. That would be seriously brave.....Or stupid.

Gina rummaged amongst the papers on her desk to find a calculator then tapped 50 x 500 followed by the = key. 25000 showed on the screen.

Shit. £25,000 if I bet £500. Shit. As simple as that. £25,000 – that's more than I'd hoped to make for the marathon

profit. And if I could find £1,000 to bet, that would win £50,000. All assuming the horse wins of course.......
Hmmm, of course - quite an important detail, that.

And that gave Gina reason to check herself. She laughed at the ludicrous proposition of betting her hard-earned charity money on a horse race. No emergency today, she was happy to put any decision off until later. Right now she had a more personal task. An email to send.

To: BeckyStevens3003@gmail.com
Subject: Mummy

Dearest B
Last night I was in bed when mummy spoke to me

No, that's rubbish.

Dearest B
Something happened last night that you should know about

Nope

Dearest B
I m not sure how to tell you this but mummy visited me last night. Her spirit was in my flat. I know it was her for certain because the smell of her White Charm perfume filled the room. Then she spoke to me briefly and told me to be strong.

Gina stopped and stared at the incomplete message.

That's crap. I'll wait until I see her next. This should be like something I tell her in person.

Neither Gina nor her sister, Becky, would describe their relationship as close. Not since they drifted apart when they went their separate ways after school. Then Becky married Geoff Stevens whom she had known since university, but he now has a job in The City - something in banking that Gina doesn't pretend to understand or pretend to be interested enough to enquire about.

He's an asshole, basically, with the morals of a...a....someone with shit morals. And Becky seems to have like, adopted them. They suit one another very well now – and that hurts me to think about. But she is my sister and we only had one mum who loved us both right to the end, so I thought I should tell Becky about the visit. But it can wait.

The call came from Guy at the TV production company at about midday, by which time Gina was nervously counting the minutes. So it was a great relief when he announced that she would be allowed to mention her charity. Only a mention, the presenters would be briefed not to let that dominate the interview. They agreed the details about her hands being in bandages for dramatic effect and that she would bring her damaged bike with her. A taxi would pick her up early on Thursday afternoon. Sorted.

Dizzy was making his way to his weekly meeting with his probation officer when a white Range Rover pulled across his path just off the main road.

"Hi Dizzy."

"Jocko." Dizzy nodded politely but both men knew that there was no love lost between them.

"I'm surprised to see you. You haven't been in circulation lately. Any reason?"

"No."

"Good because I might have some work for you."

"I don't want no trouble while I'm on probation. It was my birfday last week so next stop jail now."

"Happy birthday, Diz. I hope you got some nice presents. Did you buy something special for yourself? No, don't s'pose you did when you ain't got no money."

"I've gotta go."

"The job's still open for you Dizzy - usual terms - in fact, because you was such a good worker I think we could discuss them if you're interested. From what I hear you ought to be interested. Word has it you would prefer this to be me what stopped you than Mr Bessick. Is that right? Word had it you was out of town because you don't want to bump into Mr B."

There was a long stare.

"I've gotta go," Dizzy announced. Then he did.

"Good Morning Mr Gillespie. How are you?"

"Okay."

Kathy Rawlings had been allotted Dizzy's case since his potential incarceration in a young offenders' institution was commuted to Community Service. She was an experienced probation officer with the look, tone and persona of an experienced probation officer. A general weariness pervaded her conversation even when she was trying to sound enthusiastic or reassuring. But this morning hadn't been good so Ms Rawlings wasn't making any effort. She speed-read some notes under Dizzy's true name: 'Daniel Anthony Gillespie' while Dizzy looked on from the opposite side of the lemon yellow table that was presumably intended to bring cheer into the very cheerless atmosphere of the probation team's offices.

"You were allocated time with a charity called......Watersource, for three months but you were sacked last week, only seven weeks ..."

"What?!" Dizzy interrupted abruptly. "No I weren't. Where d'you get that?"

"That's what it says here. You weren't what? Doing community service with Waterstone's.......Wateresource. Or you weren't sacked?"

"Here. This is my reference what the lady at the charity gave me."

Ms Rawlings' attitude changed visibly as she read it. By the end, she was almost upbeat.

"Mmmmm. Very good. So why was your term shortened so much?"

Dizzy explained in a tone that matched Ms Rawlings' opening address.

"I see. That's a shame. I'll amend your file but now we need to find you another placement to suit your obvious talents. I will be in touch as soon as that happens. Meanwhile I will see you here next week, same time as usual. Okay?"

"Whatever."

8

_____

Safia had tried to make time to encourage Gina out of her flat. They eventually planned an early supper close to Safia's office. A Vietnamese restaurant with some outside seating was perfect for the warm evening.

I was in two minds about Saffy's suggestion but she was right when she literally demanded that I take time off from work and get out of my apartment. That wasn't how she put it – something about Ed, her boyfriend, being away and needing a girlie catch-up – but I sensed a more benevolent reason, especially when she offered to pay. I'm getting seriously fed up with my pauper status amongst my rich friends. Saffy's on £40,000 plus, but I console myself that web-design would like, drive me totally insane, even if I could do it. Seems to like, suit her though, bless her.
And since Saffy would be literally the first of the gang that were in Devon that I've seen since the accident, this would be my first opportunity to test my memory of events.

Gina managed not to launch into her investigations too soon after finding a table on the pavement outside the restaurant. There was genuine news to catch-up - about Gina's hands and her recovery; the news about the 7 O'Clock Show and Gina's preparations (that took quite a while once Safia got inventive about Gina's wardrobe) and about the wind-down of the marathon project. Getting back to the subject of the accident allowed Gina to slip in some questions about Hilary Flik and her house.

I think I over-did 'casual'. It seemed obvious to me that I was hunting for information, but Saffy didn't seem to notice.

"I've thought a lot about the bits I can recall about the accident. There are still gaps though."

"Blimey Gee, that's only to be expected."

"Even the farmhouse and that lady - Mrs Flik - what did you make of that?"

"In what way?"

"Did she seem normal to you – nothing unusual?"

"Not particularly. A bit odd I suppose, but who isn't. There was the thing about the photos – that was a bit odd."

"Photos? What photos?"

"Of course, that was when we arrived and you were zonked out in bed. Craig was looking at photos in the kitchen and when he asked the lady about the people in them, she got agitated – well, annoyed really. And the next morning he whispered to me that they'd been like, removed from the kitchen. He obviously didn't think much about it if he didn't mention it to you."

"What were the photos of?"

"Just family I think, I didn't take any notice really. I thought Craig was just being polite by taking an interest and asking about them."

"What about the location? I'm having trouble picturing how far it was from where the lightning hit us. How long were we driving?"

"That's not surprising, you were completely out of it for the drive there. I think it was a couple of miles, maybe more – no, about a couple of miles. But you remember leaving next day - you made a note of the name as we drove away, didn't you?"

"Yeah, at the entrance to the drive, by a wood is how I remember it."

"Yeah.....yeah, that's right. The waiter'll be back in a minute, do you know what you're having?"

So, what did that teach me? Basically, nothing about the location except that Saffy remembers it exactly like I do. But the photos? What was that about? Why were they a problem to our phantom hostess?

9

Thursday was going to be a big day. Gina hadn't slept well. Her arrangements for the 7 O'Clock Show appearance were in place and didn't trouble her, unlike the thought of gambling her charity money on the prospects of an injured horse winning a feature race at odds of 50 to 1, against some of the best horses of their age.

Can you blame me? I suppose I slept at times but my recollection is that I was literally awake the entire night thinking my way through what felt like an endless list of permutations. And if it wins, what all that money could fund. I had to admit I was grasping at something to replace the charity ride money and this had come at the right time. But was it clouding my judgement too much? To be honest, I dunno. By morning I realised that my choice boiled down to: Shall I do it? Well, that was quite easy to answer, but if so, how much do I gamble? Hmmm, therein lies the big dilemma. It would have been easier had it been my money, but it's the charity's. Basically, I've got the opportunity to lift this weight from my shoulders - all my financial worries – while sending loads of water units to Kenya and that means saving thousands of lives. Or, if it all goes tits-up, I could take months to claw back the money, basically. Thinking through all the strands that linked those considerations was what had kept me awake. And throughout the night my mother's advice was constantly in my head. '...you have to take gambles in life. Be brave'.
Time to stop. Time to be brave.

As Gina made her first fresh coffee of the day, the easy decision was made. She would do it.

I'd known that for two days. I had to do it, but the sum was the stumbling block and being brave meant that I should gamble like, most of the money in Watersource's bank account. I could withdraw it this morning and walk down the High Road to one of the three big bookmakers....yes, I'd already checked them out. Basically, the worst that could happen will be a very big hole in Watersource funds. At least no-one but me needs to know about it.

Just considering the process made Gina very nervous. She knew that she must do it quickly and not look back. She opened the charity bank account on-line to check the amount that she could take. After some calculations to deduct a long list of costs from last weekend and a variety of monthly standing orders, she found herself looking at the numbers 1547.27. A little over £1,500 which about summed up the worst state of her finances for as long as she could recall. No surprise. She stared at the number for a minute then casually tapped the number 1200 into her calculator followed by 'x 50 = '. The number 60000 appeared on the screen. £60,000 prize for gambling £1,200 at 50-to-1. She couldn't be that brave, not £1,200 - that would be reckless - but perhaps £1,000, a nice round number. She pulled open the top drawer of the filing cabinet below her desk, took out the cheque book, opened it to the next page and wrote 'CASH'. Then she signed it. Then added the date. Just the sum to fill in.... Without more thought she wrote £1,200 in numbers and then spelled it out. She filled out the stub, tore the page and replaced the book in the drawer.

Gina hardly gave the cheque another glance because she knew that this was the only way she could go through with what she was about to do. The *madness* of what she was about to do. The *braveness* of what she was about to do.

The youth behind the glass at the bank checked the Watersource account when Gina presented her cheque made out to 'cash' but he didn't ask for the photo identification that Gina had taken.

£1,200 was a fortune to me, but nothing special for bank staff it seems.

The lady at the bookmaker was visibly surprised. She had to consult an older colleague behind the screen before she placed the bet for Coombridge to win then pushed a slip of paper under the screen. Gina checked it at a glance and left the shop quickly. Job done.

A black taxi arrived at her flat precisely as Guy at the 7 O'Clock Show had arranged. Two hours before the Gold Cup would be run. Gina decided not to look for, or ask anyone about the result. She should be alone back at her flat when she made the discovery. She knew that one way or the other her reaction would be extreme so it would be for her alone to witness.

Guy Tozer was waiting by the kerb outside the TV studios when Gina arrived in the taxi with a bag of clothes and her broken bike that she hadn't seen since it was loaded into the horse box in Devon. She was shocked to see its condition when she had opened the lock-up for the taxi driver to help her load it into the taxi. As was the driver who wanted to know all about the events that caused the damage.

"Blimey lady, you was hit by lightning? When you was on the bike?"
Gina explained in more detail when she realised that he was genuinely interested. Taxi drivers hear myriad stories of varying levels of interest, but this one was special.

"No wonder they want you on the 7 O'Clock Show. I've never met no-one what was hit by lightning and survived….(thinks)…Well course they'd have to survive or I couldn't have met them could I?"
He laughed aloud. "You're one brave lady."

46

Guy helped Gina to what he termed *The Green Room* that was more of a beige colour, where he offered some refreshments that Gina declined. He ran through the proceedings that reminded Gina of her visit to the hospital where staff kept telling her what to expect.

Eventually, part way through her fourth magazine, a man with headphones around his neck entered the room and introduced himself by a name that Gina instantly forgot. But she recalled him being the floor manager. He told her what to expect again then disappeared for the duration of another two magazines. When he returned he had a lady with him who introduced herself as Emma without a title. Emma stared at Gina and decided that what she was wearing was perfectly fine so she didn't need to change her clothes but her complexion would need some powder. Emma seemed to be content with that so Floor Manager was also content with that.

This is boring. If this is like, the magic of the movies - or the tele - I'm not very impressed? It's totally boring.

Suddenly there was a flurry of activity. Guy was back to take her to the studio. Her twisted bike wouldn't wheel as the tyres were burnt away, so he carried it as Gina followed him to a holding area near the set that Gina had checked on-line. It looked very familiar and very brightly lit. A make-up lady with a big smile approached with an open powder compact and a brush. She inspected Gina's complexion briefly before wielding the brush over her entire face in a few deft strokes. Then she was gone. Floor Manager now appeared and stood beside Gina and spoke in a hushed voice.

"As soon as we go to the video about a bird sanctuary, we'll move you onto the seat nearest us."

For the first time, I felt nervous. Really nervous. How strange is that?

The bird sanctuary video appeared on the screens around the studio and Floor Manager and Guy ushered Gina and her bike into position. The video ended and Gina heard her introduction described in terms suggesting that she was lucky to be alive, let alone interviewable here on television for the delectation of the 7 O'Clock Show audience.

Actually, it was really good, surprisingly. I was suddenly a little more relaxed and the questions were respectful and logical and polite and very like those I'd rehearsed and, most importantly, provided me with the opportunity to talk about Watersource. Basically, the two presenter people were really good. They were really interested in the work and didn't stop me reciting the web address. I couldn't have asked them for more, really.

Then it was over and I sat contemplating my performance while another report was introduced from a boat in somewhere about something. A video came on the screens around the studio and I was ushered away.

Guy was really nice, in a cocky public schoolboy sort of way. He took me and the bike back to the Greenish Room until he was sure a taxi was waiting; then we made our way to a side door. I seem to have made a good impression on him at least. I hope he's typical of the viewers because he was like, fascinated by my description of Watersource's work. He was very sweet about it. He made a passing suggestion that we meet up sometime; I think I instinctively said that would be good but did nothing more as I climbed into the back of the cab. Anyway, he had my contact details. I might have thought more about it had I not been literally shocked by the taxi driver.

"Call me Lighnin' dum-dum-dum-do-day. That's a turn-up innit?"

Gina was looking at the back of the same head that had brought her to the TV studios earlier.

"How did it go?"

"It was good, thanks. Have you been waiting all that time?"

"Nah. Not for TV companies these days. They wouldn't pay for that. I just got a call from my big fat controller because I was nearest. Coincidence, that's all. Camden innit? Via the lock-up again?"

"Yes please."

An easy banter with the cabbie helped the journey pass quickly despite the heavy evening traffic. Gina was trying not to think about her bet or the outcome. She knew that the horse race was over. By now she would be hero or villain and could do nothing about it either way. Someone had left a copy of London's freebie afternoon newspaper, The Evening Standard, on the seat of the cab. Perhaps it would have the result if this was a late edition. Gina glanced at it but refused to be drawn. Perhaps the cabbie had noticed in his mirror because when he pulled up outside Gina's flat he suggested she took the paper.

On reflection, he sort of insisted that I take it. If I thought about it at all, I assumed that it was like he wanted it gone from his cab because it was making it look untidy, so I took it. No big deal at the end of the day.

Immediately Gina was in her flat, she knew that she must check the result of the race. She dare not leave it to build up in her mind - that would be a way to madness for her. She walked into her office, sat down and opened her computer then immediately tapped '*ascot gold cup results*' into the default search engine. The page filled with options. At the top:

BBC Sport
50-1 WINNER OF GOLD CUP

Gina hardly had to read further but she opened the page to see the full report.

I cannot tell you the relief I felt in that instant. Yeah, relief....huh. The shock and excitement and utter amazement would follow but in that moment, I felt pressure literally drain away from me. I hardly recall the rest of the report but it was basically a potted history of Coombridge's accident and recovery. I think I read enough to convince myself that no mistake had been made before a mist descended.

I had just won £60,000. Un-fucking-believable. It had been a good day. a very good day.

10

Dizzy was having a bad day. His probation officer had ordered him to join a painting team that was refurbishing railings around a local park. He could handle the boredom, but he was in full view of anyone walking past the park - or driving. That's how Charlie Bessick spotted him. His black Jaguar pulled up after passing Dizzy who, by chance, had looked up to watch the car go by. He couldn't see the driver through the windscreen but Charlie Bessick could see out. The car screeched to a halt and started to reverse back down the road at speed until a following car blocked its way. Most of the paint team had noticed the reversing Jaguar, but only Dizzy recognised the bulky frame that clambered out of the driver's door.

Dizzy took off. He wasn't going to wait for the shouting or worse that was about to ensue.

"You better run, you black shit!" Charlie Bessick shouted in rage. He certainly wasn't in any shape to run after Dizzy, but he didn't need to. It was enough to know that Dizzy was back at home; he would catch up with him whenever he wanted. And Dizzy knew it.

11

It was soon apparent that Gina's appearance on the 7 O'Clock Show was achieving everything she had wanted. Her personal email, Twitter and Facebook in-boxes were soon filling with kind and generous praise. Plus a few leg-pulls about her bandages. Her friends all knew that she didn't need them anymore, but their comments were in good humour.

Funds started to arrive in the Watersource bank within minutes of the live broadcast. They continued next day and were to accelerate over the weekend.

What a difference a day makes. From pauper to...... whatever's the opposite of 'pauper'. This is such a lovely feeling. Literally within about a day after the 7 O'Clock Show, Watersource had £10,700-worth of new donations. And a load of new contacts. A couple of companies asked if they could like, sponsor Watersource – I didn't expect that – I still have to think how to handle them.

My contact with Kenya's a man called Eric Wilammi. Basically he masterminds the operations to turn my funds into the kit that gets out to Kenya from me and some other charity sources around the UK. I told him about the 7 O'Clock Show in advance and he was one of the first to send a really nice email congratulating me. So I wanted him to know that I was getting a result. I'd only ever sent a few grand at a time, like every few months. I didn't know that there's a sort of hierarchy. As soon as I told him to expect a big contribution in the next few days, he responded with descriptions of the new bigger purifying systems that we could supply. Literally big enough for a whole village, even a small town, he said. My little systems were only good for a homestead or two. I suppose Eric didn't want to embarrass me by suggesting that my contributions before were minimal. But now....well, now I could like move up the rankings to another league to supply mega systems. That's great. That's what the race winnings will buy. This is so great – I'm loving having some money at last.

Getting £60,000 from the bookmakers was an entirely unfamiliar process. Gina put it off until the following week when she could open a new bank account. The money would be paid in her name by the bookmaker but she didn't want it in her personal account, so first thing on Monday she walked to her bank and sat with a girl who looked too young for such responsibilities. Gina explained enough to get the new account opened then walked to the bookies to ask advice about claiming her winnings. The teller recognised her, so did her colleague who looked around the room furtively before speaking in a hushed voice.

"How did you know?"

"Know? Know what?"

"£1,200 at 55-to-1. How did you know? We hardly ever get bets that big on a rank outsider."

"I just got lucky, I s'pose....What did you say?"

"What?"

"The odds – what were the odds?"

"55-to-1, didn't you know?" She checked the slip. "Yeah, look they was 55-to-1 when you placed the bet."

55-to-1. Bloody hell. They must have changed. I didn't notice that. Bloody hell. But I didn't expect the grilling just to get my winnings. It made me nervous that someone was going to hear. I basically wanted to know how to get them to pay the money into my new account once it was open. It got sorted eventually, but our High Street is not somewhere to like, bandy around the figure of £60,000 without someone taking notice. But it's more now, of course.

Gina walked home in something of a daze, having mentally calculated that she had won over £65,000. An unimaginable sum beyond her experiences.

Her phone rang. The name DIZZY appeared on the screen.

"Hi Diz, what's up?"

"Hi Gee. Where are you?"

"Behind you." As she walked, she realised that Dizzy was standing in the street outside the door to her flat. The biggest smile split Dizzy's face as he turned to see her walking towards him. They greeted a little awkwardly. They had never been in the habit of touching or hugging except the last time that they were together. They hovered for a moment then Gina grabbed him and kissed Dizzy's cheek.

"How nice to see you. You here for a coffee?"

"Nah, not coffee but I'd like a chat please - if that's okay - if you got time now you're a famous TV celeb an' all that." He laughed one of his wide laughs.

"Piss off."

Gina made herself a coffee and joined Dizzy on her sofa. He was noticeably agitated and sucked air through his teeth as if contemplating his words.

"This is a big ask - and I know it's not likely but - you know, my mum says if you don't ask you won't get, so here goes ....Can I do some work for you in Kenya?"

"Crikey Diz. A big ask all right. Where the hell did that come from?"

"I really don't mind what I do. Anything, really. You don't have to pay me - just get me out there and give me accommodation and food."

"Woooow – slow up. Dizzy, what's this about? Are you in trouble? Are you trying to get out of London?"

"Hmmm. I won't lie to you, Gee. You never asked why I'm on probation, doing community service, so I'll tell you. I was dealing. For a few years. Only enough to get by but ….well, I got in debt to someone I don't wanna to be in debt to, if you get my meaning."

Gina nodded. Dizzy realised that this wasn't what he wanted to say.

"But don't get me wrong Gee, my time working with you and getting to know what you do was - well, it's made me think a lot about the shit I was in and my shit life and shit future and the shit people what I hang out with. What you do is…well, it's fucking important, man. No, I mean it, Gee. What you're doing is jus' brilliant. Everyone else I know does stuff for themselves. Number one. Not you. And yes, I would like to get away but I could do that by staying with my cousin in Leeds. I did that before I came to you. Leeds, man – it's not for me and just runnin' away's for a loser. I really want to do something to help you and Watersource. And if I was working for you that would be Community Service so I'd be clocking up lots of hours and that would be really cool so what d'you think?."

"That's a big speech Dizzy."

I didn't really know what to tell him. I know he wanted me to say something to give him hope and perhaps his timing was just good enough for me to do that. On the spur of the moment I just thought to be careful. I don't really know him or the people he hangs out with. Basically, warning bells were fighting the thought that 'charity begins at home'. Here's someone I care about, asking me for help – help that could change his life as much as the clean water does for people I will never meet, living thousands of miles from here.

"Okay."

Dizzy sat up with a start. His eyes were open expectantly. Gina jumped in.

"What I mean is - okay, we have to sort something out for you."
Dizzy relaxed, waiting for the soft landing as Gina brought him back down to earth.

"How much do you owe?"

"No, Gee, I know you don't have no money, I'm not asking you for money, really I'm not."

"How much?"

"With interest, about five grand…. Originally it was three, but that was six months ago. I was going to work it off by trading for the man but… well, things changed and now he wants his money or bits of my body."

Gina considered his answer.

"Would he take it like, over time – the money, I mean?"

"Gee, I know you haven't got that sort of money. And I can't repay you. No, that's embarrassin'. I never came to beg for money but I am begging to be allowed to help in Kenya."

"Here's my offer…." But her mobile phone started to ring in her office. "Sorry Diz. Let me get that and I'll be back. I think I can help."

Gina didn't recognise the incoming number on her phone.

"Hello."

"Is that Gina?"

"Who are you?"

"This is Guy from the 7 O'Clock Show. Do you remember me?"

"Oh hi. Yes of course. What's happening?"

I was so wrapped up in the results of the 7 O'Clock Show that I just assumed he was phoning to tell me that their switchboard had literally crashed under the pressure of calls with donations or maybe he wanted to know where to forward the mountain of cheques. So his invitation to meet for a drink – or dinner was like, a genuine shock.

"Oh right. Yes, I'd love to. Thank you. When, where?"

"How about tomorrow evening? I can come over to you after work if that suits you."

"Yeah, that'll be good. You know my address. Just let me know that you're on your way......See you then."

Gina clicked off and smiled as she dropped the phone on her desk and reconnected with Dizzy who she assumed had listened to the call. It was impossible to do anything secretly in her tiny flat. But when she stepped back into the sitting room she found Dizzy engrossed in the old edition of The Evening Standard that had been lying around since Gina brought it in from her cab ride. Dizzy was puzzled.

"This is some weird paper. Where did you get this?"

"It's just an Evening Standard – no weirder than it ever is. It's an old one from last week."

Dizzy was puzzled by something in the paper but he dropped it back on the coffee table as he re-engaged.

"You were saying that you had a plan."

"Yes. I don't want you getting hurt while I try to sort something for you so I want you to contact your man and ask how much would hold off his dogs for like, a few weeks. I assume he would prefer some money than some of your body parts that aren't legal currency even in Camden."

"What if he says a few grand – and he will. What if it's five grand?"

"Find out."

"Then what?"

"I'll make some enquiries. I can't make any promises and I'm worried about helping you to run away. That doesn't seem right."

"No. I know. But I can't think of anything else right now and I promise you Gee, I genuinely want to help."

57

"Hmm. Just in case I can sort something, check with your probation people that they will let you go. Have you got a passport?"

"Yeah, course."

"Okay. So, get the other answers and I'll do what I can, but don't promise anything to anyone because I'm not. Do you understand?"

"Yeah. No promises. I promise."

12

I surprised myself how much I was looking forward to the drink with Guy from the 7 O'Clock Show. Not because it's him - I've never been attracted by pretty preppie-types - but because being asked out is so unusual these days. It's been ages since a fanciable man who wasn't drunk or high showed any interest in me. Hardly surprising, I suppose. I know I don't make enough effort with my appearance, but what the hell, it doesn't bother me. I know I spend too much time at home alone these days so this is a good excuse to get out even if it's just down the road. I'll suggest we go to Trappers if the weather's good enough. We can get a seat in the garden and if we get on well enough and he's not like, too boring we can get some food to make an evening of it.

So that's what they did. Guy phoned at about six-o'clock and was waiting outside Trappers within the hour. They found one of the last available tables in the garden and Guy went off to buy a round of drinks.

So far so good. He's not quite as I remembered him. Maybe that's because he's outside work. He's still basically a bit too preppie though.

With such low expectations, the only way for Guy was up. And so it proved. The conversation was non-stop starting with the topic of Gina's hands that Guy had never seen, then onto the 7 O'Clock Show experience that led to a lot of gossip about the presenters, which expanded to include celebrities from around the world of TV - stories that Guy had witnessed first-hand or had heard about from his inner sources. That subject was so absorbing that they had both lost track of time. Time to get some food, so again Guy disappeared to the bar to order.

Yes okay, it's going better than I thought. And yes, okay, he's very good company, but so would anyone be who can trade on so much gossip.

When Guy returned to the table, he seemed to be aware that he had been doing all the talking so immediately demanded that Gina do some. He wanted to know about Watersource (although Gina had to prompt him with the name). He wanted to know how it works; what made her divining systems unique; how many people it employs; the impact of Gina's appearance on 7 O'Clock Show; what precisely did the funds buy; had she been to Kenya to see the equipment installed? Gina never needed prompting to talk about her passion so once again Guy had pressed the easy-conversation-topic button.

Two plates of food arrived with cutlery wrapped in paper napkins. The break provided Gina with the excuse to change tack to ask about Guy, but she didn't expect the profile that quickly developed after some encouragement. As he started to describe a broken home and rebellious teen years she realised how she had misjudged this book by its accent. Guy and his brother had been to a modest private school local to their family home in Wiltshire, but it was paid for by his grandmother who also provided a home for them during holidays. He was obviously very close to her and gave her credit for providing both boys with the little stability that they had known during their formative years. Their father blew all the family money and left his mother when Guy was ten. His mother became a reclusive hippy who seemed to live her life through the occult and made the barest living from selling her services as a medium.

Okay, I was wrong about that as well. Had I not been eating, I think my mouth would have dropped open at some of the more extreme details, like him being a flute player. I think he would have been a good one too if his hopes hadn't been crushed when his left hand was, in a rugby accident. That was eight years ago and he still hasn't got full use of his hand, basically.

Their conversation about their personal histories led naturally on to Gina's parents and their deaths. She seldom spoke about them or it, so her explanation was unrehearsed.

At one point I felt an overwhelming urge to tell him about my mother's visit last week and I might well have, if I'd not been fighting back emotions. I think Guy realised and changed the subject – or would have done, but the rare break in our conversation made us realise how late it was. Guy went to the bar to pay the bill. I stood up and hovered, waiting for him to return. It lasted no more than like, a couple of minutes, but as I stood watching the traffic and people passing the beer garden through the railings, I experienced a calmness that I'd literally never known before. It may have been the drink but I just felt content and relaxed and whatever the opposite of 'anxious' is – that's what I felt.

Guy walked Gina to her flat door and refused her offer of a coffee.

Thank goodness. I couldn't remember how I'd left the flat but it was probably in a mess.

During the short walk through Camden, Gina had thought to ask where he lived.

"Currently in Camberwell but I have to get out in a couple of weeks so I'll be looking for new accommodation – a cheap and

61

cheerful flat-share so if you hear of anything, please let me know. That'd be really cool. I've been looking south of the river because that's what I know a bit, but this is more convenient for my office so round here would be really cool. This is Camden isn't it?"

"That's right, but it's not cheap anymore. I'm really lucky because I've been here a long time and I have a great landlord who likes me and the charity, otherwise I'd literally have to move out much further. But I'll keep an ear open for you."

Was any of that a leading suggestion? No, don't be silly we've only just met. Sometimes, Gina, you have the most suspicious mind.

They stood for a minute talking on the pavement then Guy told Gina how much he had enjoyed the evening, leaned forward and pecked her on the cheek then immediately turned away towards the tube station.

That was nice - the evening, I mean. I hope we do that again. Probably won't though.

Gina needn't have worried. She was making up her sofa bed when she heard a text arrive on her mobile. That wasn't unusual recently so she only opened it when she came out of the bathroom.

Gina. Thank you for making 2night so much fun. Plse can we do it again soon? Guy xx

Gina replied in the affirmative.

13

Hi Eric

Please send more information about your big systms. I will have more funds soon and would like to plan how to spend the money. Thank you.

I also want to discuss the possibility of my assistant travelling to Kenya to help instal the new systems for an extended stay. I will pay for his travel if you can include him in your program when hes there.

Regards

Gina

Within a few minutes of sending the email, Gina's phone rang. The name 'ERIC' was on the screen when she picked it up.

"Hi Eric, that was quick. How are you?"

"I'm fine thank you Gina, and you?"

"Yeah, great thanks."

"Is the extra money coming in since your television appearance? That was so good, I'm not surprised."

"Thank you. Yes – literally what a difference a bit of TV exposure makes. I wouldn't have guessed how big the response has been."

That's an easy explanation. He doesn't need to know more.

"So, can you send me more information about the bigger water systems? I'd like to see if I can fund one, or perhaps more, over time."

"Yes I'll email that, but I called about your assistant going out to Kenya – I didn't know you had an assistant. Who is he?"

"Yes you do. I told you I had a young guy helping with the marathon."

"Oh, him. But you said he was a young offender."

Bugger, so I did.

"That's right. Is that a problem? He's great. I will vouch for him. Basically, the truth is, Eric, he's got a less than angelic background but he really wants to turn his life round. That's why he came here and he was brilliant. I literally couldn't have wished for anyone better."

"I get the message, Gina. Leave it with me. We couldn't pay more than expenses, maybe a little pocket money each month. And it will be general labouring-type work to start. How long would he want to be out there?"

"I don't know. If you can use him, you tell me what you can offer for how long and I will put it to him. When will you know? I want to give him a definite answer soon so he can make plans one way or another."

"I should get an answer for you tomorrow."

"Thanks Eric."

Gina had become obsessed with her in-box while the near-constant flow of mails offering money and assistance or requesting more information about Watersource, was showing little sign of slowing. Amid the kind sentiments were some heart-tugging requests, usually for financial help. Gina had formulated a few standard replies that she adapted to enable her to respond with a personalised reply to any that deserved a response. She was absorbed in the emails when her phone rang mid-afternoon and the name GUY appeared.

Great.

"Hi Guy."

"Hi you. How's your day going?"

"Oh okay – you know. I seem to spend most of them on email at the moment. Still masses of incoming from the 7 O'Clock Show."

"If you fancy a break from it later I have to check out a flat-share your side of Tufnell Park. Do you fancy giving me your advice?"

"Gosh that was quick – are you always such a fast worker?"

Oooops. That sounded clumsy.

"A coincidence. There are a few in your area but this looks cool for a price I can afford. Don't worry if you're busy though."

"I'd love to come. I'll get the tube and meet you outside Tufnell Park station. Is that okay?"

"Perfect. It looks like a five minute walk from the tube. I'll call you when I'm leaving work."

Yes, I admit it – maybe I am a wee bit smitten. Not enough to be dangerous, but enough to be very happy when his name popped up on my phone.

Gina looked around her flat. It had become a bit batchelorish in recent days.

I'd better clear up this time, just in case he accepts a coffee tonight.

It didn't take long for some cursory tidying to make an impression on her tiny flat. She took the bin from the kitchen and moved around discarding bits of obvious rubbish into it. When she came to the old Evening Standard that still lay on her coffee table, she dropped it into her bin before recalling Dizzy's reaction to something he had seen in it. She perched on the arm of the sofa and began to turn the pages, expecting to find something blatantly odd; something visibly wrong with the printing or ….. or what?

It was only when she stopped to check some of the TV listings that she noticed that BBC 2 was showing Wimbledon Tennis Tournament coverage. Coverage of an event that wouldn't start for another week. There was no mistake. Gina read the programme notes. This was coverage of the second week of Wimbledon.

Odd, or what? At this point, I wasn't sure what I was reading.

Now she went back to the cover and started reading the news items. The lead story was a celebrity court case that, in reality, had just started but the outcome was emblazoned across the cover. Inside, Gina spotted items that she knew to be wrong – about a big West End film premier; and a French air traffic controllers' strike that was in its fourth day with pictures of queues of passengers at Heathrow and Stansted Airports. Gina shook her head. Neither were happening when she found the paper in the taxi. The more pages she turned, the more obvious it was that this paper was reporting news that hadn't happened yet. Gina smiled when it only then occurred to check the date: Tuesday 14th July. Over two weeks from now.

Oh - my - god !!! …… Not again???

14

Guy was waiting at the entrance to the underground as Gina arrived. If he had given their meeting as much consideration as Gina, it certainly wasn't evident as he walked straight to her with a ready smile and gave her a brief hug. Gina was all too willing to respond.

They walked as they talked about Guy's flat hunting. He did infer that the journey had taken longer than he had expected from his office in the West End. Perhaps that should have registered but Gina was enjoying his boyish exuberance and they soon arrived at a scruffy 1930's house matching the address on Guy's phone.

The flat was disappointing. Gina hadn't been flat hunting for so long that she realised how little she had to offer with her critique. She had no idea whether it was good value or not – or whether its run-down appearance and dishevelled furnishings were what she should have expected. But judging from Guy's reaction when they compared notes whilst walking back towards the station, he clearly was no more impressed than Gina. As they approached the underground station, Gina was waiting for him to suggest that they divert to a pub or maybe go back to Camden Town to Trappers again, but he did neither. She sensed that he would have got back on the next train had she not suggested a drink. Guy looked at the clock on his phone.

"Er, yeah, okay, let's do that."

They stepped into the first pub that they saw and ordered drinks. Guy was such an easy conversationalist that Gina couldn't read him.

He's such a nice bloke – he's gorgeous, basically, but, you know what? I really didn't know if he wanted me to be there or not. He was babbling on like he always did but there was nothing more than that. Perhaps I wanted him to be interested in me like, too much. Or maybe the answer was....

"You know what? I think this may be a mistake if that's all you get for your money up here. And the journey is slower to work than from Brixton. There's someone at work who lives quite close to Brixton station who'll need a new flatmate at the end of next month - and the Victoria Line is so quick that I could be in work in half an hour."

Well that's that then. No more to be said.

Except Gina did say:
"That's a shame. I was hoping you would be closer to Camden."
"Yeah, that would have been cool. I was looking forward to pastures new - and new people, but I have more friends down south, so I would probably spend my time back and forth if I lived up here."

Well that's that then. No more to be said.

So she didn't.
They finished their drinks and set off for the station. The conversation never wavered, never felt like an effort, but Gina knew that her hopes were misplaced. She had to conclude that Guy was just a nice bloke who found it very easy to communicate his charm. It didn't mean anything, nor did Gina mean any more to him than a hundred other friends and acquaintances. Or so she assumed. Her expectations were just wishful thinking, no more than self-imposed delusions. This was not an unknown emotion. Not the first time she had fancied someone who had not reciprocated her interest. But this one lingered and she had no idea why. Perhaps because he was getting away. She tried to tell herself that he was not her type and that she was never attracted to preppies, however pretty, but it wasn't working.

She sat in her flat with the TV showing some house makeover programme that Gina found easy to ignore. It provided a wallpaper backdrop to her thoughts about her life of late. She walked away to the bathroom where she stared at her image in the mirror.

I never do that. Well, occasionally I suppose - last time was probably before the 7 O'Clock Show, but that was to see if I looked injured. I can't remember the last time I like, just looked at myself – my image – to see what other people see ...... and it's ...well... not very attractive, to be honest. Basically, I'm not doing myself any favours. I could blame the time of the month but that's not all the problem - basically, I just look shit.

15

Another day, another dollar.
No idea why that expression came to mind as I lay in bed,
but it about sums up my situation. Basically, I have the
news that won't happen for another week or so. If I can't
make some money from that Evening Standard ... well, of
course I will. Let's see if I can make enough for a mega
water system – that's about a hundred grand.

Gina refused to linger on thoughts about the weirdness of her situation. The potential to make funds for Watersource won over and excited her into action. She scrambled out of bed, snatched the paper from a side table, wriggled back under her duvet and started to scan the pages for any news that could provide a profit. By page three she realised that this was not such an easy task so she flipped the paper over to the sport coverage on the back pages.

Some football results – they'll be useful.

Working backwards, Gina started to identify various bits of sports news that she could bet on until she spotted the jackpot. It was in a report referring to an upset at the Wimbledon tennis championships when the woman's third seed had been knocked out by a teenager with a name that Gina didn't recognise – hardly surprising since the young pretender was only in the tournament because she had won a wild card entry. She was a nobody who had just made her name – or would do in five days from now.

Oh yes. Result. What odds can I get for that, I wonder?

The answer was 25-to-1. She phoned her local friendly bookmaker before realising that this was probably a bad idea. She shouldn't go back to the scene of her big win, but that thought came too late just as the phone was answered so she asked for the information and quickly hung up.

25-to-1? Fantastic. But this'll need a bit of planning so that I don't like, attract too much attention. Can't do it on-line. Basically, I need to spread the bets around to keep them small. Is this what they call 'spread-betting'?

Her mojo was back. Gina began to flick over the pages of the Evening Standard and mark any details that could have a chance of turning a tidy profit at the bookies. They numbered about twenty facts and figures but none with the potential of the Wimbledon upset. Gina was re-energised. Singing along to a nineties pop tune on the radio, she jumped off her bed with a flourish and pogoed into the bathroom - where she stopped. Staring back at her from the wall mirror was the same face that she had examined last night. She cocked her head, pulled a couple of silly expressions and…

Right. Time to sort that as well, Ginapops.

Hi Saff. I need some advice . clothes and makeup stuff. Call me when you have a mo please babe. Ta Gina xx

Text sent, Gina quickly completed her ablutions that never took very long; still shorter this morning because she was on a mission to make the next tranche of income for Watersource.

An hour and two coffees later and Gina had her plan worked out. She would make a series of cash withdrawals totalling £10,000 from the Watersource bank account over the next three days to reduce the attention as much as possible. Time was short so she would also start placing the bets starting the next day by travelling a pre-planned route to a total of more than twenty bookmakers across all areas of London away from her home stomping ground. A branch of her bank had to be located close to every few bookies' premises so that she could pay the cash into the Watersource account as she received the pay-outs. She wasn't about to carry such large sums in cash any further than she needed. At each betting shop she would place winning bets on a variety of events and sports. To add to her smoke screen she would place some very small random bets that she assumed would lose. By her best guesses, her £10,000 would be worth well over a quarter of a million pounds once all the events had taken place.

What a buzz. I can't tell you. I could get used to this - or maybe I already have. It's better than sex... Well, maybe. I should give that a try again - just for research purpose, of course... Yeah right, chance'd be a fine thing.

Gina soon got into the rhythm of the process. Travelling by foot and public transport around her planned route across London during the next three days, making notes and filing the forty five winning and random bets, she started to realise that her default facial expression was a satisfied smile.

She was about to get on the third bus of the first day somewhere in south London when her phone rang and the name SAFFY appeared on the screen.

"Hi Saff."

"Hi you - how are you?"

"Great thanks - and you?"

"I'm in shock, to be honest, babe. You want my help to buy clothes and make up?"

"Yeah, can you do that for me?"

"Gosh Gee. I'd love to – what's brought this on?"

"Well, basically, I just thought I should make a bit of an effort now Watersource is becoming like, legit."

"When do you want to do it?"

"I'm busy for the next few days. How about this weekend? Is that okay?"

"Yes, fine by me. I'll call you Friday and you can tell me what's on your shopping list. We can go to Covent Garden….. No, I know, let's go to Chelsea. I haven't been there for ages and the West End will be awful on Saturday. I assume lunch will be on you now you're in the money."

What ? !!

"How do you mean? I'm not in any money." Gina was so abrupt that Safia was silent for a moment.

"Sorry, I thought you were raking in loads of funds for the charity since your TV thing."

"Yeah, you're right, it's going great. I'm sorry but I don't like, think of that money as mine. I'll call you Friday night to sort something for Saturday. Thanks Saff - that's great. Love you."

"You too."

Back on the trail. Five hours later, job done for the day and Gina sat in another tube carriage, exhausted from the unfamiliar day's activity, but experiencing a warm sense of satisfaction. Until a chilling thought then occurred to her.

What if it goes wrong? No, I won't think about that. I literally can't do anything about it now. And if it doesn't work, I still have a shit load more money than I could ever have imagined a month ago. So, time to worry about other things til all those bets have been won - or lost. End of.

Her attention was taken by her reflection in the train windows across the carriage. She stared for a moment then checked who else might be watching. No-one was. So she slowly adjusted her head from side to side. The distortion of the glass and the moving tunnel wall beyond, left the impression of the shape of Gina's head more than a mirror image.

That's not bad. Perhaps we can do something with you, Ginapopsickle.

16

The evening was balmy and unremarkable. A typical end to a hot summer day in London town. The noises and smells and atmosphere were reassuringly familiar. Dizzy should have been relaxed but that wasn't a mood that he allowed himself of late. And for good reason. Twice he had tried to call Charlie Bessick then sent texts, intending to discuss his debt, but all efforts had failed. Perhaps Mr B doubted Dizzy's sincerity or he was making a point by not communicating, but the effect was unnerving Dizzy.

He had been playing pool with a couple of new friends from the work parties and now walked an unfamiliar route back to his mother's high-rise flat that was only his part-time home recently. He was in the habit of varying his patterns so tonight he had been off his normal patch and making his way across a small park when ahead he saw a car pull up. Immediately he slowed his pace, suspicious about a car stopping across his route out of the park, albeit some hundred meters ahead.

He walked to the next intersection of paths and turned at right angles. The car pulled around the perimeter of the park and stopped at the exit gate ahead of Dizzy, but now less than fifty meters away.

Time to get out of here. He turned and fled the way he had come into the park but the car screeched into life and raced to block the gate that Dizzy was about to use to get away. He turned from the path and raced across the grass towards clumps of bushes in front of the railings that flanked the entire park.

Dizzy crashed through the foliage, barely aware that two men had left the car and were in fast pursuit. The car raced along the road to get to the point where Dizzy would meet the railings, so as he threw himself at them and pulled his frame up to the spikes at the top, the car and the two chasers all arrived at the same point at the same time. Dizzy had no chance. If he cleared the spikes, the driver was waiting but behind him two pairs of hands were around his legs and ankles. The two men had pounced. Outside, the driver checked the street before pulling a knife.

"Mr Bessick sends his regards – and this."

He stabbed the knife into one of Dizzy's knuckles that gripped the railings.

Dizzy released his grip and an agonised scream, until one of the men slammed a fist into his mouth and the other a boot into Dizzy's ribs.

The fight was beaten out of Dizzy in a few bloody moments.

17

Dear Ms Melina
You are cordially invited to attend the 5ᵗʰ Nograim CityZen Awards.

So began an email that Gina hardly noticed as she scrolled through her inbox, but within the hour, her phone rang and a chirpy lady's voice asked:

"Ms Melina?"

"Yes," Gina answered cautiously.

"Hello, my name is Delores, I do PR for the CityZen Awards sponsored by Nograim Foods. Have you heard of them?"

"I know of them, but nothing about them."

"No matter, but I'm delighted to inform yourself that you've been nominated as one of the four finalists for the international charity award. Many congratulations to yourself. I think one of our judging panel saw you on a TV programme and checked out your website. You've made a great impression with our judges - well done.

"I would make the point that year-on-year the CityZen awards are becoming extremely well-established and highly prestigious so will be very useful to yourself and your charity. This year they will be held at the Guild Hall here in London and we've got live coverage by Radio London and local TV News will be there, so that's a great opportunity to raise the profile of….Watersource. That is your charity isn't it?"

"Yes, that's right."

"Brilliant, so can I confirm that you'll be there on Thursday 23rd – later this month starting at six-o'clock in the evening?"

"Twenty-third? I don't know, let me come back to you. I think I saw an email from you, didn't I?"

"That's right. All the information is there or on our website. Please do come. I will call to confirm in a few days because we need people like yourself at this great event."

"Okay. I'll see. Thank you."

Gina tapped the name 'CityZen' into a search engine and arrived on an expansive website. The sponsor's bi-line: *'Eat Calm And Carry On'* raised a moment's concern but Gina's attitude changed when she scrolled through a gallery of photos and more impressive testimonials in which various award winners claimed that their companies' and personal profiles had benefitted immeasurably from their involvement with the awards. She skipped back to the photos of the prize-winners at previous events and recalled seeing some in the press – or were they familiar because all celebrities-at-events pictures look so similar? Whatever the reason, Gina found herself imagining an award, a photo, the resulting high profile for Watersource and for herself and that was very appealing. She had to admit that she had loved the attention created after her 7 O'Clock Show appearance and this could provide the next opportunity to attract attention to Watersource.

Hmmm. Twenty-third eh?.......... No issue with the date. I could make it. TV and radio will be there... Interesting.

Gina's thoughts were jerked away from the website and her diary by the chirruping of a text arriving on her phone beside her on her desk.

Hi Gee. I need 2 c you about the Kenya trip pls. Do you know if I can go pls. Diz.

Oh hell – where are we with this? I should have heard from Eric.

Gina picked up her phone and tapped a speed dial number.

"Hello."

"Eric, it's Gina Melina in London."

"Oh hi Gina … Oh dear, I was supposed to let you know about your friend and if I can use him, wasn't I? Sorry Gina, I clean forgot."

"Don't worry, so did I, but I have to give him an answer. I know he's desperate to help and he'll be great – really."

"Well if you pay all his travel costs and sort things at your end, we can certainly find him accommodation and he will be useful - no question - providing you vouch for him and he will be there to work, not sit around watching others doing it."

"I guarantee it - the hard-working bit, not the sitting around bit."

"Okay. If you can sort everything at your end, I'll sort it here. Oh Gina – he knows everything's very basic there, doesn't he – nothing fancy; same as his pay – you have made that clear haven't you?"

"Yeah, message received. Thanks Eric. I'll let you know our plans."

Hi Diz. Its sorted for you to go to Kenya but you hav to sort it at this end. Phone me when you have permision.

A few minutes later…

Great result. Thnx G. You R gt. I dont need nothing here if u r OK 4 me to go.

Gina was about to respond with another text, but pressed the call button instead.

"Hi Dizzy. Look, you have to sort it with the probation people. Basically, you need their permission to go or that could mean real problems when you try to leave the country, right? They won't let you fly."

"Okay," Dizzy replied in a very uncertain tone. "I'll talk to the lady today if I can get her."

"Do that and let me know – and check out what visas and jabs you….no, I'll do that. You just get her permission in writing – okay? You'll literally do that like, today right?"

"Yeah."

While it was fresh on Gina's mind, she spent the next hour on the Internet checking requirements for a work visa, injections, even the clothing that Dizzy would need when he arrived in Kenya. And the cost of flights. That was all straightforward so it was now over to Dizzy and his Probation Officer.

The fact was, Gina suddenly realised, that her life had made another major change during the last few weeks. She always seemed to have time now. Instead of racing at everything at the last minute, she was getting immensely greater results at a slower, more measured pace. This morning she had the time and nothing more pressing than to sort Dizzy's travel arrangements.

18

Dizzy took a chance and made his way to the Probation Office without an appointment. He was in luck; Kathy Rawlings was in an interview when he arrived but would be finished in a few minutes, or so Dizzy was informed by one of Ms Rawlings' colleagues.

"She's been in there for about half an hour so if you take a seat she won't be much longer."

Nor was she, emerging from a cell-like room a short time later. Dizzy jumped up and caught her attention before she could get back to her desk. He rattled off an explanation about the opportunity that he had been offered and gabbled a plea that the work in Kenya would be good for him and good for the people who he would be helping. It was an enthusiastic onslaught that left Ms Rawlings somewhat speechless when Dizzy finally stopped with:

"...so that would be good, wouldn't it? Can I go....please?"

"Well it's not that simple. There are procedures. I will have to make some checks and we will let you know."

"When?"

"As long as it takes. I don't know....Are you okay - have you been in a fight?"

Dizzy had forgotten about his bruised face, which was surprising because he was in constant pain and his swollen mouth distorted his speech.

"No."

But Ms Rawlings didn't hide her disbelief.

"So, you just walked into a door?"

"How long do you think because the people in Kenya want to know because they really need me there to 'elp now? Know what I mean?"

"Come to my desk and I'll take some notes and let's see what I can find out."

And that's what they did until Dizzy ran out of key contact details for his would-be employers in Kenya.

"I'll get them for you," Dizzy said urgently. "What else do you need?"

"Here, if you complete this form... and this one ... and this, then I will do what I can. I promise you that much, Daniel, but that's all because it's not going to be my decision."

"Yeah, thanks."

Dizzy wandered away with little optimism.

His apprehension was well-founded when the next afternoon he received a phone call from Kathy Rawlings informing him that the powers-that-be in her office had already declined his request.

"What?! I haven't got the forms back to you yet!" Dizzy was not too shocked to hide his disappointment. He shouted into his phone. "What d'you mean 'no'? What'm I supposed to do to better my fuckin' life? I thought this was good initiative and you'd think that was good. Fuck it!"

"Daniel – calm down. And if you swear at me again I'm going to put the phone down."

"Sorry Miss Rawlins, it's not you, it's...it's the f... f...friggin' system. I'm trying to help myself – that's how I saw this and I thought you people would think that's a good thing. What am I supposed to do?"

Something in his plea touched a nerve with Kathy Rawlings.

"Leave it with me, Daniel and I will see what I can do." With that, she was gone.

The first time Gina knew any of this was a few minutes later when her phone rang and a very downbeat Dizzy reported his lack of progress in an equally downbeat tone.

Gina was as upset as Dizzy.

"So, did they give a reason?"

"No, nothing."

"That's totally out of order. Ridiculous. Have you got a phone number for your lady?"

"No, they don't give private numbers."

"What's her name?"

"Kaffy Rawlins."

Gina wrote it on a pad on her desk.

"Let me call her and I'll get back to you."

"Thanks Gee."

To Gina's surprise she was put through to Kathy Rawlings' extension by an operator; and to her greater surprise, Ms Rawlings answered the phone. Gina introduced herself and explained the reason for her call in an artificially controlled voice that didn't betray her true anxiety or the irritation created by Dizzy's version of the story. Gina was cautious in case he had misunderstood the situation and she didn't want to create a problem by storming into his probation officer unduly. But Ms Rawlings confirmed the key points of Dizzy's sorry saga and the decision that had been made concerning his request for the work placement.

"So tell me this if you will please Ms Rawlings – what more is one of your charges supposed to do to help themselves – or to help you to help them? I assume you don't consider you're part of the prison service – Dizzy is not tagged or under house arrest, so how is keeping him captive, in effect, here in London, supposed to improve his situation when he's been offered a potentially life-changing experience? To help himself and to help possibly thousands of people in Kenya, eh? How's your actions supposed to help anyone?"

A moment of silence.

"I assume you *think* this call will help Mr Gillespie, but I can tell you you're wrong. We took his request seriously and discussed it in the team that know his record for drug-dealing, some other petty crimes and his violence and I believe he has been involved in a fight recently, judging by the state of his face today. And his left hand was heavily bandaged. All these factors were considered and that's what we based our decision on."

Gina had been thrown by the reference to a fight. She had no idea if it was true or not.

"........So if we have both made our situations clear, Miss Melini, I don't think there is more to discuss. I will say goodbye. Goodbye."

Gina immediately phoned Dizzy. She was still evidently upset.

"Have you been fighting?"

"What?"

"I have just been told by your probation lady that you've been beaten up? Is that right - have you been fighting?"

"Sort of....but it wasn't much of a fight."

"Bloody hell Dizzy. That was a great help, well done. Because I had no idea, I didn't know what to say when she just told me. Thanks for that"

"That's why I wanna get outa here. It was a warning from the guy I owe the money to."

"Well I think you've just fucked up, Dizzy. Like badly. I don't know what to tell you.....Leave it for now. Don't go back there til your next meeting date and then be on your very best behaviour, right? I'll try to think what we can do."

"Thanks Gee..... Sorry."

The problem must have been niggling Gina more than she realised until the next morning when, for the first time in several months, she woke with the memory of a dream fresh in her thoughts. Dizzy had ridden his bike into a quagmire on a moor. He was sinking but Gina couldn't get to him to help.

That didn't take much interpreting. Bollocks. I don't need this right now but I need to sort something for Dizzy.....silly sod that he is.

It niggled her all morning as she set about her daily routines, so imagine her shock when she answered her phone to:

"Is that Miss Melina?"

"Yes."

"Hello, my name's Tracy Rufina, I work for the Probation Office and I've been handed a file for Daniel Gillespie who I believe you know – is that correct?"

"Yes," Gina answered cautiously.

"Good, so I think you're up to date with his application to travel to Kenya to help with a charity with which you are involved – is that correct?"

"Yes, I think so...."

"Good. Well, I've checked into the credentials of your charity….. Watersource, which I have to say is very impressive."

"Thanks."

"…So if you can confirm to me that he will be travelling under your auspices and you will cover all related costs including providing accommodation and a salary, then I can give permission for him to travel........." And so the conversation continued.

Gina could not believe the result of the call as she hung up – or her excitement to tell Dizzy – or his burst of exuberance on hearing the news (although that should have been more predictable). She was overwhelmed by the feeling of relief and immediately began making plans with Eric for Dizzy's journey to a village called Nantuni, east of Nairobi, which would be his new home for the foreseeable future.

Huh – what a difference a day makes - twenty-four little hours.

19

The Kings Road, linking Chelsea and Fulham in central London, earned its reputation for fashion during London's swinging sixties when an eclectic mix of independent shops resided along its entire length, playing their role in the sixties fast-moving fashion scene. Times long gone, but still a good street to find a mix of fashions, provided these days by the multiples that can afford the rents.

Gina and Safia arrived on Saturday morning with a list of clothes that Gina thought she needed on her image-changing mission. Safia had reviewed the list on the train and replaced half the items with her suggestions. Since Gina had virtually no clothes-buying experience and Safia had more than enough for the two of them, Gina was only too happy to follow her friend's advice.

They had so much fun. For Gina, the experience was a novelty that she decided was long overdue immediately she witnessed her abrupt change of image in the first of the many shops they would visit today. For Safia, the exercise of spending someone else's money on clothes was second only to being given the funds to buy her own.

The experience was so unfamiliar to Gina that all aspects of the adventure brought surprises. The price of clothes was truly shocking, the energy that the process sapped and Safia's suitability for the task were revelations.

She had obviously given the trip and my needs so much consideration. Literally, I couldn't have done the trip without her. Well, not to get anything like the same result in one day. Safia was brilliant. She had literally researched the shops to work out where we go as soon as we left the underground. And she thought of things that I would never have considered. Like underwear and make-up. Ha, she was brilliant, basically.

Gina was also very pleasantly surprised by the passing glances she was attracting after wearing a new raincoat and some Dandy-Rock ankle boots out of one of the shops. Even as she re-educated her posture after years of shuffling in her beloved Doc Martens. And when she and Safia ducked into a small bistro out of the drizzle to stop for some lunch, she was convinced that a group of teenagers watched her make her way to an empty table while Safia made haste to the toilets. Gina reflected on the attention and had to reluctantly admit to herself that she was revelling in it.

That was the greatest surprise of the day. I loved being noticed......And attractive....... And girlie, for want of a better expression. How about that then, Ginapops? Never thought you'd hear yourself admit that, did you?

By mid-afternoon, both ladies were almost burnt out, so sitting in the perfume department of a large department store while an over-fake-tanned lady in a white uniform gave Gina a facial makeover, was very welcome. She just let the lady work under Safia's direction.
Another transformation. Gina loved the face looking back at her in the hand-held mirror. And at that point Safia had a fresh idea.
"You need a new hair style."
"What?"
"Yeah, really Gee. It's totally obvious. That would be the final touch – essential. It'll be a tall order without a booking on a Saturday but we could get lucky."
And they did, at the second hairdressers they tried just off the main road.

If Gina had thought that her new wardrobe had achieved her wildest ambitions for her self-esteem, the new hair style surpassed it by an unimaginable distance. For most of her adult life, Gina had cut her own hair into its post-punk spikey style, although even Gina wouldn't have used the word 'style' to describe it. At *'Heady Daze'* off the Kings Road, Sonya assessed Gina's hair from a few angles before she announced that she advised Gina to have an urchin cut.

"You have such a lovely elfin shaped 'ead, darling, that you can take it. So on-trend since Candy Ravel had one. It'll look fabulous on you."

Gina and Safia exchanged approving, if bemused, glances which Sonya noticed.

"Right then, let's get started."

An hour and £75 later Gina was in shock – marginally more at the staggering effect than the staggering cost. Her appearance had been transformed and she could not have been more delighted with the result.

Safia didn't recognise the very pretty lady standing in front of her when Gina went back to the reception to collect her friend.

"Good God, Gee !.... I can't believe that's you. Huh....... You look fantastic......Look at you."

And Gina felt as well as she looked.

Immediately she arrived back at her flat she started trying on her new wardrobe. She relocated the one large mirror that she owned and propped it on her sofa bed to show her torso. Everything that she tried on brought another smile; mostly at the transformation of her own image. The final outfit was to be for the awards event which brought the task of finding her 'plus one' partner for the evening back to her thoughts.

She found six eligible companions in her address book and composed a group email invitation with a connection to the CityZen website.

During the course of the next two days, she received four responses, but none of them was the one she wanted. After her initial disappointment, she decided it was time to put Guy out of her mind and future plans. That should not be too difficult, she reasoned, with so many distractions in her life right now.

Only a vague acquaintance called Solomon, admitted to being available on the night of the awards. His acceptance was charming and chivalrous. He would be delighted to accompany Gina to the event and suggested that he pick her up by taxi because her flat was between his house and the venue in the City of London.

The pair only knew one another through a part time job when they both served in a Rialto Coffee Emporium two Christmases ago. They subsequently exchanged bits of news infrequently and Solomon always remembered Gina's birthday (which she didn't reciprocate) but they otherwise had had no contact for almost two years. Gina was glad of the offer of company and the more she thought about the Solomon whom she had met at the coffee shop, the more she started to look forward to this almost blind date.

20

The speed with which Dizzy's affairs were sorted with the Probation Service was surprisingly brisk. Within a few days, his visa and all the plans were in place. Gina had bought an open return airline ticket to Nairobi. His accommodation was never likely to be a problem, but Gina did worry about what Dizzy would find in rural Kenya – certainly nothing akin to his life in London, but Gina reasoned that this was part of its attraction.

I just hope that's how it looks to him when he gets there .... Oh well, you know what? I can't do more – it's literally over to you now Dizzy.

Dizzy hadn't seen the new-look Gina until he dropped over to her flat to say goodbye the day before his departure. His reaction when Gina answered the door was akin to frozen fear. He was paralysed for several seconds, staring at her, taking in the face and persona of someone he barely recognised. He said nothing until...

"Holy-moly, Gee.... you look... different." Then he rushed to add: "A good *different*, I mean. You look well fit, Gee."

"Thanks Dizzy. I thought it was time for a change, basically. Come in."

Gina fiddled with a cup of Earl Grey tea while Dizzy fumbled somewhat incoherently to say goodbye and how grateful he was for everything that Gina had done for him.

"I don't mean just getting me the work in Kenya, I mean how you like, changed my way of looking at me and my life and what I can do with it. I don't think you quite know how much difference you've made to me, Gee, and I want you to know that."

"Thank you Dizzy. That's like, reward enough, just knowing all that. Now you have to make a success of this next bit of your life story, yeah?"

"Yeah – and I will, I promise you that."

This was a natural place for him to make his exit, but he evidently had something more to say, or do.

"Gee, I wanted to get you a present but you know I don't have no money so ....well, I got you this card and wrote you a poem to say my thanks and to show that I really care 'bout what you done for me. It seems a bit silly now, but anyone can buy chocolates an' stuff, but I think a poem is more like, special. I hope you like it." He awkwardly handed Gina a card in an envelope.

Gina looked down on Dizzy's outstretched hand as tears arrived in her eyes. She took it then pulled Dizzy's arm until they embraced for only the second time since they met all those months and adventures ago.

Gina took a moment to gain enough composure to break away.

"Dizzy, you are special – you're a darling - you remember that. I'll treasure this and the memories of the shy person I met earlier this year, one day when I'm reading news about how you've succeeded at something or other. You will, I know you will make something – no, you're going to make *a lot* of your life from here on, I just know it."

Gina stopped for long enough for the pair to exchange true affection in their smiles.

"Go on now. I want to read this when I'm alone because I think it'll set me off again."

Gina reached up and cradled his large face in her right hand for a moment. Dizzy smiled his 'goodbye' and turned away down the stairs for the last time.

Gina pulled the card from its envelope when she heard the front door close. The atmosphere had already changed and she was dispassionate when she read his poem. It brought a sympathetic smile until the last lines that were confusing. Was she reading more into it than Dizzy intended or was this a coded message?

I was lost in darkness when you rose in my east
Spredding warmth in the chill of my frosted life
Melting me.
Enlitening me.
I was looking for something that was outside my
reech
Beyond me, but not you.
Hot you.
Spreading mid summer heat
In a flash
A crash
You saw the future
For me and for you

Gee - THANK YOU is to small for
what I ow you.

Dizzy X

Gina reread the words repeatedly and was about to text Dizzy until she couldn't think what to write, so she decided that it was best to do nothing.

21

Wimbledon Tennis Championships arrived with a day of summer thunder storms. It crossed Gina's mind that it might be an omen for the week ahead; a week in which her gambles would realise a fortune or wash away some £10,000.

Exciting though.

Gina realised that she had been distracted from Watersource of late.

Well, apart from all Dizzy's shenanigans, but yes, the daily affairs have slipped a bit. And there's some issues I need to sort out, basically, but by this time next week .....O-M-bloody-G.... can you imagine what a quarter of a million quid will buy? Two of the biggest purification systems – that's what – with money to spare. That's going to be quite a welcome present for Dizzy's arrival in Nantuni.

The game was scheduled for the third day of the tournament and would be televised live. Gina was ensconced in front of her TV the next afternoon and flicked between the BBC channels to find the match that would result in an enormous pay-out.

I was surprisingly nervous to start with, but you know what? By the end of the first set when I realised the game was going exactly as it was reported in the Evening Standard, I don't think a smile left my face for about an hour, basically. It literally just happened in front of me. I can't tell you how made up I was. As the commentators became so excited about the upset, I just watched it unfold like the paper said.

By the end of the afternoon....

It was job done. None of the other bets mattered then because I'd just won £250,000. Aaaaaaah! Unreal!

Within a few days, all her bets did exactly what was planned and prophesied; all apart from two of the bogus small bets that she only placed to create a smoke screen, but instead of losing, they won £43. It amused Gina who by then was in a daze of confusion combined with a sense of inevitability. She had no control over the premonitions, but she took credit for maximising the opportunities they were offering.

Gina now began to think about her return on these 'investments' as she started to consider them. She had taken the risk that had paid off, so she was entitled to keep some of the money. This was a new sensation – a fresh viewpoint that had never occurred to her previously. And the thought excited her.

Even with Gina's very limited experience of betting odds, a little time spent tapping the numbers from the betting slips into a calculator confirmed that the winnings would be more than £260,000.

Unreal. I can't wait to tell Eric that I can fund two new middle sized systems.

Only then did Gina realise that she would need to keep some of the winnings to make new investments if and when the next opportunity presented itself.

Of course. How stupid. Basically I need to keep a lot of the money so that I can make it into more. But I can buy one of the largest units and pay for it to be shipped. I'll get Eric to involve Dizzy with its installation – yes that'll get him involved as soon as he gets there. That'll be great.

Gina spoke to Eric about supplying one large system. He was thrilled and only too pleased to agree to Gina's request that Dizzy help supervise its installation so that he was useful immediately he arrived on site.

Eric promised to calculate the total cost so that Gina could move the funds.

An hour later Eric emailed the total. It took Gina a few minutes to calculate that the payment would leave more than £210,000 in the account. Gina stared at the total in near-disbelief.

22

As Gina prepared for her night at the awards, she tried to recall the last time that she had been excited by the getting-dressed-up procedure. It was a long time ago – perhaps when she was a teenager. But now she was enjoying every part of the process – even washing her hair that she normally hated, but with so little to dry, the task took less than half an hour. Then on with her make-up as she had been instructed by Safia and the lady in the Chelsea store; and finally getting dressed in her crisply-ironed dress. The first time she had seen the total look without labels hanging from her outfits.

And I loved it. I can't tell you the joy this gave me. And confidence that whatever happened this evening, I was ready for it. Oh yesssss.
Bring it on.

If that wasn't enough, when Solomon arrived at her door his evident shock at his first sight of Gina served to reinforce her confidence.

And some. He was so charming ... and lovely .... and very complimentary. I'd forgotten that he's quite a good looking bloke in a quirky way. Not sure about the pony tail ..... hark at me, suddenly I'm Miss Fashionista. But this had all the makings of a very good night out.

As it proved to be. From the moment the taxi pulled up at the venue, to the return journey home, the evening could not have been more perfect for Gina. She had thought a lot about what would happen at an awards show, but with no experience other than watching such events on television, she was intrigued to see it first hand from the viewpoint of a short-listed award winner.

Gina need not have worried. Whenever she was unsure, Solomon was there with his support. He was the perfect escort, apart from the attention he attracted from male and female guests.

He can't help being attractive. And after all the flirting, he was with me, so that was okay ….. Very okay.

Eventually, after the Champagne reception and meal, the awards ceremony was hosted by a cable TV newsreader; or so Gina was told when she asked if she should recognise her. But she was very professional and confident and did a great job of maintaining interest in each of the ten categories.

The International Charity Award was near the bottom of the list and as we got closer I started to get so nervous that I desperately needed a pee. I timed one of the awards to work out if the next three would allow me to get to the loo and back, basically. I decided I had the time, but I didn't think about any waiting time for a cubicle so my heart sank when I found two ladies in a queue when I got into the loo. By now I was so desperate that I dare not go back without emptying my bladder. Fortunately one of them offered to let me go ahead of her when she saw that I was uncomfortable but only when the other lady had shot into a vacant cubicle after someone left it.
I raced through …. anyway, let's just say I hurried as fast as possible but when I got back in the room I noticed Solomon was agitated and as I took my seat I heard the TV lady say: "…….. Gina Melina of Watersource."
There was a lot of applause and some whooping and Solomon pushed me out of my seat.

"You've won. Go on – collect the award."

I sort of composed myself and made my way through tables and got to the stage for a man from the sponsor company to hand me the award that was like, really heavy. I thought I could smile for a photo then get back to my seat but the man said that I should say something and gestured to the podium. So I turned to look at the audience but the lights were literally so bright I could only see the people on the front tables. I had thought about a speech in case I had the chance to mention Watersource for the radio and TV coverage, but now I wish I'd rehearsed it more. My heart was in my throat and my mouth was dry with a sudden hit of nerves. Shit.

The audience saw a composed Gina handling the situation with more ease than she was feeling.

"Um....I have literally, so many people to thank, but mostly the wonderful British public that must have like, the biggest hearts in the whole world, basically. I'm amazed how generous the Brits can be when like, disaster strikes anywhere in the world. Literally, the disasters that my charity, Watersource, is sorting out's not like, short term so they don't get in the news headlines, but we are tackling the need for clean water in Africa where like, two million people die literally, every year from water-borne diseases, basically. So with the public's continual support, we are literally doing our tiny little bit to like, help reduce those tragedies. So thank you very much for this award and recognition."

More applause. Was it even louder than previously? Solomon insisted so when he welcomed Gina back to their table with a broad smile and evident pride. Gina was still shaking with nerves.

The public relations lady arrived soon afterwards to congratulate Gina before whisking her away for photos with the other winners, posing with their trophies in front of the sponsor's logo.

Then the BBC had booked her for an interview for radio followed by one for local TV. It was all rather hectic back stage but Gina had calmed her nerves so managed to mention Watersource at every opportunity.

By the time she returned to her table she was reflecting on what she thought was a good evening's work with the media. But it wasn't over and she wondered how it would develop with the highly attentive Solomon. Thoughts of another date with him had crossed her mind several times during the evening, but she was not going to embarrass herself by taking the initiative if he wasn't forthcoming.

Okay, old fashioned, I know, but so be it. Less embarrassing than a rejection and I'm not like, that confident yet.

When Solomon kissed her on the cheek at her front door before getting back into the cab for his journey home, Gina was none the wiser about his intentions. He could be in little doubt about Gina's, however, when, after more wine than she would ever consume in one evening in normal circumstances, Gina's flirting became the source of some shame when she woke the following morning and reflected on her night out.

Oh dear ..... And I was trying to avoid embarrassment. Huh. I need to thank Solomon and apologise. I'll do that later.

She knew that this was the ideal excuse to contact him again and as she contemplated that thought, she was aware of how she was changing in more ways than her make-over portrayed. She had never given men more than a cursory passing interest – considering them to be an unexciting distraction from her true passions. But now, Guy had left his mark and she was starting the day by calculating how to get back in touch with her escort from last night.

Last night. That was such fun. Solomon was such a gentleman – the perfect escort .... Not Guy, but .... great.

She pondered that though for a moment until she realised how pointless it was then scrambled out of bed to retrieve the trophy from the kitchen table where it had unceremoniously spent the night surrounded by detritus from the event. Gina took it through to her bedroom (as it was at nine-o'clock on a Saturday morning) and placed it on a book shelf.

Perfect.

She decided.

By mid-morning, Solomon had come into Gina's thoughts so frequently that she decided to call him. She should thank him and a text or email was a little impersonal – or so she convinced herself.

In for a penny, Ginapops.

Solomon's number rang too many times, so Gina was expecting to leave a message just before he eventually picked up, except it wasn't Solomon. Another man's croaky voice answered:
"Hello, Solomon's phone."
"Hello." In that moment, Gina wanted to hang up but pressed on. "Is Solomon there, please?"
"Yes." Then the voice became muted, but Gina could just hear: "Are you awake? It's someone for you....Yeah, here on your phone."
"Hello." The voice was barely discernible as Solomon's.
"Solomon? Sorry, this is obviously bad timing. It's Gina – I just phoned to thank you for last night, but I will go – I'm sorry, I've obviously woken you."

"Gina – no, please it's no problem – it's lovely of you to call. It was a lot of fun. Thank you for inviting me. I will call you when we can get together again soon."

"Yes, that'll be nice. Sorry again for waking you. Bye."

"Bye."

Shit!

Gina chuckled to herself when she thought about the telephone conversation as she made coffee later and reflected on any tell-tale signs suggesting that she had probably not been Solomon's main sexual interest last night. Perhaps the looks that he had received from those other men were *initiated* by Solomon. No matter. It was of no importance now.

Gina had the perfect distraction. She had to plan the process of collecting her Wimbledon and other winnings that would be waiting at betting shops around London. She had deliberately put off the task, worrying about what reception could be waiting for her at each or any of the bookies. The more she thought about how to repatriate a total of more than a quarter of a million pounds, the more the task took on the character of a military operation. The timing; the route; what to wear; what to say if challenged; or just, what to say about winning a lot of thousands of pounds.

By lunchtime, Gina had assembled all the weapons that she could identify. *Operation Cash Collection* would begin on Monday.

23

Gina had a very bad night's sleep, disrupted by waking repeatedly during the night and sleeping lightly between, so when her alarm finally woke her at eight-o'clock she would have preferred to go back to sleep, but she was on manoeuvres in an hour so she struggled into life with a fresh coffee as she washed then dressed in drab clothes that wouldn't attract attention, topped with an old stoker's cap with a peak to hide her face from surveillance cameras in the bookies. She put an alternative jacket and a selection of baseball caps in a rucksack to change her appearance during the morning as she visited different branches of the same bookmaker chains.

I had no idea if all this planning was overkill, but there was no harm in taking sensible precautions to be as anonymous as possible, basically. I wasn't like, doing anything illegal, but the last thing I wanted was for someone to challenge me for literally knowing about the results before they happened.

She checked everything for a second time, reasoning that this is what anyone on a military exercise should do.

Right, 'time to stop spitting on the handle and get on with the digging' as my grandad used to say.

Gina was wide awake and starting to enjoy the prospect of the enormous windfall when she entered the first bookmaker's premises. Her nerves were apparent when she handed over her slip and waited for the money to be produced, but it went to plan without a hitch, as did the next six of the morning. The first scheduled bank drop came after Gina's third collection by which time the haul had totalled almost £20,000. She deposited it in a branch of her bank in Streatham, but that took longer than she had planned, so Gina worried about the time the process would take to complete. That was the least of her problems during the afternoon at the thirteenth bookie on her list.

The now-familiar routine began well with the usual exclamation from the teller at the size of the win, followed by his request that Gina to wait by another window while his manager retrieved the winnings from the safe. At which point, to Gina's shock, the manager arriving with bundles of cash was none other than one of the ladies from her local bookie in Camden who had paid her the winnings for her Coombridge bet.

I was paralysed for a moment. My instinct was to fain illness and leave but I couldn't because they had my winning slip and that was worth more that £5,000. But my new look – she won't recognise me....

Except Gina had covered her new hair style with a baseball cap and was wearing her old cloths, so her make-over wasn't evident.

Shit, you're right.
I did my best to avoid her eyes but she seemed to want to see mine so it was only a matter of time before...

"I know you don't I?"
"Probably, I come here a lot."

I was speaking with a sort Irish-Scottish accent. Where the hell did that come from?

"Really, but I've just been moved to this branch. Don't I know you from Camden?"
"Camden? No, never been there – it's out west ain't it?"

"North London."

"Uh-huh. Do you mind if we do this so we don't attract attention?"

"Yes of course, sorry."

The manager completed the rest of the transaction in silence, but it was clear that she was still trying to place Gina as she passed an envelope containing the bundles of notes under the reinforced glass screen.

Gina slipped the envelope into her rucksack and checked the room before leaving. What neither ladies noticed was the elderly gentleman, sitting nearby peering at the sports pages of a Daily Mirror newspaper whilst listening to the conversation. He now folded the paper abruptly and followed Gina out of the betting shop without drawing her attention that was still reeling from the encounter with the cashier.

That just freaked me out. I felt like a criminal. When I got out of the shop I needed some time to catch my breath and calm down. My notes showed that there was another bookie nearby in the same road before I had to do another bank drop at a branch literally at the end of the same street. I didn't feel like going into another bookies, but what are the chances of that happening again? Literally zero, basically. Okay, let's do the next one then the bank drop then I'll stop for lunch.

Gina was still shaken when she entered the next bookies, but to her relief, it went to plan and after some pre-rehearsed banter about how she was winning back the money she had spent there over the years, she left the shop with another envelope of cash. Almost. In fact she didn't quite leave the premises because her exit was blocked at the door by the elderly man from the previous bookies. Gina had no idea who he was or why he was deliberately standing in her way. In the moment it took to assess the situation, she realised that he was holding his mobile phone full in her face to photograph her. In that split second, Gina dropped her head and forced her way past him.

"Pervert!"

She shouted so loudly that people on the pavement turned to see who was shouting at whom. That might have been the reason that the man made no effort to pursue her, but stayed anchored as Gina scurried away. She was so shaken that she sat in the bank at the end of the road, composing herself while filling in another paying in slip for her latest total from four more collections.

You know what? I'm starting not to enjoy this. What was that last dickhead all about? Hopefully just an oddball who takes photos of people in the street. Yeah, perhaps that's it – a nutter.

The more Gina considered the events of the morning, the more she had to conclude that she was creating the drama, almost certainly because she was so sensitive about how she had won such an enormous sum of money.

Why am I feeling so guilty literally, all the time? I'm trying to help people who need it for God's sake, but I just feel so guilty at having all this money because something weird's happened that I couldn't control – can't control. I'd normally not like, let a nutter in the street upset me. God knows I've had enough practise, but this one freaked me because I'm .... well, because I'm feeling so guilty, I suppose. I totally didn't ask for it to happen but now it has, I'm making the best of this weird situation. What else should I do? What if I literally passed up the opportunity to make the money that'll make such a difference – what then? Now that would be a sin.

Nothing about this process or my life lately is what I'd call like, 'normal'. At times I know I'm having trouble identifying normal. I'm doing 'weird' pretty well now –

*that's what my life has become ... Weird's the new normal
for me.*

After banking the last tranche of winnings and buying an egg on
toast lunch in a local café, Gina felt more like continuing with her
mission. She would have preferred to go straight home, but there
were only two more bookies to visit in this area then she need not
come back this far south. So she steeled herself and set off re-
energised.

To her relief, the rest of the afternoon and the next two days followed
a pattern without upsets akin to the earlier problems. By the end of
the entire exercise, Gina totalled the winnings minus the losers:
£268,612.00.

Result!

24

Dizzy's journey to Nantuni was long, but straightforward. He took a direct overnight flight from London to Nairobi where a man called Tambo would meet him.

As Dizzy left customs, Tambo was standing with a hand-written sign: 'MR DIZY' that he missed on first passing. That brief panic over, Tambo drove them both back to Nantuni that was the current centre of local Watersource operations.

Everyone in the village seemed to be aware and excited that Dizzy was coming, but a variety of stories had arrived ahead of him. He was a member of the British royal family; a millionaire philanthropist coming to see how his money is being spent; and a mix of all the stories combined with some nonsense about building an airport for the village.

Dizzy heard them during the next few days and relished the friendly banter that made him feel welcome and comfortable in the company of the locals. More so than his accommodation that was basic in the extreme and made him wonder what a true member of the British royal family would have thought about his corrugated metal hut without running water and the crudest of toilet facilities. But the good outweighed the less-than-good by such a margin that Dizzy adapted within days, sorting his few possessions to make his hut feel as homely as possible. One day's travel but a million miles from his life in London and just what he had hoped and needed.

He was there to work and was well prepared to get stuck in with a shovel or pickaxe, but that was not to be. Tambo and his wife, Shani, were supervising the installation of one of the smaller Watersource purification units, but as soon as Dizzy was shown around the site, even to his untrained eyes, he identified inconsistencies in the way that the makeshift workforce was handling the task. At first, as the new boy on the site, he was reluctant to say too much, but it quickly became apparent that Tambo and Shani were expecting Dizzy to provide advice. That gave him licence to voice his concerns to a point at which his knowledge ended. He needed to do some research.

The most precious possession in the village was a single satellite telephone which was evidently for emergencies only, due to the cost of using it. Dizzy authorised payment for its use to be taken from the Watersource budget so that he could speak to the manufacturers of the new purification system to get advice about its installation. That call was invaluable and accelerated the work threefold. Dizzy knew exactly what to do and with so much ready and willing labour at hand, Dizzy could sort a work schedule for the entire installation.

He would later report to Gina and advise that sending the money or the modular systems without the infrastructure to get them installed properly was madness; and wasteful. It had to stop, so he volunteered to visit the other two local sites over time, to check on progress to ensure that Watersource's and other charity funds were being used efficiently.

25

In London, Gina was riding the wave of fresh interest in her and Watersource since receiving the award. Not the same scale as that following her 7 O'Clock Show appearance, but an appreciable influx of emails, website hits and, most important, funds.

I should be getting used to the power of celebrity but it still surprises me how it works so well. And with social media, it's so fast. Literally, a few blogs and tweets and Watersource gets like, instant funds. Ha, it's fantastic.

Gina was musing whilst sitting at her desk forwarding the link to the local TV coverage of the awards evening, to all the press outlets in her address book. She then thought to check the radio coverage and couldn't believe her luck when she found that her acceptance speech could be played in full. She ran it:

"Um….I have literally, so many people to thank, but mostly the wonderful British public that must have like, the biggest hearts in the whole world, basically. I'm amazed how generous the Brits can be when like, disaster strikes anywhere in the world. Literally, the disasters that my charity, Watersource, is sorting out's not like, short term so they don't get in the news headlines, but we are tackling the need for clean water in Africa where like, two million people die literally, every year from water-borne diseases, basically. So with the public's continual support, we are literally doing our

tiny little bit to like, help reduce those tragedies. So thank you very much for this award and recognition."

As it played, her expression changed from mild amusement to concern. She played it again.

I had no idea I sound so ... so juvenile, really. All those 'likes' and 'basicallys' - that's crap. It's so strange that we photograph our lives – and video bits – so we know what we look like but I've never heard myself speak....well, you know what I mean – not formally, like that. I didn't know I sound like that or speak like, so badly.

She played it once more, by which time she had her head in her hands and added 'literally' to her *words-to-be-banned-for-the-future* list. She was too embarrassed to forward a link to the speech and decided in those few minutes to make an effort to sound more 'grown up' as she phrased the process of ridding her speech of oddities.

Her thoughts were tugged away from her self-castigation when a text dinged onto her phone and the name GUY showed on the screen.

Guy? Bloody hell! I was really made up to see his name, of course, but I shocked myself at the reaction it like, gave me. Oops. I said 'like'.

Hi Gina. Saw your award in the paper. Brilliant well done. Hardly recognized your new look photo but its great. Should celebrate with a drink sometime soon if your free. Best Guy

Hi yourself. Thanks. Yes free as a bird lets do that. G

Now what? Should I have suggested a date like, this week – bugger, that was a 'like'.

110

Her phone rang and the name GUY again displayed on the screen.

"Hi Guy."

"Hi, is this convenient?"

"Yeah - yeah, it's good, I'm working at home."

"Counting all the funds coming in, I hope. Congratulations on the award. I saw the coverage in the paper and looked it up on our local news. That was so cool. You did brilliantly – well done."

"Thanks. How are you - how's your flat-hunting?"

"Don't ask. Badly. The Brixton flat-share fell through."

"You'll find somewhere, won't you?"

"Yeah – it'll be fine…..It hasn't helped that I've been out of circulation for a while. A bit distracted, because my gran died."

"Oh no. I'm so sorry."

"Yeah, thanks. She was only in her seventies. Some form of heart attack. Tragic."

"That's awful. I know what she meant to you, Guy - I'm so sorry."

"Yeah – thanks." Then he changed gear. "But, life must go on – what d'you think about a drink some time?"

"Love to – if you want to do that. When? Not too far ahead because I can't plan too far ahead these days."

I hope that doesn't sound as obvious to him as it does to me.

"Okay then, how about Thursday this week?"

"That'll be good."

"Cool. I'll check during the day and if you're still okay, we can sort somewhere for the evening."

"Yep, that's fine."

"Must go – catch up then, then."

"Yep – and sorry again about your gran. Bye."

Gina felt a mix of emotions – and a reassurance that Guy's loss might account for his recent absence. She became aware of a warm feeling that she hadn't felt since her last date with Guy. That hadn't

111

gone to Gina's plan, so she should keep her expectations in check this time. Instinctively, she left her desk and ducked into the bathroom where she checked her appearance in the mirror.

Yeah, that's not too bad.... Well, a good start for Thursday. A helluva lot better start than the last time we went out, at least.

It was later the same afternoon that the email arrived. The email that would trigger a series of events with a lasting impact on Gina's life. It may have been sitting in the Watersource inbox for a while when Gina eventually noticed it with two attachments from 'L Sid'.

Subject: **'Streatham High Rd 28th July'**

It took a moment to register. Then it did and Gina felt the grip of fear in that instant. She would normally not have opened such a cryptic email, assuming that it was a phishing scam, but she immediately knew the significance of this more dangerous mail. And so it proved when she opened the attachments to find two photos showing her entering and leaving one of the bookmakers in Streatham three days earlier. She was unrecognisable in the wider view that showed a figure in fatigues wearing a baseball cap entering a well-known bookmaker's premises, but the close-up shot of the very same figure was unmistakably Gina in the doorway of the same bookie's shop. It was the photo taken by the elderly stalker who had followed her when she was collecting her winnings.

Gina sat back in her desk chair and stared at the photos for several minutes while she tried to assess the full significance of the pictures and the resulting impact of the revelation that Gina had been gambling with charity money.

I had no doubt this was blackmail. I just assumed that was a fact – but maybe not. I tried to imagine there was some other reason for this bloke, L Sid, sending me the photos and using the location and date to catch my attention ... No, this has to be like, some sort of blackmail. Fuck it! Fuck – fuck – fuck it!

So, how will that work? 'You give me money or I take them to the press who will pay for a story about award-winning charity-organiser gambling with charity money'. *But how can he prove I was using charity money? He can't ..... can he? But smoke and fire and all that – at the end of the day, mud sticks. They'll make a story – that's what papers do ..... Shit it!*

I could deny all knowledge – so, this person in the photos just happens to look like me .... yeah, that could work. He can't prove it's me.

Gina looked at the close up photo and her optimism dissolved. It was such a clear view that she knew that this would be a very difficult defence.

But not impossible. You know what? He would have to prove it's me and not someone who looks like me. I'm innocent until he like, proves beyond doubt that these are photos of me, basically.

The longer Gina thought about this defence, the calmer she became. She was still shaken, but the initial impact had softened a little. Now she had nothing more to do until L Sid got back in touch. So, move on.

26

My day starts with a cup of Earl Grey tea and a think. Sometimes in the opposite order if I can't be bothered to get out of bed to make the tea. But the thinking time for me to plan my day in my head is a habit of old. Usually as I stare at the ceiling.

So, my schedule was due to be uneventful – the usual like, business .... oops .... The usual business stuff for Watersource then my drink with Guy. That's great.... well, I hope so. I decided not to get my hopes high after my last outing with him – that wonderful evening of unbounded fun and merriment and uncontrolled exuberance, checking a flat followed by a single drink. So tonight could be the same, especially if poor Guy is still upset about his gran. At least I have an excuse to get myself made up with one of my new outfits.

Gina pondered that thought for a while, contemplating her options for her look for the evening.

Her day then took the pattern that she expected. Nothing too demanding. Keeping her social media identity and press releases updated, then clearing incoming emails to Watersource always took longer than she expected but most of the correspondence was positive and supportive and a pleasure to read; but not all. And mid-morning one such email arrived with a subject that changed Gina's mood in a moment.

'Streatham High Rd 28th July'

Oh no! I didn't want to open it but knew I had to, basically. Get it over with.

Gina clicked it open with a sudden flourish.

You won over 60k on a horse in the ascot gold cup the manager remembers you in camden. And you a charity. Good story for the papers unles you speak to me.   Sid

That was all it contained. But that was all it needed to hit Gina with such impact that she froze with chilled dread. She closed the email and looked away, not wanting to see the words or absorb the meaning. But she had. And it frightened her. A lot.

What would I do if that wasn't me in the photo? How would I react? Would I react or just bin it? I think I would ignore it – a nutter who thinks I'm someone else basically. He doesn't even know that I've opened it .... does he? No, he can't do. So, if I do nothing - just bin it - what will he do next?

With that thought, Gina immediately deleted the email along with the previous photographs. The act had a surprisingly cathartic effect. Gone - for the moment at least. She knew it wasn't the end of the matter but right now she could ignore it because there was nothing to remind her that a blackmailer had tracked her down and meant to do her harm.

A more immediate problem became apparent about lunchtime when Gina felt the unmistakable warning signs of a migraine. She only gets them very rarely these days but the signs were all too apparent. She had never worked out what caused them during the years that they were so frequent, but she had perfected a formula of antidotes to reduce their impact. That began with a particular herbal tea that Gina kept *'just in case'*. It was a bit old and dry but hopefully it would still work as a first line of defence. Gina drank two large mugsful during the next hour but the symptoms demanded her second plan of attack – two pain-killers, a hot bath and a strong spliff. Gina's use of drugs was now so infrequent that she barely remembered where she kept the remains of a stash of marijuana resin. She made the spliff very strong to compensate for the age of the hashish. And the process seemed to work.

Thank goodness. As I lay in the hot bath the pressure literally drifted away. With a lot of other pressures I think. I forgot what a nice feeling a spliff can make and this one in the bath was exactly what the doctor ordered.

Gina laughed aloud.

Can you imagine?.... " Well Miss Melina I recommend a course of marijuana for you. Here's a prescription." .... *They should – this is brilliant.*

She was at peace. Total relief. The migraine was replaced with a spacy drift towards sleep.

Gina woke with a start in barely-warm water almost an hour later. She summoned her thoughts but she was still dazed. Very dazed. And she was now running late.

That was the least of my problems. I was totally spaced out when I tried to stand up. Maybe I stood to get out of the bath too fast but I was all over the place.

Gina wrapped herself in a towel and sat on a stool in the bathroom with her head down until her senses felt more controllable. Then she slowly uncoiled and stretched her neck….and felt better.

Well enough to make the date with Guy, that's the important thing ….. er, where? We haven't arranged that …. Or what time.

Gina checked her phone for texts. Nothing from Guy. Then her emails and there was a short note suggesting:

Trappers at 6.45, is that good for you.

Gina responded and was about to close her emails for the afternoon when one amongst the many caught her attention.

Subject: **Advance notice for Watersource funding**

And below it:

Only open the attachment in private.
This top tip is for you alone, Gina. With a little effort, it will lead to your next opportunity to raise money for Watersource.

That subject line and short message were enough to catch Gina's attention and prevent her from deleting what could so easily have been a scam.

It can wait. Probably a scam. I'm not in the mood to think about it now.

She closed it down and prepared to make ready for her date while still suffering the effects of the pain killers and marijuana combination, but without the nagging pressure of a migraine. That at least was gone.

Gina studied her reflection in the bathroom mirror as she applied lip balm and approved the image that smiled back at her.

I just hope Guy does. If not, well, it won't be for my lack of effort. Careful Ginapops, you are becoming obsessed. And if your new look's the only reason he fancies you, what then? Is that the sort of man you want in your life, eh? .... Well, is it? .... Err, I'll come back to you on that one. Right now I'm so spaced, I can't give a fuck .... be nice if he could though ..... Gina! What're you like? I said 'like'...... like, like, like!

Shoes on; new £95 shoulder bag packed; keys; wallet .... with cash; checked – and Gina left the flat.

The summer evening air was warm and friendly and welcoming on the street. But the man who stepped forward from the next doorway certainly wasn't. In truth, his demeanour was unthreatening, but his intentions were counter to his smiling persona.

Thank God I was so relaxed that I know I handled the situation better than if I wasn't as high as a kite. I saw him coming but couldn't place the face for a moment. He was smiling when he called my name and for a moment I thought it was someone I knew from round here. By the time he got close I'd recognised him as the weirdo from the bookies in south London. But thank God I had the presence of mind not to run or scream or over-react. I just stared at him while I tried to collect my thoughts.

"Hi...Sorry, do I know you?"

"Not exactly but we sort of met in Streatham last week. I took your photo in a bookies."

"No, not me, I don't know what you're talking about."

I think I was handling it okay. I started to think as if I really didn't know what he was talking about. If some bloke used my name and then confused me with someone else what would I do? Leave – that's what.

"Sorry, wrong person. I've never been to Streatham High Road – must have been someone else. Must go."

"I never said 'High Road'......."

118

Fuck! Stupid.

".......But you're right, that's where you were collecting your big winnings."

Gina had already turned away and now quickened her step, but the man was on her shoulder. Gina turned briefly.

"If you don't stop pestering me, I will scream very loudly right now."

"Like you did last week?..... Okay.... But you know I know who you are and about your charity so you better answer my emails or I'm going to sell the photos to the papers."

"Go to hell!!"

I was in a right state when I reached Trappers. Only a five minute walk but that asshole had really screwed my head. I hoped Guy wouldn't be there so I'd have time to calm down.

But Guy was standing by the entrance reading something on a Kindle, looking the image of calmness.

Which I clearly wasn't.

Guy's first reaction when he recognised Gina was to praise her appearance. He was about to extoll gallantries describing how gorgeous she looked, until he realised that Gina was upset.

"What's wrong?"

"I just got approached by a weirdo ..... who .... threatened me."

"That's dreadful. Did he touch you?"

"No – just threatened me with something far worse."

That remark threw Guy for a moment.

"Worse? What's worse?"

"Nothing. Don't worry about it – let's get a drink – that'll calm my nerves."

I could see that Guy was confused. A crap start to the evening – that pissed me off more I think. A drink will get it back on track ….. or so I hoped.

And it did, at the outset. It was evident that Guy didn't want to ponder the loss of his grandmother, so the subject quickly moved to the CityZen Award and the awards event and Gina's new look and Guy's flat-hunting. Guy explained how much he had been impressed by Gina's passion for Watersource in her acceptance speech. Gina winced at the thought, unnoticed by Guy who quizzed her at length about how her charity money was being spent. An easy conversation for Gina, even in her heady state.

It was going okay. I was still spaced but holding it together. And I sensed that Guy was happy in my company tonight. He hardly looked away from me as we sat in a window with plenty of distraction around us, but he was very attentive – I remember that much.

What Gina hadn't realised was how quickly she was drinking her spritzers on an empty stomach. She offered to pay for the third round as Guy stood to replenish their drinks. Had she also walked to the bar to get them, she would have realised how much effect the alcohol was having on her senses, but she sat people-watching as she waited for Guy to return.

The thing about spliffs is that they're uppers while alcohol's a downer. That's what they do to me – way up on weed and depressed as hell on too much booze. So maybe they cancelled themselves out because I was feeling mellow. Very mellow and at peace with the world. Not silly up or down. That weirdo had almost gone from my thoughts but when I was alone, waiting for Guy to bring the drinks, my mind went to the start of the evening and it upset me again for a brief moment – like a shudder, basically.

Guy returned at that moment and again noticed Gina's mood.

"You're not okay are you? You still shaken up by that guy earlier?"

"Sorry. It just came back into my thoughts."

"Can I ask what a stranger can do to you that's worse than a physical assault?"

"Is this a pub quiz? I don't know – you're going to have to give me the answer."

"Very funny. I'm just worried about what you said when we met – that that guy had done something worse than assaulting you."

Gina thought about Guy's question; and assessed his motives; and what he would do if he knew.

You are so sweet .... Is this a big mistake?

"Threaten me."

"Threaten you? With what?"

"Blackmail."

Oh dear. Too much?

"Really? Gosh. How? So you do know him? What have you got that he can blackmail you with?   Sorry, that's not my business....Unless you want to talk about it."

Gina stared into her drink as she assessed the situation. For the first time she became aware of the effect of the cocktail of drink and spliff. But she had to say something.

"It's nothing. Not your problem. A bit of something about nothing."

"You know that I don't believe you don't you? It's obviously enough to upset you, so that upsets me. So the next thing I will tell you is that I would really like to help. If you need someone to help you, I want to be that someone. Do you understand?"

You're so sweet.

"Thank you – you're very sweet – do you know that?"
Gina reached across the table to hold Guy's hand. He responded with a squeeze as sensitive as the loving look in his eyes that were trying to read Gina's emotions.

I think we knew in that moment that something special was happening. I totally felt it and I sensed that we were both in the same place.

The tone was set for the rest of the evening. A closeness that shut out their surroundings as they drew close to one another. Guy sensed it was not the time to pursue the many questions he had about the blackmail threat, but there was much else to explore, so they did. Early life, family, school, loves and hates, jokes and politics.
Gina was in a daze. Eating food mid-evening helped to offset the effects of the earlier cocktail, but she knew full well that she would not otherwise have been as relaxed or talked so freely about some of the more sensitive aspects of her life. That was not normally her default position.

I should admit that I hoped that by sharing confidences with Guy, I would like, draw him to me. I hadn't thought that the reverse would also work. Totally silly – it's obvious really – except the obvious could have been staring me in the face and I probably wouldn't have noticed that night. But he admitted some time later that it was that evening that Guy went from liking to seriously fancying me. For me, I think I went from fancying him to wanting him in my life – okay, falling for him big time.

The incident at the start of the evening was one subject that remained unexplored by the time Guy walked Gina home. He considered mentioning it again, but thought better of it. He had made it transparently clear that he wanted to be there for her if Gina needed his help, so Guy decided it was best left at that. However, the prospect of meeting Gina again was starting to linger in his thoughts; he wanted to make an arrangement before they said goodnight, but eventually it was Gina who took the initiative as they approached her flat. They had discussed Guy's broken family at some length during which conversation Guy had mentioned that he had to drive down to his mother's home in Wiltshire to see her the following weekend, a few days prior to her birthday. A duty more than pleasure, so he was dreading the visit.

"Would you like me to come with you to see your mum at the weekend?" Gina asked out of the blue, catching Guy unaware for a moment.

"Er, yes, that'd be really cool. It's not going to be much fun though – she can be funny peculiar. But I'd love the company – *your* company," Guy quickly added.

"It's down and back in a day isn't it – you're not staying over?"

"No, no chance."

"Good. If you want me to come, I'd love to."

So that was sorted.

Good one, Gina.

As they arrived at Gina's front door, Guy took her hand.

"Thanks for this evening. I've really enjoyed it – but I think you know that don't you?"

Gina smiled sheepishly and nodded.

"Good – glad you noticed. I loved it."

Kissing passionately seemed the most natural reaction. They both made the move in the same instant. Guy cupped Gina's face as she closed her eyes. They parted slowly and both reconnected tenderly,

Guy caressing Gina's top then bottom lips with his. Gina, still in her dazed state and eyes closed, was lost in those moments.

"I'll call you about the weekend," Guy whispered as he released his grip, but took Gina's hand and kissed it before he turned in the direction of the tube station, leaving Gina on her doorstep as rain began to fall.

27

The after effect of last night - that's the memory of my evening with Guy and that kiss, not the drug and drink cocktail - was going to get me through another odd day. Some good, some less than ideal ... okay, some really shitty bits, to be honest. You can probably guess the bad bit. Yeah, Sid Weirdo sent another email overnight that was waiting to upset my mood as soon as I opened my mail. The usual subject title didn't shock me as much as it had before.

'Streatham High Rd 28th July'

Perhaps I was getting used to it. But the message .... well, that was upsetting.

Time to stop messing about. You buy the photos for £5000 at weekend or they go to the pres on Monday. If you ignor this I will now you want me to sell the photos to the papers insted of you.   Sid

Fuck! Time's running out til I have to make a decision to call his bluff or pay the money. But I haven't done anything wrong and he still can't prove it was me who he photographed in Streatham.
I should do something. Doing nothing's a bad idea.

Gina tapped 'Reply'.

I don't know who yu think I am but you have contacted the wrong person and your email today is obviously blackmail. Thats illegal so if you contact me again or repeat this threat I will contact the police with the email.

It sat on Gina's screen while she thought about the consequences as she percolated a small pot of coffee in her kitchen. By the time she sat back at her desk, she was confident that this was a good option. How could this, her first written response, do any harm?

Gina tapped 'Send' and poured a cup of fresh hot coffee.

Before it had cooled enough for her to take her first mouthful, a reply arrived from L Sid:

By monday or the photos go to the press

Gina was upset by the apparent confidence that this email conveyed. Those few words popped her conviction that she was on top of the problem. Sid was not backing down so she had to think of a different approach – a new line of defence – or, perish the thought, she pays. If that was the end of the matter, it would buy her privacy; her protection from the press on her doorstep; staff in all the other betting shops coming forward to reveal the total of her winnings on the same bet; and the obvious conclusion that she had tried to hide the scale of her win. Then there was the inevitable question about how she had the confidence to bet all that charity money on an outside chance of a wild card player beating the third seed at Wimbledon. The word 'conspiracy' came into Gina's thoughts and the consequences of that accusation made her still more upset.

Can you imagine what the press will make of that? Oh my god. Weirdo Sid doesn't know how strong his threat is – he just knows about two of the bets. But if I pay, will that really be the end of him and the threats?

This train of thought racked Gina's head and body. She sat slumped at her desk in a stance that summarised her depression, her head dropping so low that it was resting on her desk.

Enough! Come on, you can't sit here like this all day.

She straightened her posture and began to busy herself with other more familiar tasks to divert her attention. And to ponder last evening and the trip to Wiltshire with Guy tomorrow. Anything to fill her thoughts.

Eventually, her activities drew her back to her computer and the usual wealth of emails that had become the norm in recent weeks. Gina had grown proficient at clearing the dead wood to leave the few that were worthy of her time and a response. Only as she neared the bottom of the unopened mails from yesterday's influx did she arrive at the mail that had caught her drug-clouded eyes briefly before she left to meet Guy yesterday.

Subject: **Advance notice for Watersource funding**

Only open the attachment in private.
This top tip is for you alone, Gina. With a little effort, it will lead to your next opportunity to raise money for Watersource.

Just one among the dozens. Another to be deleted, or the next step to more wealth, more funds for Watersource - more money, plain and simple? Gina couldn't open it. She couldn't take the chance that this was just a well-worded opportunist scam that would carry a virus that

127

could cause untold misery if she invited it into her computer. But nor could she bring herself to delete it.

28

The weather on Saturday was due to be perfect for a trip to the country. Gina was tired from the turmoil of a restless night, but she made herself ready in crisp new clothes for her day out with Guy, summoning more enthusiasm than she had managed for anything to do with her 'worklife' as she collectively described all things non-social.

Gina arrived early at the prearranged meeting point near Hammersmith underground station. Her mood was out of synch with the fresh autumnal morning that seemed to be making such an effort to play its part in Gina's special day; hers and Guy's first date since their unspoken declaration of love two nights ago.

Love? Hang on. Let's take one step at a time. I never used the word 'love' ... Affection isn't quite right – not strong enough. Infatuation maybe ...?.... No, that's not right either. I admit I fancy the pants off him and yes, he's gorgeous and seems to care about me now, so let's just say there's every possibility that this could develop into something. But I sort of thought the same thing after our first date at Trappers and I got that totally wrong. Let's see how it goes today. Note-to-self Ginapops: take it slowly or you could embarrass yourself.

The thoughts had provided a brief distraction from the stone-in-her-shoe worries about Sid's threats that were now in or never far from her thoughts every waking hour, niggling her to make a decision before Monday. Immediately her thoughts drifted away from Guy and the day ahead, she became aware of the stone again. If only she could shake it out of her shoe, her head, her stomach. Would paying Sid £5,000 achieve that relief? Or would that be stupid? The more times she thought about it, the more she questioned her own judgement to make the right decision.

Beep – beep. A silver hatchback car swung out of the traffic into the layby, stopping beside Gina. At the last moment she recognised Guy as he reached across to open the passenger door.

"Wanna lift, lovely lady? I'm going west – any use for you?"

"Depends on your intentions, sir – will I be safe?"

"Probably not – not with you looking as gorgeous as you do."

"That's okay then."

By now, Gina was in the car and instinctively leaned across to kiss Guy on the lips.

"Morning. How are you?"

"Oh I'm okay, thanks," Guy replied with little enthusiasm, then cheered as he added: "Thanks for coming today, I've been so looking forwards to seeing you again. If it all goes pear-shaped we can escape early, I promise."

"It's not going to be that bad is it?"

"Could be a bit bumpy. I never know with my Ma - let's see."

A little under two hours after they left west London, Guy turned the car into a short drive in front of a scruffy Victorian red bricked cottage on the edge of a nondescript village. Only then did Gina think to ask:

"Your grandmother, was she your mum's mum?

"No, my dad's. Best not mention it."

"Okay."

There was no activity in the house, no-one greeted them at the door. Gina deliberately hung back when Guy took a bouquet of flowers from the back seat then left the car to ring the doorbell. After a prolonged wait, the door opened and a slight female figure dressed in a very colourful full-length kaftan opened the door cautiously.

"Hi Ma."

"Guy?"

"Yes Ma – you were expecting me weren't you?"

"I was?"

"I phoned last weekend to tell you I'd be here for your birthday." He brought the bouquet from behind his back and handed it to his mother.

"It's not my birthday."

"Not today, but it is on Tuesday. I've brought a friend with me who wants to meet you."

Guy turned to see Gina starting to leave the car to join him on the doorstep. As Guy's mother watched her walk the few metres towards them, her expression became pinched and her attitude hardened, so when she greeted Gina, it was with a far from convincing:

"Hello."

"Ma, this is my friend, Gina," Guy added as he sensed his mother's tension. Gina was oblivious.

"Hello Mrs Tozer – I'm very pleased to meet you." Gina was charm personified but Guy's mother was reluctant to shake hands. Guy noticed and stared at his mother trying to read her reaction.

"I think Gina can call you Sheila can't she?"

But Sheila had already turned into the house leaving the others to follow. By the time they arrived in the little kitchen, Sheila had discarded the bouquet and was fidgeting about tidying away papers and dirty cups from the work surfaces. It was apparent that she was not expecting visitors.

"Sorry Ma – I should have called to remind you. I totally forgot – sorry for that."

"Yes, well I'm sure you're busy at work with better things to do. More important things to do."

Guy and Gina exchanged 'oh-dear' expressions.

Salvation came in the garden. Coffees made and the three moved to a table and chairs on the patio overlooking a lawn in need of cutting.

Guy led the conversation as he and his mother caught up on news, some of which Gina knew from their car journey. But it became apparent that Sheila was not registering Gina's presence. At points where the conversation would naturally lead to her asking about Gina - her work, her background, any connections with Wiltshire - instead there were silent gaps that Guy filled with another question or a bit more news that he was deliberately releasing in drips. When Gina asked about the house and garden, answers came in single words or short sentences. It started to become embarrassing.

"May I use your loo please Sheila?" Gina needed relief from the atmosphere more than for her bladder. Guy answered for his mother:

"It's by the front door on the right."

"Thanks. Excuse me."

Immediately Gina was out of earshot, Guy turned on his mother.

"What's wrong?"

"Wrong? With what?"

"Stop it Ma. You're embarrassing me. Why are you being so rude to Gina?"

"How long have you known her?"

"A few weeks. What's that got to do with anything?"

"She's evil."

That had the impact that Guy assumed was intended by such a vitriolic statement. He physically sat back and stared at his mother who didn't look away from his eyes.

"I mean it. I sense evil, or something close to evil."

"You're totally wrong. You don't know anything about Gina – and don't seem to want to know about her. She runs a charity. She's amazing – and passionate about helping people in the third world. How's that evil?"

Sheila appeared to doubt herself.

"I'm telling you Guy, that there's something wrong about her. Are you in a relationship?"

"Not exactly….Not quite…But I like her a lot. You've got this all wrong. She's amazing and lovely. She hasn't got an evil bone in her body. And I'd like you to be polite to her…please Ma – yes?"

The loo door handle clanked.

"Guy's just told me off for being rude to you. I'm sorry." Sheila spoke the words dispassionately with the same delivery as if she had just asked Gina if she wanted another cup of coffee. Gina's shock was evident. Guy looked to the sky and shook his head.

"May I ask why?" Gina enquired after a pause.

"Did Guy tell you that I'm a clairvoyant?"

"Yes, but I don't really know what that means."

"It means I have what some people call a 'sixth sense'. I can see beyond your outer persona."

"So what do you see that upsets you about me?"

Guy interjected before his mother could answer:

"I don't think this is the time or place." That broke the pattern of the conversation. "Well is it? You know you aren't always right about these things Ma."

"I am. When was I ever wrong?"

"Enough. I thought we could all go for lunch at The Feathers. Would you like that?"

"Okay. Have you booked? You'll have to book to get a table in the garden on a Saturday."

"No but I will now, for one-o'clock, okay?" Guy stood to get his phone from his coat pocket in the kitchen, leaving Gina alone with his mother.

"I'm sorry you're worried by something about me."

"Hmmm, me too. You seem like a nice person and Guy speaks highly of you…..I can't help it you know? I just sense these things. Perhaps I shouldn't have said anything."

"About what? What can you sense?" Gina was genuinely intrigued and unsettled by Sheila's accusation.

I didn't think of it so much as an accusation – more of a prophesy, but you can imagine how it hit me in my super-sensitive mood – especially about anything supernatural or weird like that. I felt sick, to be honest. I really wanted to get away from there, she was scary, but I also wanted

*to know what she could tell me, but just when she might
have told me something useful, Guy came back out and
that was that.*

"It's okay for one-o'clock. We should leave soon."

*Thank goodness we could sit outside in the pub garden -
in the fresh air. There was enough distractions to distance
myself from Sheila's intensity and weirdness. I could let
Guy chat to her, only occasionally did she acknowledge
my presence without Guy drawing me into their
conversation. I didn't mind, I just wanted to get through it
and get away. I couldn't use the loo excuse again so I sat
it out and smiled and pretended to listen to their
conversation while I worried about Sid. One train of
thought that I hadn't considered in any detail before, was
the consequence of paying him. I could afford £5,000 for
sure, but how could I be sure that the one payment would
be final .... I couldn't, basically. And I had to somehow
move from 'you've got the wrong person – fuck off ' to
'okay, I'll pay you'.... but I suppose that's not like, my
biggest problem.*

"Back in a minute." Guy stood and left the table to go to what
Gina assumed was the toilets. She had immediately reconnected with
the conversation, except there wasn't any now that she was left alone
with Sheila.

In for a penny....

"I'm sorry you don't approve of me. Really. I'd literally like you
to like me because I think Guy is special and at the end of the day, I
want to be his friend so ..."

"I don't dislike you." Sheila interrupted abruptly. "I didn't say
that. I just sense a bad aura around you that could embrace Guy if

you are too close. That's bad. I'm his mother you know, so I worry about him and you may be a danger to him. I hope not, but you could be."

"What's an aura mean?"

"It can mean various things." Sheila immediately transformed into a meditative state, head slumped with her eyes closed. Gina watched her then checked that people sitting nearby were not taking an interest, which they weren't. Sheila was almost silent but animated. Despite her eyes being closed, she seemed to be looking around a scene in her imagination. She eventually spoke.

"You are in a strange place. I think you know that. I sense you are unhappy....No, worried or upset. You're very tense. It's a bad aura. There's something powerful influencing your life. Not for the better."

Over Sheila's shoulder, Gina noticed Guy returning from the pub. She caught his eye and signalled for him to wait, unseen by Sheila who had her eyes closed again as she spoke, her face conveying stress. Gina watched her contorted expressions, trying to read something into her twitches and grimaces. Whatever Sheila was experiencing, was causing her obvious discomfort. Gina found herself sharing the pained expressions until Sheila's moist eyes opened then raised to meet Gina's. Sheila unclenched her fists and slowly reached across the table. Gina watched her hands approaching her arm, not certain whether to recoil or accept the physical contact. She froze. Sheila's touch, then squeeze, was surprisingly sensitive.

That's the bit that nearly freaked me. Even more when she said nothing. I waited for her to say something about what she'd seen or heard but she just stared. I could see her eyes filling with tears – literally welling up. So we just stared at one another for – I dunno – a long moment. Then she slowly removed her hand from my arm. Bloody hell, it was seriously scary.

135

When Gina looked away from Sheila's eyes, Guy was walking back to the table. He sensed that their conversation had run its course.

"We ought to be going soon. I have to get the car back this evening."

Gina was relieved to break the mood with the prospect of leaving.

"It's not your car?" she asked.

"No, I can't afford to own a car in London – nor do I need one. Car-pool. Ideal for odd occasions like this."

Sheila remained transfixed to Gina.

I pretended not to notice but it was seriously unsettling. It was like she was still thinking about whatever it was she was seeing before.

From Guy's position, he could flick a signal to Gina with his eyes without his mother noticing. The signal suggested that they should make their escape.

"Is it okay with you Ma if we drop you home then head off?"

Sheila returned to the conversation.

"Yes, I didn't know you were coming, if you recall. I always have things to fill my day."

So charming.

During the drive back to London, Guy was more animated than on their outward journey. A weight had evidently lifted from his shoulders. Job done, responsibility met.

I, on the other hand, felt… well, I felt physically sick. The weight of Sheila's prophesies on top of her seriously scary behaviour was still upsetting me, but I didn't want to talk about it now. I should never have gone there today. I felt dreadful.

I've told you before how difficult I'm finding it to handle this weirdness, so today stirred up a sense of

helplessness – like there's nothing I can do to stop it. It's
something way beyond my control. Sheila seemed to
know that.

Guy sensed Gina's mood and thought he understood why she was so quiet.

"I did warn you. I'm so sorry, though."

"For?"

"For? For everything. I'm so sorry about Ma. She has better days when she can be lovely and charming – yes, really she can. I never know which one I'll find. I'm so sorry. She was unforgiveable."

"Don't apologise."

"What were you talking about at the end there that you didn't want me to hear - if you don't mind me asking?"

"It wasn't that – I didn't mind you hearing, but I was worried she would stop talking if you came back to the table."

"So at least you were talking. About what?"

"Oh nothing of much interest – just about why she was ..." Gina had to consider her phraseology then settled on: ".......unsure about me." Gina knew this was only part of the truth but she didn't want to discuss the more frightening silences.

"Any conclusions?"

"No." Gina was reflecting as she watched the countryside. "What did she tell you when I escaped to the loo this morning?" Guy was on the spot. He couldn't tell Gina that his mother called her *'evil'*.

"You can sometimes see kites near here. You know, the big hawk bird that they re-introduced. You see them gliding on thermals – can't miss them, they're really big with a forked tail."

"How very interesting. I assume that means your mother told you something that could upset me – yeah?"

"Let's just say she was a little concerned about something that she sensed about you," Guy offered with apparent caution. "You know that she's a clairvoyant and she gets these things about some people. They usually come to nothing."

"Usually?"

"Yeah – something of nothing – as you say. But she was very embarrassing and so rude. I can't apologise enough for that. I'm so sorry."

"Stop apologising." Gina reached across and squeezed Guy's thigh and tried to lean to kiss his cheek until the seat belt locked to stop her progress. They both laughed then Guy leaned towards Gina to take up the space between them so that Gina could plant a smacker on his left cheek.

Such a simple act, but it immediately changed the atmosphere in the car. I suddenly relaxed and felt very close to Guy and his reaction suggested he felt my warmth ... Is that the word? No, not enough ..... 'passion' ... no that's not right either. Okay, a bit horny. But that may have been something to do with the two large spritzers during lunch. Whatever the reason, the change was great. So stroking his inner thigh seemed sort of .... well, right.

"Hey, I'm trying to drive here." A smile beamed across Guy's face.

29

Oh....my.....god.
I will relive that night for a very long time. Every time I think about it, it gives me a warm glowy feeling. Sorry, I'm not about to share that night with anyone else - it was just mine and Guy's, but I will say that everything Guy did to me was perfect. His touch, caresses, kisses....He just seemed to know how to, when to, where to touch me to send me to somewhere I've never been before. I was.....it was epic. And that's all I'm going to say – except my residing thought was: 'I can't believe you learnt how to do this at an all-boys' school'.

When Guy had driven past Hammersmith on their way back into London, Gina briefly questioned what he was planning, but they both knew that they would spend at least the evening together. Then after a Chinese supper, during which neither Sheila nor her prophesies were mentioned, Guy drove Gina home to Camden, then parked the car in a side street around the corner from her flat, where it remained overnight.

Something very special happened last night. I have never felt like this about anyone in my life before. I was so close to Guy that I wanted to wrap him around me so he'd never let me go. I know, I know.... yes I'm very vulnerable right now and sensitive and weirded out, but that doesn't change how I feel about him. I feel so close and safe and in love. And that scares me a bit in case I do something stupid. And get hurt.

Gina had woken first and lay in bed listening to Guy's rhythmic breathing. She could only see his smooth, muscular, eggshell shoulders and neck, but stared at them, wanting to make physical contact – to touch him again. She leaned close enough to smell his skin and breathed in as if inhaling his body, his love, his very being.

Gina lay with Guy and her thoughts for a short time, then slipped out of bed, found her oversized tee-shirt that she was using as a night dress and wriggled it over her head.

I could taste Chinese food from last night. I had no idea how the morning was about to pan out but I wasn't about to let my dog breath play a part.

Guy was awake, lying on his back watching Gina when she left the bathroom.

"Good morning." His smile was reassuring.

"Hi." Gina matched Guy's smile as he gestured for her to come back to bed. Gina was about to slip back under the duvet, but Guy stopped her while he slid his hands from her thighs up her body to remove the tee shirt over her head. He ran the back of his fingers down the side of Gina's breasts as she sat on the edge of the bed feeling the tingles of his touch once again. She closed her eyes to enjoy the sensation and reached out to touch his chest, then his torso and down to meet his erection coming up to meet her hand. Guy gently grasped Gina's wrist.

"I haven't got another sheath. Have you got one?"

"No - sorry."

Too right I was. Note to self: get some as soon as possible. Then must sort something better.

Gina snuggled down until their two naked bodies were entwined. Guy pulled the duvet over her shoulders and they both slept for another hour.

I don't think Guy was awake when I woke up. I could hear his rhythmic breathing and feel his naked body tracing the shape of mine behind me. As I lay there with warm sun filtering into my flat, I felt more secure and comfortable and content than I had for the last two months – probably more. I started to worry that this was stupid – Guy might leave this morning and everything would go back to my weird normal.

No, I won't think that.

Gina slid out of bed and slipped on her tee shirt as she made her way to the kitchen to make tea or coffee. She had no idea how Guy started his day but hoped that this would not be the last time she needed to know.

Guy woke to the sound of Gina pouring out-of-date milk down the sink. He couldn't understand the glugging sound. Was she being ill?

"Are you okay?"

"Yeah." Gina reappeared in the bedroom. "Good morning again. I'm making tea or coffee – what do you want?"

"Tea please. White, no sugar."

"I need milk." Gina was hunting for her fatigues under a pile of clothes on the back of a seat.

"Don't worry about it – it's not that important," Guy insisted.

"It's no problem – I need some anyway and it's only across the road."

Gina was tugging on the trousers then pushed her oversized tee shirt into the waist band.

"Are you going out on the streets of London like that?"

"Yes. Why not?"

"No reason. But if you notice any horny men rubbing against you at the checkout, don't be surprised – that's all I'm saying."

"This is modern-day London, not nineteen-nineties Wiltshire." She flashed Guy a smile, picked up her purse and keys and was gone.

Guy spotted his boxer shorts and pulled them on then wandered into the kitchen where he splashed cold water on his face and wiped out his eyes.

He was drying two mugs from the draining board when he noticed Gina crossing the road from the minimart directly opposite the flat. She disappeared from view so he expected to hear the door at the street open a moment later, but nothing happened. That seemed strange. He leaned over the sink to look down to this side of the road below the flat where he could see Gina in conversation with a man wearing a hooded parka. Guy smiled, assuming that he could now boast that she did attract attention as he had warned, but as he was about to look away, the conversation on the street became a confrontation. The man in the parka was prodding Gina's shoulder very aggressively, forcing her back along the pavement. There was no mistake, it was aggressive. Guy turned away to find his clothes so that he could get down to help but then heard the outside door slam shut and Gina pounding up the stairs. He opened the door to the flat and Gina almost fell into his arms. She tried to make light of the incident when Guy challenged her for an explanation, but she couldn't disguise her upset.

Gina sat in silence on one of the two high stools in her kitchen with her head bowed as Guy made two teas. He placed Gina's infusion on the counter in front of her and perched on the other stool with his tea in his cupped hands, waiting for something to happen.

The silence was protracted. Guy broke it with a question.

"Do you want to talk about this?"

"No. Sorry." Gina looked up, tore off a sheet of kitchen towel and blew her nose.

"It's not your problem." She barely got the words out before she broke down and cried openly despite her apparent efforts to hold it in.

I knew at that moment that I was about to lose Guy. And so I should. His mother had warned him and I was proving her right. I couldn't think what to do for the best and that

142

upset me more. I thought I had it controlled..... Then I
didn't. I lost it. Fuck it.

"Your mother was right. I'm damaged goods basically." Gina could hardly speak through the sobs. Guy tried to put his arm around her, but she pulled away.

Why would I do that? Now I was just feeling sorry for myself. What a fucking mess. I really messed up. Poor Guy – he didn't deserve this.

Gina blew her nose again and managed:
"I think you should go."
Guy seemed to accept that and after a few moments of consideration he stood and walked back into the bedroom where Gina could hear him getting dressed. Or so she assumed until she heard the familiar creek and clunk of the sofa bed being put away. A moment later, Guy reappeared, still only wearing his boxer shorts. He picked up his cup of tea, put Gina's in her right hand and took her by the other and led her back into the sitting room in silence. He placed the two cups of tea on a small table between them and sat Gina down at one end of the sofa while he sat facing her from the other.

"Give me credit for knowing my own mind. I will decide if this is over or not. You don't have to tell me anything but I want you to – as I told you before. I want to be here to help, but right now that's up to you, Gee."
There was a pause. Gina was obviously assessing how much to say.

Obviously.

"This? What's this?" Gina asked without looking at Guy.
"I don't understand."
"You said you'd decide if *this* is over – what's over?"
"Our relationship."

"I didn't know we had one – not more than something in passing."

"Yeah, I suppose that's right, but I live in hope that it could be more than passing - something *much* more." He thought for a moment then added: "I don't know right now that I'd use the expression *'in love'* – not at this moment – but .... but .... last night I made love to you. It wasn't sex, it was love. I hope you sensed that because I tried my hardest to make you realise it. It was special and important and wonderful for me and I wanted you to feel something similar. . . . . . Do you understand?"

Gina couldn't answer. Guy's statement had set her off again and she jumped up to take a tissue from a box across the room. Guy watched her mopping her eyes then blowing her nose until she was composed. When she turned back, her face conveying something akin to a smile, she came to Guy, cradled his head in her hands and kissed him passionately. He responded in kind and both sensed a relief for their own reasons. Still standing, Gina held Guy's head to her chest then turned it up so that Guy looked into her eyes.

"Are you sure you want to know everything? Are you sure you want that?"

"Yes."

Gina moved away, slowly drank two mouthfuls of tea, sat back down on the sofa and began her explanation. Guy knew a little about the start of Gina's story from the charity cycle ride on Dartmoor and the lightning strike, but of course he knew nothing of the detail or how her life had developed during the last two months – nor about the premonitions or winning bets – or L.Sid's blackmail threat.

Gina spoke almost uninterrupted as she chronicled the saga in detail. Guy listened, only occasionally asking for clarification of a point while he hung on Gina's every word until she ended with their visit to Guy's mother's house.

A lengthy silence followed. They both drank their teas without making eye contact. Guy was first to speak.

"Shall we go out for brunch?"

144

30

_____

That morning would change more than I could ever have expected. Short term and much longer. Of course the instant result was to have Guy on my side and in my life and …. well, just there. I can't tell you what a difference that made – what a weight that lifted. Even just telling him everything, was fantastic. Whatever the opposite of stress is, that's what I suddenly felt like.

Huh, at one point, Guy thanked me for telling him everything and suggested that 'it couldn't have been easy'. Well he got that totally wrong. It was the greatest relief imaginable. A problem shared is halved, or whatever that saying is.

By the time we left the flat, Guy had convinced me that I mustn't pay Sid any money under any circumstances. His take made a lot of sense. He reckoned that the fact that this bloke Sid was door-stepping me was a sign that he didn't think he would get any money without force and even if he sent the photos, no paper would print them without checking the story. And I have a great profile by comparison with that of some drop-out. I could just deny everything, then what? That was Guy's take and it made like, so much sense when he said it. Easy said, but Sid scared me and I didn't want that every time I leave my flat. Guy was convinced that he'd just get bored. I hope that's right because I was prepared to make him an offer to make him bugger off – maybe £2,000, but I knew in my heart that wasn't going to be the end when I'd effectively admitted I have something to hide, basically. Talking it through with Guy was like hearing my conscience talking back.

So Guy was at my side as we left the flat together to go into Town but Sid was nowhere to be seen, thank God.

We went to Spitlfields for brunch. The buzz and crowds and noise suited me perfectly – well, having Guy there was the perfect bit. We found a corner table in a small café that Guy knew would serve all-day breakfasts and we ate and talked and talked and talked. Nothing seemed to be off the agenda. Of course my story was the main topic but our lives to date and families and his mother's reaction to me and work and friends and relations and favourite music and films and people we can't stand in the media and cars – that was quite a short subject, to be honest – and favourite holiday destinations. We covered everything with hardly a breath or mouthful of food interrupting the flow.

It was mid-afternoon when Guy remembered that he had to get the car back to south London that evening. They had travelled into The City on the Underground, so they had to get back to Camden for Guy to collect the car. Both he and Gina were glad that he would see her all the way home although neither mentioned the unfinished business with Sid despite his end-of-Sunday schedule having almost run its course.

Neither Gina nor Guy noticed Sid as they approached the door from the street into the flat. But then they did. He was loitering a few metres from them and obviously would have challenged Gina had she been alone. Gina saw him first and turned to Guy who was at her shoulder.

"That's him," she whispered loudly.

Guy had noticed but was unsure until Gina's confirmation. Sid was evidently nervous and turned away, but Guy immediately confronted him.

"Oi! Yes you!"

Guy may have misunderstood the man's intentions as Sid turned with his arm raised to defend himself against Guy's forceful approach, but the result was that Guy's momentum brought him so close to Sid that they were face-to-face with Sid's arm still raised. To Gina's shock, she watched as Guy brought his head down onto the man's face in a furious head butt. Some pedestrians had already stopped on the street when Guy had originally shouted at Sid. They seemed equally surprised at Guy's attack. Sid fell on his knees holding his nose that was now bleeding profusely.

"If I ever see you here again, it'll be even worse than this – you little shit." For good measure, Guy kicked at Sid's huddled frame – not making a heavy impact but Sid was so disorientated by the head butt that Guy's blow pushed him over into a crumpled pile on the pavement. Guy turned away and ushered Gina into the flat, watched by a small clique of pedestrians who then moved to help Sid.

Once upstairs, Guy slumped on Gina's sofa. Gone was the bravado of a few minutes earlier. He was visibly shaken and shaking. Gina sat beside him and put her arm around him. She sensed that he needed it.

"I feel dreadful," he confided. "I'm not violent. I hate violence. I don't know what happened then. I felt so sorry for him I almost apologised."

You know what? I know it'll sound daft but I was relieved – and probably not for the reason you're thinking, but because Guy was upset. He scared me for a moment to see him so violent. I was relieved that he didn't take it lightly and could behave like that without worrying about the consequences – or about the bloke he hit. It took him a while to recover.

"I'm going to deliver the car back, collect some clothes for work tomorrow and come back as quickly as possible…If you'd like me to do that, so you're not on your own tonight."

"Would you? Please."

"Cool."

When Guy left I felt a strange sense of loss. Even though I knew he would be back in a couple of hours. What a day. What a weekend.

31

A bigger week was due to follow. It started well enough; Sid was nowhere in evidence so Gina assumed that Guy's threat had served its purpose. What she couldn't have anticipated was the knock on the door by two police officers on the Tuesday. Gina was at home and invited them in when they explained that they had received a report of an assault that they were now investigating.

They assumed Guy lived in my flat and when I told them about our relationship they still wanted my details. Taking them up to the flat gave me a couple of minutes' thinking time. I couldn't say too much about the blackmail but I had to defend Guy so I explained that the weirdo - Sid - had been pestering me and threatened me on Sunday morning.

"Threatened you? With what precisely?" asked the female officer, then noted Gina's reply.

"I don't know. I assumed he thought I was someone else that owed him money."

"Why would he do that?" asked the male officer.

"No idea."

"Do you owe him money?"

"No. I told you I don't even know him."

Are they listening?

"Where was the confrontation?"

149

"On the pavement outside the flat, down there, when I came back from the shop. He came up to me and told me he wanted his money, then he pushed me about and upset me – well it would wouldn't it? My boyfriend was in here and saw it from the kitchen window, but the bloke wasn't around when we back got down to the street later. Then on Sunday afternoon he was back so my boyfriend warned him off, sort of – told him to clear off and keep away from me."

"The man who reported the attack to us said that it was unprovoked."

"He provoked me in the morning for no good reason. And physically pushed me about and literally threatened me - so that was provocation, basically. My boyfriend isn't violent – he was very upset afterwards. Really upset. He sat right there and had to calm down. He's not a violent person."

"Was he injured?"

"Not badly. I suppose about the same as the other guy."

"The other guy had a broken nose and cracked cheek bone."

Gina was visibly shocked.

"No. We had no idea. That's dreadful. I'm sorry."

"Didn't it occur to you to report the confrontation in the morning?"

"No."

"I haven't got the name of your boyfriend in my notes – what is it?"

"Guy Tozer."

"Job?"

"He works for a TV production company."

"We have your address of course but I need a contact phone number for you and address and contact number for Mr Tozer."

Gina provided the details on the assumption that it would be best to appear to want to co-operate.

"Thank you. We'll contact him directly. Thank you for your co-operation Ms Melina."

They closed their note books and stood to leave.

"Are you employed?" asked the woman as an after-thought.

"I run a charity from here."

"I thought you looked familiar. I've seen you in the paper haven't I? You won an award for your work recently. Is that right?"

"Yes."

That exchange changed the atmosphere a little for the better.

Immediately after they left, Gina sent an email and a text to Guy warning him that the police want to interview him about his confrontation with Sid. But no reply came until lunchtime when Guy phoned Gina, very concerned.

That concern proved justified when just two days later, Miguel, who owns the mini mart across the road from Gina's flat and seemed to be at its check-out whenever Gina shopped, furtively waved Gina aside when she had paid for her groceries. He took a copy of the local Camden paper from a pile and slipped into her bag as he whispered:

"I think you should check it, Miss Gina. Page four I think." He waved her away when she offered to pay for it.

Back in her flat, Gina immediately flipped the pages, not knowing precisely what she was looking for, but she wasn't going to miss it. A short item with a photo and the headline:

STREET BRAWL LEAVES MAN HOSPITALISED

jumped off the page at her. Gina knew in an instant that it referred to Guy's fight, but making it worse was the photo, apparently taken on a phone by one of the onlookers, showing Guy with a snarling expression kicking out at Sid's crumpled body. Guy was unmistakable.

Shit it ! Instant nausea. Even more when I read the article that named Guy, mentioned his TV production company and made reference to me and my charity work with a clear inference that I was hanging out with a thug who picked on some innocent old man and beat him up so badly that he was taken to hospital. God - that's so unfair. It was only later that I realised the only people that knew

151

all the facts in the report were the police. Even Guy's full name and that he worked in TV. I wanted Guy to be with me but when I thought that, my next concern was about telling him - and what his reaction would be. Shit.

That turned out to be the least of Gina's worries. Things moved quickly after that.

I can't remember the details exactly but the end result was that Guy lost his job. Poor Guy. I felt so guilty. He was trying to help me for God's sake. All my bloody fault. Aaaaaaaah!!!
Once the story got back to his jerk bosses they called him in and put him on some sort of warning for his violent behaviour. For God's sake. Guy – violent behaviour? If they took more interest in their employees they would never come to that conclusion. What a load of............
Guy told me later that he lost his rag with his boss - I can't imagine him starting the argument - which is a bit ironic now I think of it - but I know he thought that some of his managers were akin to pond-life (his expression, not mine) and apparently one of them was lecturing him – laying into him and not listening to him .... Well, whatever. The result was, he walked out. No redundancy or anything. Just walked out that afternoon. Shit ... it ! Jobless and about to be homeless .... So he came to live with me.

That created a dilemma for Gina. She hadn't lived with anyone since sharing with her best friend for almost two years after leaving home at twenty-one. But the mixed emotions of guilt over Guy's circumstance and no little passion for him, compensated for her concern and the adjustments to her life. Guy travelled lightly with clothing and possessions that would fit into a large rucksack and small holdall, but once they came out of the bags, he needed some storage space that wasn't available in Gina's tiny home-cum-office.

No matter – we made it work – sort of. I admit now that I was unsure about it. First time for years that I had to worry about anyone else in my space, but having Guy there all the time was just wonderful. He made it wonderful. He was considerate and apologetic to a fault. He knew that this was a test and seemed to want to make it work. So it did. Okay, I have to admit to you and myself that I was all loved up but it had been such a long time that I cared for a bloke like this. I had to learn the rules of falling in love – or maybe I was already in love – okay, yes I was in love with Guy and I loved it. Loved being in love with someone who loved me. Then there was the sex......my god. How can I not have missed that? I suppose you have to know the real thing before you can miss it. I can't remember when I last wanted to go home because someone was there waiting for me – or wanted someone to come home because I was missing them. In fact, I can remember and it was when I was a teenager for God's sake. Ten years ago – more. And that was when my cousin lived with us during a holiday and I was infatuated for a couple of weeks and heart-broken when he left. He was five years older than me and hardly noticed I was there but it was a big deal for me. Sort of my first big crush. And now here I am with the real thing. All mine.

Within a few days, the couple had settled into a workable routine. Gina ran her schedule as she always had; they shared household responsibilities and Guy spent much of his time job-hunting.

After ten days and two interviews during which his 'dismissal' from the TV production company came to light, Guy started to worry.

He wasn't dismissed. He left because of a....... a disagreement.

Unfortunately, when the HR personnel at the TV companies where Guy was applying for work checked his CV, they received his last employer's version of Guy's story as *'dismissal due to unprofessional conduct'*. Further investigations revealed a dark story of violence which sealed Guy's fate. And that quickly started to take its toll on his confidence.

I could see it happening and it ripped me apart. He really didn't deserve this.

Guy applied for other jobs outside the media industry over the coming weeks but with little enthusiasm.

He was losing his mojo and I felt helpless. It was horrible. Meanwhile my work continued to provide a distraction and one mega result came as a long email from Dizzy – with loads of photos of his activities in Kenya. We had exchanged a few short sentences now and again to keep in touch so I knew that he was okay. His emails didn't give much away – just that things were going well with the new divining and extraction system. But one morning when I opened my email there was one with his name with some attachments that were photos of the opening of his first water system. With all the villagers. I can't tell you how much it literally cheered me up. Brilliant. It gave me such a boost. I'd sort of forgotten why I was doing all the work. With all the distractions over recent months and the last few weeks, I was sort of just doing my daily routine Watersource stuff without the end in my thoughts. The photos of Dizzy looking like he so fitted in with his dreads and the widest smile and all the villagers....It was wonderful. What a legend he's turning into. I sent an email

154

straight back telling him how much it had cheered me up and I copied in Eric. I wanted him to know that Dizzy was doing great.

Guy had been making breakfast for them when Gina squealed from her desk. He scurried through to her office, thinking she was upset, but when he realised what had happened, he shared Gina's excitement as she scrolled through the photographs to show him. They both needed the lift from the downbeat routine that had set in during recent weeks. The news led to a conversation on a topic that they had not mentioned of late; Gina's funding for Watersource and her bizarre ability to raise so much money since the summer. Nothing odd had happened for quite a while, so her life had settled into a new rhythm without the interruption of the absurdities of the forecasts. It was during their conversation that Gina recalled the email that she had seen in passing a few weeks previously. She mentioned it to Guy who showed considerably more interest than Gina.

"What do you mean? What kind of email?" His sense of intrigue intrigued Gina.

"It arrived a couple of weeks ago. Maybe longer. I don't think I deleted it. It was probably nothing. Now I think of it, it was more likely another scam, but I think it mentioned Watersource which was why I didn't dump it straight away. I can look it up if you want."

"Yeaaaah." Guy was openly excited. And impatient. "Now?"

"Okay, if you want."

Gina wandered back to her desk and opened her email with Guy closely in tow. She started to scroll down through reams of mail in her inbox.

"Do a search for 'Watersource'," Guy suggested.

That produced another lengthy list that Gina started to scroll through until she found an unopened mail that stood out from the crowd. They both read the subject:

Advance notice for Watersource funding

155

And below it:

Only open the attachment in private.
This top tip is for you alone, Gina. With a little effort, it will
lead to your next opportunity to raise money for
Watersource.

"I don't want to open the attachment." Gina was emphatic.

"Why not?" Guy was genuinely shocked – as was Gina.

"It could be a scam, of course. God knows what it could do in my address book."

"Well I'll open it. Send it on to me."

"Really?"

"Yeah - that's cool."

Gina forwarded the email and watched it arrive on Guy's laptop beside her. He immediately opened it with little regard for any adverse consequences.

They both watched the attachment open to reveal ...... a few words of instructions in black type on a white page, followed by a series of number and letter combinations set in several short lines. Quizzical looks were exchanged.

"There I told you, it's a scam."

"What is?"

"That. They just wanted you to open the attachment and now they've got their squirly-wirly-virusy-thingy trashing the inside of your computer."

"That's not how they work....is it?"

"I dunno. But it's all gobbledegook anyway."

Guy was studying everything in his screen.

"Is this normal?"

"Normal? Normal what?"

"When you got your leads in the past, did they look like this?"

"Oh, that normal?" Gina chuckled, then laughed aloud. Guy seemed oblivious.

"What?"

"Guy, darling, there is nothing remotely normal about any of that stuff. To answer your question – no, my previous leads, as you call them, happened….Well, you know how they happened – the radio broadcast and Evening Standard paper both existed weeks earlier than when they really happened. I've never seen anything like this. It's totally dodgy and probably doing something dastardly right now."

"Well it's too late now, but I don't think it's a scam. Look at the headline, that's directly to you – and names Watersource."

"That's not clever. That's like how the Met Office weather forecast website knows that I was looking for shoes at Humble & Keen the day before and shows me more Humble & Keen ads every time I check the weather forecast for the next month. Black magic spooky-wooky web stuff. That's all."

"Algorithms."

"Yeah, whatever. The work of the devil, that's what that is."

"If you say so." And with that, Guy picked up his laptop and left Gina to carry on her routine in her office. He set up on the coffee table in the sitting room and stared at the cryptic instruction, followed by the lines of numbers and letters.

For you to become Lord or Lady of this thing,
you need to use a pompom dog,
but only when you exchange equine slang
for its daily allowance

Guy dabbled at lightweight crosswords occasionally, but professed no particular talent. After a few minutes of analysing the various parts of the clue, he thought to copy it for a Google search, but that generated nothing of any use.

He randomly copied one of the lines below the clue for the same treatment.

5753-177

That search provided a link to a newspaper article about the '@' symbol and a lot of phone number permutations. Useless. Guy was getting frustrated but tried a Google search of another of the letter-number combinations:

M33 7

His hopes were raised for a brief moment when a map of Manchester appeared, but it was so non-specific that he quickly concluded that this wasn't working.

Back to the cryptic clue and a light came on. Guy suddenly thought of his mother. She was an inveterate crossword fanatic.

"Of course," he exclaimed silently with some surprise that it had taken him so long for the penny to drop. He copied the clue into a short email, then sent it and forgot about it; for about an hour, after which he was so frustrated that he phoned his mother to ask if she had received his email.

"No idea darling. I haven't switched on my computer for a couple of days."

"It's a cryptic clue that a friend has been sent. I'm sure you can crack it, Ma."

Sheila promised to look at it later so Guy put it aside and went back to his daily job-hunting.

"Do you fancy going down to Trappers for a sandwich for lunch?" Gina called through from her office. "My treat," she quickly added.

"Cool," was Guy's response, but only because he was conscious that his financial situation was becoming a boring topic. He hated having to worry about money but with no job or prospect of one soon, he had little choice but to be frugal. Gina was aware of his frustration so tackled the topic head on when they sat down at Trappers, each with a soft drink and a sandwich.

"Babe, I know you don't like taking my charity, as you see it, but it's not like that. I don't want you to worry about money. Or to think you owe me for your accommodation. I have more money than I could ever imagine and you know how I got it – not by working long hard grafting hours, that's for sure. I want to help for the few days – or weeks, til you get sorted. So let me. It's nothing to me to have you at the flat... No, you know what I mean. It's everything that you're there, but what I mean is you like, cost me nothing."

Guy smiled and took Gina's hand across the table and kissed her palm. He didn't need to say anything to convey his thanks.

"You're right that I'm not comfortable not paying my way. Old fashioned I suppose, these days, but well, that's just how I expect to be in a relationship. The money-earner, bread-winner. But you're right, it's temporary. I feel it in my waters, as my grandma used to say." Gina smiled her agreement as she took a swig of her Diet Coke.

The couple were preparing supper when Sheila phoned.

"The answer to your clue is Google," she announced with casual satisfaction.

"Are you sure?" Guy asked with evident surprise.

"Yes. Pompom dog is a poodle. A daily allowance is a per diem – or a PD; and a 'gg' is slang for a horse. So, replace the 'p' and 'd' in 'poodle' with a 'g' and 'g' so poodle becomes 'Google' the computer search thing."

"Ma, you're a genius. Thank you so much."

After a few pleasantries, Guy hung up and carried on preparing a salad.

"Well...?" Gina asked.

"She said the answer to the clue is Google but I tried some searches this morning and nothing came up. Perhaps you're right, it's all bollocks."

So it was with little enthusiasm that Guy went back to the puzzle after supper with Gina taking only a casual interest as she flipped the pages of a colour supplement at the other end of the sofa.

Guy took each line of the clues in order and wrote down the results of a Google search on a note pad. After six searches of the letter-number combinations, he had summarised the results with various nondescript words.

O ring   Feature film 'FOUR'   4
Manchester   ~~Guardian~~   @ North London
Seven Sisters Road   ~~Greek phone nos~~

"See what I mean." Guy turned the pad for Gina to read his notes summarising the search results. Gina was as confused as Guy.

"Sorry babe, load of bollocks, as you so eloquently described it." But then Gina took more interest, put down her magazine and slid along the sofa to look at the original clue on the laptop screen.

"The first part of the clue – *'For you to become Lord or Lady of this thing'* does work with *'ring'*." She pointed at Guy's first note: 'O ring'.

"Lord of the Rings."

Guy was suddenly engaged.

"That's so cool. What about the next lot of numbers?"

VI1693755673 had led to a trailer for a film called 'FOUR'. Guy repeated the search and arrived at the same destination. The plot about four relationships criss-crossing on the night of 4th July in the US, provided no apparent clues.

"That could be the start of some numbers like, 'ring 4 - something'. It could be a phone number," Gina suggested.

"Yeah, could be." Guy was now showing a modicum of optimism that they were on a track that could lead somewhere.

"Or maybe we should read it as 'ring for something' like 'an explanation' or 'ring for help'. That sort of thing."

Guy added the word *'for'* to his jottings on the pad; then put the next clue into the Google search window which again arrived at a map of Manchester. The postcode prefix **M33 7** dominated the first page of results on his screen. Guy opened the map and moved around it hoping to find a street name or a word that looked appropriate or perhaps a lead to another number, but only found repeated references to the Sale area of Greater Manchester.

"Sale....bloody Sale!" He exclaimed. "Of course." He added the word to the pad to give them *Ring for Sale*. He almost fell over himself to add the @ symbol that he had found previously for the next clue on the list; then on to search the next number-letter combination that he had already discovered to be a house number and postcode that took him to a property on a street in north London. A blue pin landed on the same property when Guy repeated the process. He clicked Street View and a moment later he and Gina were looking at the image of a jeweller's shopfront. The couple gasped aloud in unison. Guy turned to Gina, wide-eyed and chuckling with overwhelming excitement.

"And the last number must be some reference for the ring," Guy added.

Once his excitement at cracking the code had subsided, Gina offered her more sober reaction.

"But so what? So there's a ring for sale in a jewellers called Rushou on Seven Sisters Road....."

"Yeah," Guy agreed sceptically. "But if someone has gone to this much trouble to provide this much clue to a specific ring, I think we can assume it's for some good reason." But whilst Guy believed what he had just said, the more he thought about it during the rest of the evening, the more he puzzled about what to do with the information.

32

Guy woke early and lay in bed thinking. He picked up from the point where he had left off the previous night, but this morning, things seemed much clearer. By the time he sprung out of bed soon after eight-o'clock, he had a plan.

At nine-thirty, Guy phoned Rushou Jewellers.

"Good morning. Can I speak to you about a ring you were selling recently, please?"

"What about it?" The response was gruff and abrupt.

"My girlfriend tried it on and took what I think is a reference number for it. Can I give that to you?"

"T'would be a good idea if you want me to do anything about it."

"The number is six, zero, three, dash, twenty, dash, forty – that's four, zero."

Without a word, the phone clunked down and Guy was left with his pulse rate increasing. He now knew that the reference number was one used by the shop, but the email had originally arrived almost three weeks earlier, so Guy was dreading the response that the ring had already been sold.

"So, a costume jewellery ring with a large paste diamond with five smaller ones set in an ornate white gold ring. Second hand – is that the one?"

"Yeah, that sounds like it." Guy's heart was speeding so much that he thought it was discernible in his voice.

"How much is that please?"

"£48."

"Will you put it aside for me please? I'll collect it later today."

"Until five this afternoon. Name?"

Guy responded with as much control as he could muster, then hung up.

"Yeessss!"

Guy arrived at Rushou Jewellers within the hour. He rang the doorbell for entry then made his way to the counter where a dapper man wearing a black suit and topped with patent black slicked down hair was studying him closely.

"Yes?"

The resonant voice was recognisable from their telephone conversation, but the petite man with paper-white complexion was nothing like the mind's eye impression that it created.

"Hello, I phoned earlier about a ring that you were going to put aside for me." Guy spoke with a determination to remain upbeat despite feeling anxious and somewhat disturbed by the tense atmosphere created by the creepy unsalesmanlike salesman.

Mr Creepy reached under the counter and produced a large ring with a price tag hanging from it. Guy took it and inspected it as if he knew what he was looking at.

"Thank you. I'll take it." Then he thought to add: "May I have a receipt please?"

"Of course."

'Get me out of here', was Guy's thought. The atmosphere was brittle, but briefly lightened as His Creepiness turned away from the counter to get a pad of receipts and dropped down some six inches as he apparently stepped off a small box platform behind the counter that had brought him almost to Guy's eye line. As it did again when he resumed his position with a pad and pen in hand.

"Who are you?"

"I beg your pardon?" Guy was genuinely confused by the emphasis on the *'are'* that made the question sound like an interrogation.

"For the receipt. I assume you want me to add your name."

"Oh yes. Thank you – Guy Tozer."

Guy pulled some notes from his wallet then watched the man fill in the details on the pad with a neat script hand-writing that suited his character precisely. Guy wondered how the man with a near-baritone voice could be so hermaphrodite in appearance. The skin on his hands and face was so smooth that it appeared any hair had been surgically removed.

The man reached under the counter again and produced a small bag with a Rushou logo printed on the side. From it he pulled an envelope.

"Is Gina your girlfriend?"

Silence. The two men starred at one another. Guy was too shocked to speak.

"You told me that your girlfriend, Gina, had tried on the ring. I was going to put a personalised gift card in the bag. But if you prefer…"

"Yes. Thank you - that would be cool," Guy interrupted. Anything to speed up proceedings. The man wrote a message on a card, placed it and the receipt in an envelope that he dropped into the small bag with the ring in a red box then gave Guy his change from £60 and watched him leave the shop.

Guy walked straight back to the Underground station intending to make his way into Hatton Garden, the centre of many of London's jewellery businesses. No need to change that plan, but he was now preoccupied and quite shaken by the encounter with Alabaster Man. The more Guy replayed his original phone conversation with him this morning, the more convinced he was that he had not mentioned Gina's name.

'Why would I?' was his residing thought. Why would he have told a man on the end of the phone the name of his girlfriend? He knew he hadn't.

'No way.'

Guy had researched Tallow, Young and Blank - TYB International - being one of the companies in Hatton Garden that specialised in diamonds and boasted a valuation service on the company website.

At the counter, Guy asked for a valuation for the ring then sat down to wait while the charming assistant took it to a small workshop just off the reception to see if anyone was available to do the valuation immediately. For the briefest moment, Guy worried that he couldn't see it, but casually moved to position himself in direct line of sight with a man who was examining the ring through an eyeglass. He lowered it, thought for a moment then examined it again. Then called an older colleague over to do the same. By now, Guy was confident that the ring was worth more than the £48 that he had just paid for it, but he had no expectation of what would come next.

"Good morning, sir," said the second examiner when he came back into the reception holding the ring. "My name is James Blank, I'm one of the company partners and chief valuer of precious stones. And this is rather precious. Very striking and I'd say, unique." He held it up to the light as he spoke. "May I ask, is this an heirloom?"

"No, I ….I acquired it recently."

"Do you know its history?"

"No, sorry."

"That's a shame." Mr Blank pondered that response for a moment. "I understand that you have asked for a valuation, but it's a little difficult to be precise - that's why I ask you about its history - so I need to do some more research if you will kindly leave it with me. We will of course give you a receipt and I assure you that it'll be kept in the safe here on these premises. Will that be possible please – just for a couple of days, three at most?"

"Yes, I suppose so. Can I ask why it's difficult to estimate a value?"

"Oh, I can estimate it within a range, sir, even now, but I would like to be more precise because I suspect that this ring may well be one with a rare history. If I'm correct, that could as much as double its value."

"From what, may I ask?"

"Without the history, these diamonds – particularly because of the quality of the large centre one - collectively have a value in the range of ..." He thought for a heart-stopping moment. "I'd estimate a range of about £100,000 to £120,000."

Guy stared speechless whilst trying desperately to think of something to say not to embarrass himself.

"Cool."

33

"Welcome to my world," was Gina's first, somewhat measured response. Guy was still beside himself with excitement. He had returned to the flat by bus, hardly noticing the route or other passengers. His heart was bursting with adrenaline and his brain with thoughts about the consequences of making the money. Numerous times the annual salary that he had just lost with his job.

By the time he reached Camden he had calmed down and started to consider what had just happened; the bizarre process from cryptic email to the likelihood of being gifted a lot of money. Gifted by whom? He had almost forgotten the creepy episode at Rushou Jewellers. Relating the story to Gina brought back the memory briefly, but he had moved on because the valuation had wiped the anxiety that he felt when he bought the ring, from his emotions.

Guy was aware that the process that he had just witnessed had been intended for Gina. He only now connected with her mad, mad, mad, mad world of recent months. He was struggling. He loved the idea of the money but, rather like a nonbeliever seeing a ghost, Guy was having to make an enormous adjustment. He had listened with sympathy and assumed some empathy with Gina's story, but now, having been involved first hand, he was unprepared for the impact of what had happened over the course of a few hours. It was all too sudden and it would need time for him to put it into context.

Once he had reported the morning's activities in a breathless gush to Gina, their conversation moved to a more measured analysis of the events that Guy had just witnessed.

"So now you can maybe understand a bit of what I've been going through," Gina suggested.

"Yeah." Guy answered with obvious sincerity in that single word.

They say money can't buy happiness, but they're wrong .... Well, in this case they were. Guy was a changed man – even before he received a penny from his new fortune. I don't think I realised how much his confidence had been knocked over the last couple of weeks but now, with the prospect of an enormous windfall of cash, he was re-energised and upbeat and bubbly like his old self. Once he'd bounced around for a couple of hours after getting back to my flat on that first evening, he took a breath and got real... Well, in his terms.

"Gee, it's not my money. At best it might be *ours* but I think of it as yours. You got the lead. It was obviously intended for you and, I assume, for your good work with Watersource. We both know it's something to do with your weird life at the moment and I was a ….a sort of facilitator. I think I…"

"Babe…" Gina interrupted, "…I wasn't even going to open the email. I wouldn't have done anything with it. Really, you know that. You made it happen. It's your money. I don't want it – I don't need it."

"You don't know that. You don't need it now but you will. These crazy leads could… *this* could be the last one. They could get even more obscure than this one and you won't even recognise them so they pass you by."

"Good. This whole thing scares me. You know what you're feeling now – the weirdness that you've just experienced – that's been happening to me for months now and I really won't miss it. Yes, of course having the money is fantastic but I've felt like some spirit or something spooky-wooky has been like, watching my every move since getting back from Devon. That's not nice or comfortable or anything I'll miss. If I can get my life back to normal, I'll be only too happy."

Guy contemplated Gina's statement.

Yeah, that seemed to have struck a chord because we didn't speak about whose money it would be again. I assumed Guy had accepted that it would be his. But - or maybe because of that - he was just lovely to have back. He was excited and fun and spending the money in his head before the jeweller contacted him a couple of days later. He was bubbling with ideas about how to help me with things I needed for the flat and personally - and suggested we take a weekend break to get away. The topic dominated his thoughts - he even wanted to know if he could buy something for Watersource. I repeatedly told him get real and stop being extravagant and to lower his expectations from the £240,000 he was expecting. I told him it was best he assumed the ring was only worth the lower price - £100,000.
Hark at me - 'only £100,000' - huh.
Round about the point where it was becoming a little too intense and to be honest, a bit boring, the jeweller sent a text asking Guy to call him about the valuation, which he did an instant after seeing the message.

"Thank you for calling, Mr Tozer, I've completed the valuation so you can collect your ring at any time that suits you. I will post the written valuation to you today."

"Thank you, can I ask what you discovered - you were going to make some investigations?"

"Yes - and fascinating they were. Unfortunately, not quite as conclusive as I hoped, but your ring's history has certainly increased its value appreciably."

"Really?" Guy was trying hard to sound relaxed and not gush his questions. "Are you able to tell me the value you've put on it?"

"Certainly. Well if I was to sell it, which is how I think it best to come to the final valuation, I would put a price of £225,000 on it."

"Gosh. That's....that's ...seriously cool. Thank you."

"Indeed, sir. As you say, rather *cool*." Mr Blank's tone betrayed an apparent smile as he spoke the words.

"And its history - what did you discover, may I ask?"

"Certainly. Well, your ring looked familiar as soon as I saw it. The ornate white gold ring is probably unique so that rung bells for me immediately. It's not one you forget once you've seen a photograph of it. I couldn't remember what the story was, but suspected that someone of note had owned it in the past, which was the case. It was originally owned by the opera singer, Norma Fritzen, when it was given as a gift by a wealthy suiter in 1965. After her death, it was sold with her estate and was bought by a wife of one of the late Kings of Saudi Arabia. All this we can prove – I even have a photograph of Miss Fritzen wearing a ring that could well be this one. How it got back into the public domain no-one seems to know. But we do know that it has never been reported stolen or lost so there is no question about it being legally yours - subject to proof of purchase, that is. Hence my confidence about a valuation over £200,000 should you ever want to sell it."

"And if I do want to sell it, would you do that?"

"It's not a service we would normally offer but for such a unique piece of jewellery I'm sure we can make some introductions, sir. I have at least three customers who I can approach directly who I think would be very interested in your ring. Are you considering selling it, may I ask?"

"Yes. I assume you would take a commission on the sale - is that correct?"

"Precisely. I would need proof of ownership and I will need to see you here with some proof of your identity. It's all to do with money-laundering legislation - sorry about that sir. But once we've completed that simple procedure, I will make enquiries and, assuming I do make a sale at an agreeable price to yourself, we will charge fifteen percent of the sale price for our service."

Guy was calm and collected by now. He took instructions about the paperwork required to verify his identity then arranged a visit to the shop the next morning.

All of which went disarmingly smoothly until James Blank studied the receipt. Guy had already considered the potential awkwardness in admitting that he had only bought the ring on the same morning as his visit to TYB for the valuation. He hadn't studied the bill of sale, so was confused by...

"So you purchased it in 2005... for £48?" Mr Blank was wide-eyed staring at the price. "Gosh. Someone at Rushou Jewellers hadn't done their due diligence." He was amazed. Guy was puzzled.

"Can I see the receipt please?" Mr Blank turned it back across the counter where they were sorting out the formalities. Guy read the date for the first time. It clearly stated '29/09/2005' in Mr Creepy's dapper script handwriting. James Blank had turned away to tap at a keyboard below the counter then, a minute later, announced:

"No wonder it's gone out of business. Never mind, no problem. The receipt is fine and the stamp has the company certification, so that's all in order."

"Sorry - did you say that it's gone out of business?"

"Yes, I've just tried a search for it online but the name doesn't bring up anything. Not a problem - it existed in 2005 and the receipt is fine."

Guy had stopped listening for the moment; he was pondering the fact that the company didn't exist. But he now reconnected as Mr Blank asked if he could photocopy the documents that Guy had brought with him.

"Yes, of course, please do."

Guy was anxious to do his own search for the phantom jewellers, which he did on his phone as he sat on the top deck of a bus making his way back to Camden. He started with the name that found nothing; then the address, including another search using property number and same postcode that had previously resulted in a Street View of the front of Rushou Jewellers. But no jewellers was to be seen, just a couple small shops and a double fronted supermarket. Guy began to doubt himself. He moved the image on his phone up and down Sever Sisters Road for several blocks, but found no jewellers of any name. Guy shut down the phone and stared out of the bus window in a daze. More puzzled than upset; not certain if he wanted answers to the questions that now started to worry him.

He had to steel himself to get off the bus at the next stop. It was an easy diversion back to Seven Sisters Road on another bus where he could prove for himself if the jewellers existed.

To his surprise, the shop came into view as he walked along a pavement on the opposite side of the street. By then, Guy had convinced himself that it wouldn't be there. But as he waited to cross between the traffic he could see that it was closed. All the window displays had been removed and a blind was pulled down inside the glass door. When he arrived in front of the shop, he could read a printed note taped inside one of the windows at eye height that stated: WE ARE NOW CLOSED FOR THE FORESEEABLE FUTURE. SORRY FOR ANY INCONVENIENCE. Guy reflected on what had happened to him during the last few days - his bizarre introduction to Rushou, his visit to the shop and the encounter with Mr Creepy and now the significance of the closure. As he stood alone, staring into the distance, he became aware of a woman brushing out the entrance to the pet shop next door. He wandered over to her.

"Excuse me – do you know anything about the jewellers next door?" He gestured over his shoulder towards the shop. The woman carried on her chores as she spoke without looking up.

"Not really – like what?"

"Like, when it closed."

"Just a few days ago. You haven't got anything to pick up, I hope."

"No, nothing like that."

"It only arrived a few weeks back. Must have been one of those pop shops."

172

"Pop-up."

"Yeah – whatever. No wonder it's gone – it hardly ever opened. No chance it was going to work."

Guy thought to ask more questions but stopped himself. Why? What would be the point? Instead, he wandered away deep in thought when Gina's words came back to him, *'welcome to my world.'*

34

I shouldn't have been so surprised about how much Dizzy's email changed things. But I was and it did. A lot. Firstly it focussed my attention on why I was plodding through my daily routines - and it gave me a new target – the next water system – a bigger one. Dizzy couldn't just send emails whenever he wanted so we saved our contacts and news for infrequent exchanges but Dizzy was back in my inbox within the week to ask when I could send a new system. He had it all worked out – where, what, how much. That gave me another target. I didn't tell him that the money was there because I thought he would literally ask for more, and more often, if I made it look easy. So I told him that I would do my best to sort it out.

That exchange reminded me about his Probation Officer and I hoped Dizzy had sent a report to her about what he was doing - and with some of the fab photos. I couldn't ask him easily so I took it on myself to send a report – well, I was the sort of sponsor of his trip. I attached some of the best photos that illustrated my report and sent it without much expectation of a prompt response, although I would have been miffed if I hadn't got one at all. But the same morning, Kathy Rawlings replied with the nicest email. It was really touching and went on about how glad she was for Dizzy and that his success had cheered her up a lot and so on and on. I was made up as well. So I sent the exchange to Dizzy, not knowing when he would read it, but that wasn't important. I think a Probation Officer's life must be hellish for ninety-something percent of the

*time, so any small victory must be something to cherish. I
was so glad I emailed her.*

*One big change that had happened to me over recent
months that I think I may have previously mentioned in
passing, was how my attitude to raising money had
changed. I used to be a tin-rattler and charity bike ride
organiser. But my brief appearance on the 7 O'Clock
Show and my CityZen award had shown me how powerful
a bit of good exposure in the media can be. And that
carries over into my social media stuff. Then people seek
you out without you having to keep chasing. Me with my
tiny little voice in the great morass of charityland was
always having a helluva struggle to attract attention – and
attract funds. But after the 7 O'clock Show I got loads of
approaches from all sorts of good guys and oddballs
offering to help. Most were selling their fund-raising
services for a percentage, but they were easily dismissed.
I've always been very principled about getting maximum
bangs for anyone's buck. If someone gives me a pound
for Watersource it's to help people in Africa, not to pay
agency fees or for advertising. A few years ago Oxfam
paid more than half a million pounds to have its brand
redesigned. £550,000 to be exact, or so their press-
releases admitted. That's obscene – unforgiveable. So
what did the thousands of volunteers manning the shops
for free and the bucket-shakers and the people that put a
few quid in them, get for the £550,000? The typeface was
changed on the logo. Seriously. I wonder how much
support they lost when that news got out – which it did –
big time. The CEO should have been sacked, or
something worse. What a monstrous abuse of
responsibility. It makes me angry even now thinking about
it. The thing is, I know I think small time because
Watersource is just me and that's probably why I've never*

understood how the big charities justify having hundreds of staff working in Central London premises. A wages bill of £millions a year plus the cost of the offices before any money goes to the causes. That includes one of the highest profile charities doing what I'm doing to fund water projects in the third world. Anyway, that's never going to happen to my supporters, or my sponsors. And after the 7 O'Clock Show there were lots of companies that wanted to sponsor Watersource. That was difficult for me to handle. I've never been in that position before. There were some odd ones that I couldn't understand why they approached me. Some offered serious money, like the tobacco company offering an obscene amount. I think it would have totalled nearly £60,000 a year if I agreed to their contract. I assume because they wanted to change their image by associating with a clean-water-provider and Africa is still a cash cow for cigarette companies that are long gone here in Europe. Anyway, I politely told them to take a hike. But after a lot of consideration I did allow a couple of companies to sponsor Watersource. Both are suppliers – one makes the plastic piping and something called 'extrusions' that our new system needs; and the other is a chemical producer that some of the systems have to use for purification when they start-up, basically. Ooops, damn, I'm still doing it. Anyway, I negotiated the deals, so I don't know if they're the best, but they suit me. £20,000 each for links between our websites and an obligation for me to use their logos on all correspondence etc. And I have to make up to four personal appearances at suitable events during any year.

Well, the first event happened to be one that both companies were going to attend so I was going to kill two birds with one outing. And I could take a 'plus one' guest which was great because I had been inventing stuff to get Guy out of the flat where he was spending more time than *ever. Too much, I think. The money had been paid to him for the ring so he didn't seem to be making much effort to find permanent work. A couple of passing references in his conversation suggested that he thought there would be more chances of windfalls of 'easy-money' as he called it. But I knew that the episode with the jeweller's shop had upset him more than he was admitting. I would catch him reading the evening paper or doing something on his laptop then realise that he hadn't turned the page or moved his screen for a long while. I knew that he was reliving his encounter with the jeweller, basically. (Damn it - I've got to stop that). But Guy would occasionally mention it out of the blue when he would suddenly ask a question or make a statement relating back to Seven Sisters Road and sometimes to my weird world in general.*

"Have you ever wondered why it was you?"

"What?"

The statement had come out of nowhere one evening at the flat.

"Why *you* were chosen for the leads and all your good fortune?"

"Er....No, not particularly. But you obviously have."

"Yeah. But you think about it – there was loads of people on your ride that day – loads of people on the moor who *could* have been hit by lightning then met Mrs Whatever-her-name-was…"

"Flik."

"Yeah, right. Then heard the lottery news and got the lead with the horse, but no-one else did, just you."

"Your point is? I sense you have one."

"Yeah. I think it's because you are…well, you. You're driven, you have a cause in Watersource. And you have spirit. You're a climber not a stander…. At which point you go – *'yer wot?'* And I explain that escalators have people that get on and stand and wait for it to deliver them to the top in a minute or so – they're 'standers'. Then there's the 'climbers' who don't slow their pace from walking or running and keep moving up the left side. Climbers don't let the

177

speed of a machine slow their lives down to a crawl. And you're a climber, right? Can you imagine if everything that's happened to you had happened to, say – sorry, what's the name of your girlfriend on the ride?"

"Do you mean Saffy?"

"Yeah, right. From what you say, she's definitely a *stander*. She'd have fallen apart if it all happened to her. She wouldn't have chased down the leads – in fact, she probably wouldn't have noticed them."

"Stop it. Saffy's a really good friend. And she'd come all the way to Devon to help me out on the charity ride."

"Yeah, okay – sorry, but you take my point; she wouldn't have done what you've done with the opportunities you got. Dizzy, sounds like he may have done something about them, perhaps, because he sounds like a climber, but no-one else you've talked about that was connected with the event, would have got as much out of the chances that were presented to you, as you did. You know what I mean?" Gina was reflecting.

He's right, actually.

"My point is that everything you've made from the weirdo world of Weirdsville has been because *you* made it happen and didn't just ignore the opportunity and let it drift past like the ads on the escalators....That's quite a good analogy – I just thought of that bit. Okay, much of that drive was because of your passion for making money for Watersource, but whatever the reason, you picked up every ball that was tossed your way (well, until the last one) and ran with it. I was just wondering if that's why you were chosen. Have you never thought about that?"

"No babe... but I *live* with that. And maybe you should do too. As you've said repeatedly, that may be the one and only time you get the chance to make your easy money. I think you should let it go now and move on."

178

You see why I was always looking for chances for us to get out of the flat to do stuff – anything really. Sometimes no more than going down the High Road for a coffee. But tonight was a big one - we were going to a swanky night out and that was great. And, as an attendee charity, Watersource would get two percent of all the money raised on the night. It was at a very big ballroom sort of place in Central London, right by Hyde Park. So Guy and me, we put on our glad rags (Guy had to hire his but he looks so adorable in black tie evening dress, perhaps he should buy one). Anyway, a car laid on by one of my sponsors, picked us up and dropped us right outside to make an entrance in our finery. We cruised around chatting to the great and good and seriously wealthy - and being told where to go and who to have our photos taken with all night, then we danced the last hour away to a fab big band. It was such a fun night. Oh yes, and there was an auction for things like some footballer's Rolex watch. I think that made nearly ten grand. And a house make-over by some guru who I hadn't heard of; and an electric car that went for over twenty grand, I remember. Guy and I kept exchanging knowing looks, knowing that Watersource was going to make some of the profits. That eventually turned out to be £4,645-78 pence. This was grown-up fund raising. I was now in the big time from the very small time world of fund-begging.

We were in the taxi on our way home when Guy announced:

"I was offered a job tonight."

"Really?!"

"Yeah."

"What sort of job?"

"A sort of Mr Fixit job from what I can understand."

"Who offered you that?"

"That lady, Brigitte, sitting next to me at dinner."

Bloody cheek. Making a move on my man. I shouldn't be surprised - I thought they were a bit close for a bit too long.

"Really? Is she legit...or just trying to get into your well cut trousers?"

"Gee – how sweet – jealousy really becomes you."

"Jealous, who me? Of that gorgeous, long-legged, blinged-up, obviously-wealthy, sun-tanned blonde who was chatting you up all evening?"

Guy smiled then removed a business card from an inside jacket pocket and read the title.

"Holly Bush International.... Celebrity PR Management.... Based in Chelsea and run by Brigitte and Holly, her partner – and not only her business partner, if you know what I mean." Guy watched the penny drop for Gina.

"Oh.... Really?" Gina was surprised, verging on shocked as she thought back to the two very attractive ladies at the dinner. "Is that the Holly who was sitting two to my right?"

"Yes, the very one. Probably the second prettiest lady in the room tonight."

Gina smiled, assuming that Guy was listing her as first, but then he spoiled it with:

"It's not fair, is it?"

"What isn't?"

"A beautiful lady like that, unavailable to the hot-blooded male populous." Gina rolled her eyes. Guy snuggled closer to whisper:

"So, nothing to worry about there for a few reasons – one of which is that they are not the slightest bit interested in me – well, not sexually – but more important, because I think you look absolutely fantastically beautifully gorgeous tonight which is just one of the reasons why I am so in love with you and cannot wait to get you home to do wonderful things to your perfect body. Outside and in."

"Ah," was Gina's briefly-considered response. "As romantic as you make that sound, good sire, I'm afraid you will have to hold that thought for a few days – from lunchtime today. Sorry babe."

"Ah – right. I will. It's a date for the weekend then."

The rest of the journey home was spent discussing the job offer, or as much as Guy could remember about it.

The noise and boozy atmosphere of the evening had taken their toll on detail, but he could recall that the job would be to look after Chaz E Jones, the rapper, whenever he's in the UK. Brigitte hadn't over sold the job because it sounded a bit thankless, to be honest. Guy would be at the singer's beck and call, but I could tell Guy was flattered to be asked and a bit star-struck perhaps, so he was going to phone them in the morning to check out more details.

"Well?" Asked Gina immediately Guy came off the phone to Brigitte the next morning. Gina had listened to their end of the conversation from which she concluded that Holly Bush International was making a tempting offer that Guy was considering seriously.

"£25,000 a year for up to sixty-five days' work whether they use them or not. If it goes over, they pay £400 a day. Last year he was in the UK for thirty-eight days, but it will be more this year because he has a UK tour for about thirty days."

"And what will you do?"

"Sort of look after him – well, his almost every need."

"What, like sourcing his drugs?" Gina asked abruptly.

"No. Apparently not, Brigitte assured me that that's not a problem because he's a born-again Christian and has cleaned up his act over the last eighteen months."

"Then why are they paying you so much? What's the catch?"

"I don't think there's a catch but she says my life won't really be my own when he's over here. He owns an apartment somewhere in

Chelsea – she didn't want to say where before I agree to take the job – and I would be there or there abouts to sort his every desire."

"Men... women... boys... girls?"

"You have such a suspicious mind."

"I heard you ask something about that."

"Yeah, I did, didn't I?"

"And...?"

"Women by preference it seems - never under-age. She said that an example of how demanding he is, is he's paranoid about secrecy and keeping out of the way of the paparazzi, so no-one he doesn't know ever goes to his apartment. If he wants a pizza at two in the morning, he would phone me to get it and deliver it to him so that no delivery boy finds out where he lives."

"Are you tempted?"

"A bit. Sounds like a well-paid adventure. And I can always leave if I don't like him or the job."

"And they pay you from when you agree, I assume, not from when he arrives for his first visit – is that right?"

"Absolutely, money in my account every month plus extra days and expenses. Except he's in London at the end of next week so they want a fast response or they have someone else in mind. I have first refusal, providing it's in the next couple of days."

35

Guy took the job. So, no surprise there. That was to come a week later when Brigitte and Holly took him to meet Chaz E Jones at his apartment in a complex built around a small harbour next to the River Thames in Chelsea. Guy was excited about starting the new job, but not overwhelmed until he met Brigitte and Holly at their offices for his briefing and it quickly became apparent that Chaz E Jones was a very important client for Holly Bush. There was much watch-checking before the taxi arrived, timed to ensure that they were all at their client's apartment a few minutes before eleven-o'clock. Once in the apartment, the women were clearly ill at ease, fawning around him, hanging on his every word, offering to oblige his every wish and laughing rather too easily at his every quip. Guy had been briefed in advance and provided with a list of duties of which the unwritten rule seemed to be: do whatever is needed to keep him happy. Guy was more relieved that nothing on the list compromised his better judgment or morals. In fact they were surprisingly mundane and included buying all toiletries as and when required. Holly was very particular about this and insisted that Guy kept an inventory of the contents of Chaz's bathrooms that he checked and replenished daily as required.

The atmosphere in the apartment changed noticeably when Brigitte and Holly left to return to their offices. And Guy quickly realised that Chaz was not taken in by their over-attentive behaviour, confiding in Guy that he liked people who made things happen, which Holly Bush do, but wasn't comfortable with insincerity. Guy took that to be a warning.

Chaz was only passing through London on his way to a big event in Amsterdam and was using the trip as an excuse to do some antique shopping in London for a few of days. So that became Guy's main responsibility – to locate the items on Chaz's shopping list, track them to a particular location then to organise the shopping trips. Just the two of them. Guy had been told that a representative from Chaz's US management company was billeted in a hotel in the same complex but he (Joey, by name) was nowhere in evidence until the third day. But no security, no friends or girlfriends. A cleaning lady called Rosita visited every morning for an hour and that was it, the only person Chaz would have met for several days, had Guy not been there. And since Rosita barely spoke English, Chaz could have lived a hermit existence very easily had he so desired.

Naturally Guy had done his homework on Chaz before they met. The videos that he had studied at length, even trying to learn some of the almost indiscernible lyrics, were typical examples of rapper fare. Lots of very scantily-clad nubile ladies dancing around the main man in a studio or on a stage or a boat or executive jet. So Guy was assuming that would be the world into which he would have to fit for the duration of Chaz's visits to London. But no. His life could not be more different. Most of the time, Guy was the only other person in his life. A life that seemed more framed by his newly-adopted Christianity than unbridled hedonism.

But the warning about the long hours was entirely appropriate. The first day ended at the start of the next. Guy was in a taxi on his way home to Camden at 12.45 when Chaz called him to change his start time for the morning to seven-o'clock because he had just realised that Guy hadn't laid out breakfast and he was almost out of milk. Warning bells rang loudly, but Guy politely apologised and Chaz forgave him because they were getting to know one another.

What became patently evident was that Guy was there so that neither Brigitte nor Holly had to be. He reported to them daily and sensed that they were pleased with his performance. He supposed that they had checked with Chaz to ensure that one of their bigger clients was comfortable and satisfied and cosy in the care of their new rep. So, by mid-week, Guy assumed that Chaz must have given him a good rating or he would have been given his marching orders.

By the end of the week, Guy needed to sleep. Chaz only slept for about four hours a night and worked at both ends on composing in his bedroom studio. Before and after Guy's hours of duty, he had an hour's travel time to and from home. It was a long day and short night for someone who ideally needed seven hours sleep.

"I can hack it for a few days at a time," he confided in Gina during their first exchange all week, "but when he comes back for his tour next spring, he'll be here for a month."

"But it'll be a different routine when he's on the road, won't it?" Gina suggested.

"I don't know."

"Well you need to find out from Brigitte. If this is it, will you stay on?"

"I honestly don't know. But I must admit that the thought of a few intensive weeks' work for such a good regular salary is very tempting. I don't know where else I would find anything like it with so much time off in between the heavy bits."

"Do you like him?"

"Yeah, I do. I think he's a really nice guy once he opens up a little and the more I get to know him…. No, the more *he* gets to know *me* and confides stuff in me, the better I like him. I still think it's crazy that his whole public image is swanky and rapperish - you know - with girls and guns and lyrics about drugs and his *hood*. I feel like I'm there to keep his secret that his ideal night in is with the Simpsons or catching up with the latest blockbuster TV series."

This was the Saturday morning after Guy's first week in his new job. Chaz and his low-profile manager had set off for Amsterdam leaving Guy to arrange transit for all his antique purchases. And that would be Guy's sole responsibility until his charge arrived back next year for his UK tour.

"Let's go to The Feathers for lunch and how do you fancy a film tonight at The Screen?" Guy suggested. "Assuming I can keep awake."

"Great."

185

The afternoon had become clear and crisp and unseasonably cold when they left the pub.

"Let's cut through the park – it's such a nice afternoon," Guy suggested. Then as they turned off the road, Guy's phone rang. He took it from his pocket to read 'BRIGITTE' in the screen.

"Sorry, it's Brigitte, I ought to take it."

Gina rolled her eyes.

Blimey. If I didn't know better, I'd think she had designs on Guy.

"No that's okay - we're just on our way home from the pub ……. Thanks, you're welcome …....." Guy had stopped walking and now moved to a park bench to sit while he spoke on the phone. Gina joined him.

"…… Really? I had no idea ……….. That's nice to know – thanks for telling me ……… Well, maybe. Will it be the same hours?......... Yes, very long days because of the extra travel time to and from Camden ……. Yeah ……. Okay ……….."

Gina was half listening to Guy's end of the conversation but started to take more interest in the activities around her. A large dog lumbered past. Some boys were playing football close to a sign stating: *No Ball Games*. In the distance someone had flown a remote plane into some trees and seemed to be having trouble getting it down. A small girl on a tiny two-wheeled bicycle wobbled past with her father close behind.

"….thanks again, Brigitte, I'll call you then ……. bye."

"Well? Was that okay?"

"Yeah, she just offered me another job."

"Really? What kind of job?"

"The same thing for another artist coming over in a few weeks, but not the same hours, so not as well paid. I said I'd go in and talk it through next week."

"They seem to like you."

"Yeah, apparently. She was just saying that I'm the third person they've put on Chaz's case and he burns them out. You know the call that first night when he told me to get in early with milk for breakfast – he does that sort of thing with all the new boys and the guy before me told him to fuck off and resigned that night – huh." Guy pondered that for a moment. "So he's given me a thumbs up and seems to like me …. which means Brigitte and Holly like me. So that's good."

Gina cuddled up to Guy with as much of a hug possible in their padded coats. They watched the tableau across the park in front of them, now backlit with a milky autumnal sun low in the sky. Neither spoke for a short while until Guy broke their silence.

"I've been thinking." They both continued to stare ahead.

"Gooooood, that's nice."

"That perhaps we should consider moving in together properly."

That caught Gina unawares. Not at the thought, but because Guy had not given any hint during the last hour and a half in the pub, that he was thinking about such a subject.

"Aren't we already?"

"Yes but it's more like I've come to live with you in your flat when I needed a port in a storm - well, for want of a better expression, but you know what I mean."

"Yes, I know what you mean. But what more do you want that we don't have now?"

"I don't know… Security… Space."

"Are you suggesting something forever?"

"Of course. Sorry, is that coming on a bit strong?"

Gina had to think about that.

"This is ….. well, such a big question. Don't get me wrong, babe…." Gina turned to look Guy in the eyes. "You are the most important person and thing in my life. I love you. I love having you living with me, but we have only known one another for a few months."

"So?"

187

"So….I need time to adjust to the idea. I've been set in my ways for years – obviously too many years – but I'm a creature of routine. Are you suggesting buying a house together?"

"I hadn't thought that far – maybe renting, but yes, perhaps we should buy something – we can afford it between us."

Gina was visibly shocked. She had no idea that Guy was thinking more than days ahead, let alone what suddenly sounded like a lifetime. The very idea of buying a house together was so far from Gina's thoughts that all she could think to say was:

"Not round here we can't, it's far too expensive."

Now Guy looked a little awkward.

"Well, I was thinking about over near Chelsea."

"You're kidding! We certainly couldn't afford to live in Chelsea even if we wanted to."

"Not *in* Chelsea, of course, but over that side of town."

Gina sighed as she realised…

"Oh, it's because of your job, isn't it? Even though you may not even keep the job – you don't sound convinced about it."

"No, but I could be if it wasn't for the travel - that's the killer. It can easily add a couple hours to my day - you know that." Guy sensed that this was not going to plan - not that he had a plan, but he realised that the way that he had just presented his case had not been convincing so it was probably best to leave it for the moment. He had planted the seed.

"It was just a thought. There's no rush and the fact still remains that I want to live with you for the rest of my life. There we are, that's the bottom line. How and where and when we do things to get us to that end ….. well, you say. But, if you don't feel the same as me, I really would like you to tell me so I don't make a complete fool of myself again."

Gina threw her arms around Guy.

"Darling Guy. Please don't ever, ever, ever doubt my love. But what you've just said, that takes some thought. Let me think about it and meanwhile I promise I'll look at what we can buy or rent over that side of town – I promise. Is that okay?"

188

"Cool."

They left the bench and carried on their route home through the park. As they approached the gate to leave, from nowhere, a sudden wind began to blow up. Little more than a stiff breeze for a few steps, then it strengthened into a strong wind. Before they could locate anywhere for protection, the wind became a gale, cascading leaves and debris around them; ripping at the trees and bushes. Other people in the park hurriedly gathered their possessions and loved-ones and rushed to find any form of shelter. Gina yelped as a gust of wind, leaves and debris slapped her in the face. Guy wrapped his arms around her, pulled his great coat collar as high as he could then buried his head in Gina's neck.

Then as quickly as it had arrived, the wind blew away. An eerie calmness replaced the noise and energy of the maelstrom. People in the park were laughing at its ferocity and brevity. The prevailing mood was shock. No-one appeared to be hurt, just bemused. Gina and Guy took account of their situation, decided that they were unhurt and started to continue their walk home, when from the trees by the gate something light in colour caught Gina's attention. It was the small remote-controlled plane that had been stuck in the branches of a beech tree. It had been shaken loose by the wind and now fluttered down and landed with a bump close to Gina and Guy's feet.

"It's a drone," Guy observed.

"I saw a man and a boy flying it when we were sitting on the bench, then it got stuck in the tree."

They looked around expecting the owners to reappear to collect it from them, but they were nowhere to be seen.

"There must be a park keeper around somewhere, we can leave it with them. The owners will come back looking for it." But as Guy spoke, Gina had been examining the small aircraft. She was staring at the plane.

"Look." She held it out for Guy to read the graphic branding on the body. It read:

GINA SPECIAL : MESSAGE TRANSPORTER

They both stared at it.

"That's not a coincidence," Guy stated without taking his eyes from the words.

"I don't think so," Gina agreed.

"Message? What message? Is there anything else printed on it?" Gina turned it over and checked the drone from every angle.

"Nothing."

"Wait. What's that?" Guy was pointing at what turned out to be a micro memory card that popped out of the body of the plane as it would from a digital camera, having been inserted for the same purpose. The pair stared at it, then at one another. They seemed to know what the other was thinking. They checked again for the owners but no-one was in evidence so they instinctively set off at the same moment to walk home at a brisk pace.

36

At the last moment, as Guy was about to push the micro card into Gina's computer, both he and Gina sensed one another's nerves.

"No. Use my laptop, just in case there's a problem, we don't want it in your computer." Guy removed the reader with the card. He was still unsure. His hand hovered before pushing the card reader into the port.

I was surprised how nervous I felt. I had to resist the urge to restrain Guy. I think he felt as uncertain as me. Scared of what it was about to reveal. I was so tense when he clicked to open the folder, I think I made a sort of yelp.

She did. Guy was almost as nervous as he clicked open the single folder on the card.

The sound of conversation arrived before any image on the screen. Just for a few seconds, they only heard a man's commentary with a blank screen, then a graphic appeared showing some statistics that seemed to illustrate the narrative. The image showed a financial chart. Then a female voice:

"We can see on the screen, Radi-On's year-to-date financial growth showing a virtually flat line until the last week of April, then things changed – what caused that?"

The male voice answered.

"That was when there was industry gossip - and it was little more than that - that the company had attracted interest from Brandylion......"

Guy had looked away from the screen. He was intrigued by the man's voice.

"……You can see that it was enough for the share price to almost double, but that was only the foothill for the peak that you can see there last week when the buyout was agreed on 8th of April."

"It's probably only the digital world that can do this for a start-up less than two years old," the lady volunteered.

"That's right……"

At that point the image cut to show the man and a woman in a TV studio, sitting on high stools talking across a round table.

"………from a few cents to over ten times that."

As the image cut to a close up of the man for barely a second, Guy yelped.

"That's him. I thought so!"

But in that moment the image cut to black. All picture and sound was gone.

"Who?"

"Weirdo – the creepy guy who sold me the ring. That guy was him."

Guy was trying to control the video to rerun it, but he couldn't make it work.

"Okay, okay, but calm down," Gina suggested. Guy was so agitated by the appearance of His Creepiness from the jewellers that he was fumbling the procedure, so he popped the card reader out of his laptop, calmed himself for a moment then reinserted it to get back to the start. But the result was the same.

"It's not there," he announced after a third attempt.

"It must be."

"It's not. Here try it in your computer."

Gina took the card still in the reader and carefully inserted it into a USB port in her machine and tried to open the file that they had both seen a few minutes earlier. But her result was the same as Guy's.

"It's cleaned itself. It's gone." Guy sat back with a long sigh, then he realised the consequence. "Quickly. We have to recall everything we saw." He snatched up a pad from the desk and a pencil from a pot.

"What was the name of the company?"

"Which one?"

"*The* company with the shares that jump ten times, of course?"

"Oh, I'm not sure."

"She said the name - Rad-something."

"Sorry babe, I can't remember. It's my dyslexia."

"Are you dyslexic?" Guy was shocked by the revelation.

Gina smiled as she realised how little they knew about one another.

"Yeah, not very badly but I can't recall words or names. That's why my spelling's so bad."

"Really? I had no idea. How about that?"

"Yeah, always been a problem for me."

"I'm sorry."

"It's not an illness – just a bloody nuisance – like now."

"Okay, what can you remember about the names. Come on, we have to get it."

"Dandelion was the buyer….. No, something like Dandelion."

"Yeah Bandylion …Or Brandylion ... That was it, wasn't it, Brandylion? But the company on the chart was Rad-something"

"Yeah, yeah, Radyon.… That's right. Started up two years ago."

"And is in the digital sector. The lady said that it was only the digital market that can do this…. Brilliant. We can get it from that."

Guy went back to his laptop to search for the Radyon Inc or Radyon Ltd. He typed all permutations and clicked the *'search'* symbol. Almost instantly, there it was at the top of the search. He added *'share price'* to the search and was presented with a similar graphic that they had both seen a few minutes earlier. A flat graph with a value of 3.17. That meant nothing to either Guy or Gina - neither knew how share prices are valued, but that was of no significance – all they needed to know was that they could buy lots of cheap shares that they knew for certain were about to jump in value at the end of March with D-day arriving in early April.

"Ten times… less than six months from now?!" Guy thought aloud.

"Apparently so."

"That's it. It's going to happen – no doubt. It was Weirdo who just told us. It's a no-brainer."

But Gina was less enamoured by the revelation.

"Yeah."

"What's wrong – we can multiply our money ten-fold – how many water systems will that buy?"

"Yeah, I know, but I just wish it would stop – stop now. I have everything I want right now and I don't want this to keep happening. It's been months for me and a couple of weeks for you. Maybe the novelty will wear off for you as well in a while."

"Hmmm, maybe. I'm just coming to terms with it. You said: 'go with it'. It's happening and it's giving us super-easy money. Lots of it. Long may it last, that's my attitude. I'm more concerned that it's going to stop….Well, at the moment that's how it feels."

"Do you want a cup of tea?" Gina stood up and walked to the kitchen.

"Yes please."

Guy was staring out of the window. In his head he was making mental calculations about how much of his money he would commit to buy shares. He called through to Gina:

"If I can commit fifty thousand quid, that would make half a million and that will be enough to buy us a flat or even a house in the summer."

"What, after tax?"

"Well, yes." In truth, Guy hadn't contemplated anything as mundane as income tax. He had no idea what that would take from his pot of new-found wealth. Yet-to-be-made wealth.

Guy moved to the sitting room and met Gina arriving with two teas.

"Here's a thought to add to what we were talking about in the park. What if we look for a flat to rent soon - somewhere near Chelsea - like Fulham or Putney, by the river – just for, say, six months? Then we'll know if we like it while I have a super-short commute to work. Then if I stick with the job - and if we like the area - we can look for somewhere to buy. But if I get fed up with the job, we look elsewhere – you can choose. Or if we don't like the area, I pull stumps on my job and look for a real one near wherever you want to live. Does that sound like a cool plan?"

"When you say it quickly….. Hmmm, yes, it could work."

"It could, couldn't it? Sounds good to me now I've said it." Clearly Guy had not been thinking about it for much longer than it had taken him to convey the thought.

From Guy's position on the sofa, he could see the drone that had been standing where the couple had cast it aside when they reached the flat and were desperate to check the contents of the memory card. Now something about it caught Guy's attention. He stood and picked it up then inspected it from all angles just as they had when it fell at their feet in the park. Gina was watching with little interest, until Guy turned it to her and waved it close to her face to let her see… that the graphics were gone. The body of the drone was totally virginal white without a mark or word or graphic to be seen.

37

Christmas was soon to become more of a pressing problem than where the couple would live. By chance, both Gina and Guy were in similar positions with their relatives.

I was in the habit – and that's all it was – of spending Christmas day with my sister, her husband, Geoff, and his sister who usually goes with her boyfriend-of-the-moment – but sometimes not. It's been a duty for both of us for the last few years, but we've got used to it and it's a way of meeting up and catching up and it's only for a few hours so we can both be on good behaviour for that long. She and Shitty Geoff live about forty minutes from Camden by cab. It costs a lot each way on Christmas Day, but it's worth it not to have to spend a night there. Geoff's sister's okay – she's a vet and always has a lot of gory stories, so she dilutes the potential tension.
As it happens, Guy is in the same position. He and his brother do the same and go to his mum's house for the day. They cook the Christmas lunch for the three of them. Duty done, minimum fuss and bother for their mum, so it seems to suit everyone. I know how they feel.

So that would be the plan this year. Do their respective duties then home to have a late supper together and spend the night in their own bed.

I can't wait - for the end of the day, I mean – when it's all over. I wonder how many people across the UK – or across the world for that matter, do the same thing for the same reason and think of Christmas as an ordeal that has to be endured. I'm sure Becky and her awful husband do and only invite me out of a sense of pity because they feel sorry for me on my own. Maybe next year it'll be different.

In the meantime, Guy had accepted Brigitte's offer of extra work providing the same service for one of the agency's older clients, Morris Hardman, the crooner. His workload and requirements from Holly Bush were far more modest than those of Chaz E Jones.

Morris and his wife, Emma, had come to London to do some pre-Christmas shopping and Holly at Holly Bush had lined up personal appearances at two of London's radio stations and one on a TV chat show to make the trip worthwhile and tax-deductible.

The agency always accommodated Morris in the hotel within the same harbour-side complex where Chaz had his apartment because it was convenient for Holly Bush, but that made it far from convenient for Guy travelling to and from the other side of London. However, the hours and workload reflected Morris' more mature years and tastes. Guy arranged his calendar, sorted his and his wife's entertainment and travel arrangements and helped with locating the shops that sell the items on their Christmas present list. Guy wasn't sure why he needed to be on call at the apartment to do it as most of the requirements could have been organised by staff at the Holly Bush offices, but that seemed to be the arrangement that best suited the Hardmans so who was Guy to complain? Nor was he about to turn down the £250 a day salary for such a lightweight workload. *'Very nice, thank you'* was his take on the arrangement.

It did accelerate Guy's thoughts about moving to somewhere conveniently located on the south-west side of London so Guy would go to search online for properties that he and Gina could rent in the first instance, then something to buy if the experiment worked. He had never before been in a financial position to allow for the luxury of house-hunting with a genuine prospect of buying, let alone with a budget that could be as high as £500,000 (if he didn't need to pay too much back to the Chancellor of the Exchequer in income tax). After setting up some alerts at three of the highest profile property websites, he was getting a slow trickle of rentable and buyable properties within his budgets arriving every few days. It had been a sobering exercise to realise how little there was to buy in the Fulham and Putney areas with what Guy had assumed to be a generous budget. So Guy readjusted his expectations and budget and soon began to receive a quicker flow of properties that met the new guidelines.

"Here Gee, look at this," became quite a familiar refrain at their flat when Guy opened a new prospective property that had been forwarded to his email.

I couldn't believe how much you have to pay for property in London. It's unbelievable – to rent or to buy. I soon realised how I've been totally spoilt by my landlord. I can't imagine why he lets me get away with paying so little for my flat. I was totally out of touch with reality until Guy started to show me what we could rent for our joint budget over in the part of town where he needed to be for his job. But I have become used to readjusting my thinking about money during the last months and this was going the same way. After a couple of weeks and – I dunno, twenty properties, perhaps – I had the hang of it and could see when something was good value or a rip off. And I started to spot what sort of place and where we wanted to live for our budget. And once I'd started, I quickly realised that it was inevitable that we would do it. We could afford the experiment for six months – just, but with the windfall of cash in April we would certainly be able to buy somewhere like a nice two bed flat with hardly any mortgage.

Of course I considered what I would be missing by moving and apart from about three friends who live up here who I see quite regularly, the answer was, 'not a lot' -

in fact, next-to-nothing really. And what would I be gaining? Loads of thoughts about that, as you'd imagine, but at the end of the day, they boiled down to: 'a future'. As Guy says – a no-brainer.

By Christmas, Guy and Gina had laid the foundations for their move – the next chapter in both their lives and they were bubbling with excitement.

I don't know why it took me so long to agree. Once I got my head round the idea of the move, it was so exciting. I quite liked what we saw in Putney. We went down there to look round and I really liked the idea of being so close to the River Thames. It's a bit pseudo hoorayish by comparison with Camden's hippy vibe, but I think I'm ready for that for everything else the move would give us.

So that was where she and Guy targeted their searches and eventually found a two-bed unfurnished flat for rent that they both liked, equidistant from the tube line and the river. And a fifteen minute bus journey or ten minute cab ride from Chelsea Harbour, so favoured by Holly Bush for its clients. The flat would be available from the first day of February so Gina gave notice to her landlord. It was a sad day and she had to remind herself why she was doing it and what she would gain in return. Gina telephoned him to explain her intensions and convey her sincere gratitude for his apparent generosity towards her. He was understanding and gracious and wished her well. Another stepping stone towards Gina's new life. Her life with the love of it.

38

February arrived with few incidents of note since the encounter with the drone before Christmas. Gina and Guy had settled into a new rhythm as they lived their lives as a very happy couple; planning for their move whilst otherwise conducting their work-life balance with a new equilibrium.

Dizzy had been pestering for some more funds for the next water system to go to Kenya, but that was okay. In fact that prompted us to commit to buying the shares in Radyon while they were comparatively worthless. That was an exciting day as well. Just buying them was like being given the fortune that we would make in a couple of months. I put Dizzy off for the moment and directed him to Eric to get the funds for a small system while I earned enough to pay for the next big one. Of course I didn't tell either of them where the money was coming from, but I knew that Eric had some money in his pot from other fund-raisers so Dizzy would get what he needed to start work on a small project that would keep him and a little hamlet happy for a couple of months while I got the big one together.

Between them, Guy and Gina had invested most of the money that they had in reserve to earn the big pay out. Meantime they could live off Guy's regular monthly income so Gina didn't need to take money from Watersource for the immediate future, so she moved the small remaining fund into a deposit account. In doing so, they had unwittingly arrived at a place that suited them both very well. Guy was now the bread-winner and Gina was happy to play the nest-builder role as she set up home with a bedroom and separate office for the first time since she founded Watersource.

It suddenly felt really grown up.

Guy had completed his duties with Morris and Emma Hardman which had all gone as smoothly as his employers at Holly Bush could have hoped. Guy had learned a few more tricks of his new trade that had been passed on by some of the ladies in the Holly Bush offices. That had resulted in an over-generous tip at the end of the Hardman's stay in London. Guy realised that they liked him but he could not picture what sort of service they had received previously because what he did for them and how he behaved with them, seemed to be unremarkable. Whatever the reason, his bosses and their clients all seemed to approve of his way of doing his job.

Towards the end of February, Brigitte briefed Guy for Chaz E Jones' next visit to the UK. This would be a big one. Guy would be away from London, so away from Gina and their new flat, on and off for several weeks while on this tour of duty. There was to be a longer break mid tour when everyone would have a week-long breather, Chaz was planning to come back to London so Guy would still be on duty but would at least be returning home each night. He and Gina put the workload into perspective and were comfortable that they could handle the pressures that it would bring.

That schedule would begin in mid-March so there was plenty of planning time. And plenty of discovery time during which they walked around various parts of their new postcode. The more they found out about the riverside walks, activities and watering holes, the more comfortable Gina became. And that made Guy relax because he felt responsible for the disruption to Gina's life. Had it gone badly – however much they considered this move as an experiment – Guy would have felt extremely guilty for Gina's upheaval from the comfort of her old flat and familiar surroundings.

Yes, I think that's a fair summary. I would have been disappointed and whilst I desperately want this to work, if I sensed that it wasn't, I would have been upset and hankering to be back in my old flat in Camden, but I assumed that boat was burned the day I handed in my notice.
But it was working – and working better than I could have hoped. Having Guy there most of the time and having time to do whatever we wanted was like, just the best.

Guy was regularly offered extra work for Holly Bush - sometimes to cover for other staff doing similar jobs when they were off sick; and sometimes to add an extra pair of hands when a company or artist needed additional services. That suited Guy well; for the extra money and to get him out of the flat. He also sensed that it was good for Gina to have some time and space to herself however much she insisted that it was not a problem.

As the tour start date approached, they both had to make adjustments; and prepare for their time apart. For their own reasons, both felt a degree of anxiety such that neither was looking forwards to the day when Guy would kiss Gina goodbye and set off on the first leg of the tour away.

It was a Wednesday evening when Guy arrived home from a day's work looking after a party of Holly Bush clients in London. He collapsed on the sofa and asked:

"What you say we have a weekend in the country this weekend?"

"Really...?" Gina was instantly excited by the idea, but then thought... "Not at your mum's house?"

"No!" Guy laughed at the prospect. "A weekend break, but a nice one. We deserve it because we're going to be apart soon so I think we owe it to ourselves to spoil ourselves for a couple of days." Gina was beaming her approval.

"Where?"

"I was thinking about a certain chateau."

"What – in France?"

"That's where they have them isn't it?"

"You're kidding!"

"Yes, I am actually, but have you heard of Chateau Automne?"

"Near Oxford? Of course – you know I have. A weekend at Chateau Automne – you're kidding …… Aren't you?"

Guy smiled and shook his head.

"No! That'll cost a fortune. *The* Chateau Automne - is that the place you're talking about?" Gina was close to over-exciting herself.

"The very same. I have provisionally booked us in – well actually, I got the ladies at Holly Bush to do it because they use it as a venue for their clients so they got a very special deal. But that's the last time we talk about the cost. It's my treat, I can afford it with the extra work I've been doing at Holly Bush, so don't think about it."

Gina and Guy had discussed the venue in the past but only in the context of *'one day we'll treat ourselves to a slap up outing there.'* Now it seemed that Guy had decided that day had arrived.

"So shall I confirm the booking?"

Gina walked over to Guy, cupped his head in her hands and kissed her confirmation with such true passion that it aroused them both. Guy picked up Gina in his arms as they remained locked in an embrace; he negotiated the furniture to get them both to the bedroom where they made love for so long that the room was in darkness when they eventually fell apart in exhaustion.

"I'll take that as a *yes* then."

39

The plan was to drive to Oxford early on Saturday morning, do some site-seeing and maybe some shopping, then arrive at the country house hotel mid-afternoon ready to relax before a long evening of pre-dinner drinks and one of the meals for which the Chateau and its Michelin-starred celebrity chef were so famous. Then they would leave after a leisurely breakfast and drive back into London or maybe stop for late lunch at a pub on route. After so much good food, that part of the trip was uncertain and probably unnecessary.

Guy hired a car for the weekend which he parked around the corner from the flat for a quick getaway in the morning.

Earlier in the week, Gina had walked into Putney High Street to find a dress for the Saturday night but that had not worked out. When she realised that one of the bus routes through Putney would take her from there to the very same shops where Safia had organised her make-over day in the Kings Road, Chelsea, Gina planned a return trip that included an appointment at the same hairdressers.

I was loving this. Well, you don't do Chateau Automne or anything like it, very often so when you do, you have to do it properly.

That is precisely what Gina did. Embracing the mood of the moment and indulging herself.

But, you know what? If I had to choose between this weekend's mega treat with Guy going away soon, or not having a treat but him staying, I'd rather have Guy at home. No contest. I'm going to miss him so much while he's away. I suppose that means we're okay and it's working out okay and we'll be okay. I thought that on the bus back to Putney and it gave me a warm comfort.

Guy was at the flat preparing Spaghetti Bolognese when Gina arrived home with her newly cut hair and two bags containing the results of her shopping trip.

"I thought we should go easy for supper tonight – save our stomachs for the weekend's onslaught."

"Good idea. Did you get the hire car?"

"Yes, it's parked round the corner so we can get away by nine in the morning. Are you going to show me what you bought?"

"Nope. You'll see it tomorrow."

"Can't wait. This'll be ready in about ten minutes."

So followed an already-familiar pattern in the Tozer-Melina household.

Gina was so excited about their outing that she was awake at seven o'-clock the next morning, agitating to get moving. Guy was sound asleep as she slipped out of bed into the bathroom.

Half an hour later, Gina couldn't contain her exuberance and woke Guy with a cup of tea and an order to get up...

"Now!"

They left the house with their small weekend bags and a laundry suit-carrier and walked around the corner to where Guy had parked the car. This was to be the first surprise of the day for Gina.

"Can you guess which one is ours?" Guy asked as they walked.

"I don't know...That one?" Gina pointed at a silver hatchback similar to the last car that he had hired for their trip to Wiltshire.

"Nope, try again, but be quick because we're nearly there."

"I don't know, tell me."

Guy raised his hand holding the car's key and pressed a button on its side. Just ahead of them, Gina saw the indicator lights flash briefly with an accompanying 'beep' sound coming from the largest sports car in the street.

"No! You're kidding. What is it?"

"Aston Martin. I've always wanted one so this was my opportunity, well, for a couple of days, anyway."

And that set the mood for the blissful day ahead. First stop Oxford for a mooch around the town in the sun, a bit of very light retail therapy and an even lighter lunch then back to the car for the drive to the hotel. Guy didn't mind what he did as long as there was plenty of driving involved so he had pre-planned a route to the hotel that he tapped into the satnav that would take them on some fabulous driving roads across country, so avoiding the London-Birmingham motorway. He was only too happy that it would double the journey time. Gina sat watching the country fly past, only occasionally suggesting that Guy should slow down. Inwardly, Guy had a smile as wide as his chest.

The last mile to the hotel was along a smaller country road. The satnav was having trouble finding their position at times but there were finger signposts pointing the way to the village on the hotel's address. Gina watched for them at each junction while Guy was hoping that the satnav would find their position again, which it eventually did. As it popped into life, it drew Guy's attention. He flicked his eyes to it just as they approached a bend too quickly. Guy controlled the car, but as his view of the other side of the corner was revealed, so too was the tractor. A tractor with a mechanical problem; driving near the middle of the road; carrying a single round hay bale hanging on a rig at its front end. It was slowly falling towards the ground as the hydraulics malfunctioned. The driver was unsighted, his view now blocked by the giant bale as he tried to control the front-heavy vehicle and bring it to a halt.

The collision was inevitable – unavoidable – inescapable.

There was nothing Guy could have done.

The car plunged into the bale that was now just off the ground, but inside the bale were two reinforced iron spikes that aligned perfectly with the height of the Aston Martin's windscreen.

40

I woke on the Monday morning. Not that I knew that then. I was in hospital with a tube dripping liquid into my right arm from a clear bag on a stand by my bed; bandages like a turban were round my head and I ached a lot; but that was as much as I knew for sure. I couldn't recall anything about the cause. What's happened to me? I lay in bed with early morning light filtering into my magnolia room. The distant noises and smells were those of a hospital - well, there's nowhere else like a hospital ward, but why I was there was beyond me. I could remember Guy and I were driving to somewhere in a big car. It was fun. Where were we going? What's that got to do with me here?

Gina soon arrived at the inevitable conclusion, but only by deduction, not from her memory.

If there was an accident, where's Guy? How is he? Is he hurt? Is he here in the same hospital? Now I was worried – really worried.

Gina called out and a nurse was in her room within a few seconds. She calmed Gina and seemed genuinely not to have any answers to Gina's tirade of questions. She could see that Gina was getting over-anxious so pressed a button on the wall which summoned a man in a white coat with a stethoscope in a pocket who Gina assumed was a doctor.

By now I was scared silly. Petrified, more like. I just knew that something horrific had happened. I knew that the nurse would have known if Guy was in another room nearby or if he had been admitted with me. I kept telling her his name, I remember that. It was a nightmare. Worse. Whatever's a million times worse than a nightmare, that's what I was experiencing.

The doctor sensed it and tried to calm Gina. Perhaps to his disappointment, he knew the answers to her questions, but she was firing them at him so fast that he had no time to answer one before Gina blurted out the next. The young doctor just watched Gina and let her burn herself out, then with his eyes full of tears he answered slowly, with a shake of his head and as much sincerity as he could manage.

"I'm so sorry."

The scream that Gina released would have been heard throughout her floor of the hospital.

Soon the room was full of more nurses. The doctor administered something into Gina's arm through a syringe and a few moments later she fell back into a deep unconscious sleep.

41

I was in Oxford General Hospital, or whatever it's called, for a few days then they moved me to London. St Thomas's right by the river. But the pain didn't go away. That came with me. I don't mean the pain in my head or my cracked ribs – I mean the dread of life without Guy. The bigness of that prospect just overwhelmed me. It was there every waking hour, literally. Remorseless, unremitting, gnawing pain.

The police came to interview me in Oxford and again at St Thomas's and the story gradually pieced together. About us hitting a tractor head-on in the lanes and the police were going to prosecute the tractor driver for murder .... No, that's not right, the other one ..... Manslaughter, that's right.

The farmer was in a bad way after the accident because he had no seat belt on and the accident did a lot of damage to him. They say he may never walk again, basically. I don't mean him any more harm ... well, I didn't until the police told me that he was trying to deliver a hay bale into a field a bit on from where the accident happened. He was carrying the hay bale – one of those big round ones you see in fields - on something on the front of the tractor that had two huge spikes to hold the bale on. Something about the hydraulic system that was holding it up, went wrong and warning lights flashed in his cab, but he was trying to get to the field before the bale holder thing collapsed because it was a Saturday and he wouldn't get any help if he stopped on the road. But the bale, that was supposed *to be up in the air, was dropping down towards the road in front of the tractor so he couldn't see when our car came round a bend and hit the thing on the front of the tractor with the big spikes. The hay bale slowed our car's speed a bit but not enough. The police said the combined speed was about fifty miles an hour – for our car it was like hitting a solid wall at that speed. The front of our car sort of ripped through the bottom of the bale but the spikes came through the windscreen. One of them grazed my head but the other......... Aaaaaaaaagh.*

Gina was of no help to the police investigation. Her memory ended with shopping in Oxford. Nothing came back to her by the time of the police's second visit more than a week after the accident. Gina took the opportunity to find out what had happened by quizzing the WPC who checked with Gina that she really wanted to know the detail before telling her almost everything that their investigations had revealed. That included the grotesque detail of Guy's cause of death.

"I don't think I should tell you this. It's really not nice," the policewoman admitted as she found herself painting herself towards the gruesome part of the story that she knew would be hard for Gina.

"Tell me," Gina insisted. "I need to know if I'm ever going to move on. Please – tell me – I must know." Gina was adamant.

So the policewoman told her an abbreviated version about the second spike in the hay bale that had killed Guy. She didn't mention that it penetrated his right eye and ripped into his skull, but she was insistent that Guy would not have felt anything and would have died instantly.

I wanted to think it was all about someone else. I couldn't remember anything about the accident so I tried to tell myself that she was like, telling me about someone else. But it didn't help. It was all horrific and I was living it and it was about me and about Guy and my future with the man who I wanted to spend it with and ..... and I .....I wish I'd died. I don't want to be here.

Gina was in hospital in London for seven days during which time a slow trickle of friends and family came to visit. Her sister Becky was sympathetic and the closest to loving that either had experienced in several years. Gina was grateful for the visit but Becky sensed the emptiness of Gina's broken spirit so promised to come down to Putney when her sister went home. The prospect of returning to the empty flat that she didn't know, in a part of London that she didn't know, had not occurred to Gina until that conversation. How she would handle it, she didn't know.

Safia and Craig, from the bike ride, came with fruit and cards from other friends and cheered Gina more than she could have expected by being upbeat and frivolous. They had reasoned that everybody around Gina would be solemn and perhaps morbid, so after the inevitable conversation about Guy, they made a concerted effort to talk about life after the accident with as much energy as they could muster. It was an approach that worked. For the first time since the accident, Gina started to think positively about things to fill her time. But she would be in Putney, not Camden, so how that would work was starting to concern Gina as her discharge approached.

The bandages on her head were removed after four days. The doctor announced that Gina would need some specialist support to ensure that the impact so close to her brain had not left any lasting damage. The metal spike had grazed the side of her temple and broken the skin above the hairline, so cosmetically, the scarring would eventually become invisible. But the cosmetics were the least of Gina's worries.

On the day before Gina's discharge, a special delivery of a very large bouquet of flowers arrived unexpectedly. There were two cards attached.

Gina opened the first to read a touching hand-written note from:

Brigitte, Holly and all the team at Holly Bush

Gina was immediately taken aback.

To Gina. Our most sincere regrets for your tragic loss. Guy was a very special person that we grew to love in the short time we knew him. Only the good die young, it seems. We send you our love.

Gina wept aloud.
Eventually she turned her attention to the second card. She tore the envelope open as her eyes still streamed tears, so for a moment she couldn't focus on the message or signature.

I have just heard the shocking news about Guy's death. He spoke of you often in the most loving terms so I hope you are finding God's strength to get through this dark time in your life. Christ works in mysterious ways and has a reason for everything, you just have to find it to find strength.
You are in my prayers. My love to you,
Chaz E Jones

cej@chazejones.com

Gina read the note repeatedly.

I couldn't believe Chaz E Jones had bothered to write to me – I've never met him or even spoken to him on the phone. That's such a nice thing to do. And Brigitte and Holly, of course. I was really made up with their generosity. I'll send them a card when I get time to get one. Mustn't forget ..... Note to self.

Only on a later reading did Gina take note of the email address at the foot of Chaz's card.

I don't think it's polite to send a 'thank you' note by email, but why add it if he didn't expect me to use it – it's in his handwriting like he was saying 'you can keep in touch here'.

So that's what she did.

Dear Chaz
I am Guy Tozer's girlfriend. I want to thank you so much for your card with your best wishes. It ment so much to me in my darkest hour that you took the time to send your card with the most magnificant boquet of flowers. I am in a very dark place right now but your generosity brought some light and was a great boost for my low moral.
Thank you again,
Gina
PS   please forgive me using email to send my thanks.

Within the hour, there was a response.

Dearest Gina
Thank you but don't forget that true release will only come when you embrace Jesus Christ.
My very best wishes
Chaz

By the time the ambulance drove her home to her flat in Putney, Gina was starting to find strength with the prospects of getting back to work. She was listing, rehearsing and inventing activities to keep her busy. Gina was drawing deep into her strength of will to contain the darkness. So when she opened the door to her flat for the first time since she and Guy had left in such high spirits almost two weeks previously, she was moderately confident that her immediate future would be okay.

That's true. I thought I had it under control, but within two, maybe three days, I realised I hadn't. And the biggest problem was that this was Putney and not Camden. My sole reason for being here was gone. I sat in a lovely flat with no purpose or excitement .... No Guy, basically. Nothing was familiar, everything reminded me of why I was here. It got worse. Each day became more of a battle to fight the black dogs.
I think it was about day three that I phoned Mr Dasheral, my old landlord. I expected he would have already rented my old flat out but I was gutted when he told me the contract was literally only signed the day before I called him. No! That was like a kick in the gut. I knew by then that the quickest way for me to get back on my feet right now was to get back to familiar things and surroundings. Just going to the minimart and passing a few minutes with Manuel – or dropping into Coffeeteria or Trappers where I knew half the staff .... Or .... Shit-it.

As Gina explored the idea, she knew without a doubt that this would be the right move. She had to get back to familiar surroundings. It soon became a passion. Mr Dasheral promised to keep in touch and call Gina if he heard of any flats that would suit her. But Gina knew that was unlikely so she started to search the online agencies to find a one-bedroomed unfurnished flat within a very small catchment area. They were not plentiful or attractive or within her budget. The sense that she had burnt the very lifeboat that she now needed above all else to save her sanity, was becoming overpowering.

Another black cloud approaching at speed was Guy's commemorative service to be held at the church local to Guy's mother's house. There was no question that Gina must go - or wanted to - but the prospect filled her with dread. Safia promised to go with her which was a great support.

Bless her. Saffy is such a dear friend – and given that Guy thought she was probably a bit shallow, I felt a little guilty about asking her. But she agreed without question. Of course she would be there .... Except she wouldn't. The day before, she phoned to cancel. Something she couldn't get out of at work, basically. I tried to make light of it but the prospect of doing it without Saffy as a crutch, suddenly seemed so awful that I wasn't going to go. That's all there was to it, I wouldn't go. Then by good timing or fortune or something, Guy's brother, James, phoned me out of the blue. I hadn't even had an email from him before. He was very nice and really sensitive and seemed to know how I would be feeling. He offered to pick me up from Swindon rail station which was great because otherwise I would have to catch a very slow bus or a very expensive taxi to their village .... If I was going.

The night before her trip, Gina found some dark clothes in her cupboard which she tried on with no emotion or commitment. Rather as she was approaching the day. She just had to do it. And get through it.

I treated it like a challenge. Like a fight I had to take on and win. I would do this and I will get through it and it will all be over by this time tomorrow. Those thoughts helped me come to some sort of terms. I was so relieved that James had called. I was picturing the church full of people who I don't know but they all know that I was Guy's girlfriend – not knowing what to say to me but thinking

they should say something. And then there was Shirley ....
not Shirley, Sheila Bloody hell, don't do that. She must
think I'm the devil incarnate turning up at her Christian
service to gloat over her beloved son., Okay a bit strong,
perhaps, but .... I dunno anymore.

Gina broke down and wept. The weeping became a torrid outpouring. She let it flow until she was teared out.

42

The train arrived a few minutes early at Swindon Station. Drizzle was blowing in a chill wind creating an atmosphere to match Gina's mood. As she walked along the platform, Gina heard the ding of a text arriving on her phone. It was from James to inform her that he would be at the station in ten minutes.

As she stood near a taxi rank where she could be seen by cars arriving at the pick-up point, she thought to note down the number on the side of the taxis in case she needed their services for the return trip.

Gina and James had never met so she hoped that her black coat would identify her, which it did. A nondescript silver version of the taxis pulled up by the kerb and through a descending passenger window, the driver asked:

"Hi, are you Gina?"

"Yes – James?"

"Yes, hi."

He didn't look much like Guy with his longish, gingerish hair, but his mannerisms were remarkably similar. It was a bit odd, really.

A little to her surprise, as she sat into the passenger seat, James leaned across and kissed her on the cheek.

"Nice to meet you at last. Heard so much about you from Bro of course."

"Thanks. And thank you very much for coming to collect me. I really appreciate it."

"It's nothing. The least I can do for family....Sort of, family."

He had the confidence that reminded me of Guy .... But I don't want to think about that.
I hadn't thought about what you talk about in these situations – after all, James and me, we were both grieving, both bereaved, so saying sorry wasn't like, appropriate. But thinking about what was to come, I suddenly thought to ask.....

"How's your mum?"

"She's not so good...... No, really, not very good at all."

"Sorry."

"Yeah. And you?"

"Not so good."

"Sorry."

"Yeah, thanks ..... And you?"

"Oh, you know. We weren't so close as brothers these days, but this news has...Well, you know."

"Yeah.....Err, no, sorry, I don't really. I have a sister that I've grown away from but this seems to have brought us a bit closer."

"Every cloud has a silver lining, I suppose. Like us meeting."

"Yeah, maybe. I can't see any silver bits yet though – not unless relations with my sister is the best I can expect."

A long silence followed as they drove through what would have been idyllic Wiltshire countryside on a brighter day. That took Gina's thoughts to her previous trip to see Guy's mother. The day before the night when she and Guy consummated their relationship. Those thoughts occupied Gina for a while until James broke the silence.

"Maybe when you get through this we can meet up for a meal. I'd like to get to know you better." Then to Gina's surprise, as if to emphasise the point, he reached across the car and squeezed her arm, for a little too long.

"Yeah, maybe."

There was just something about him and that comment – and the arm-squeeze - that I didn't feel comfortable with. I don't know what.

Gina thought about that through another spell of countryside-watching until it dawned on her.

I know what it is – he reminds me of Geoff, Becky's husband Geoff. Yes, that's what it is. I think the word might be 'gauche' – but maybe not – he's inappropriate – yes, that's it – maybe 'boorish' is better. He shouldn't have asked me out, that's not appropriate. Or kissed me when we met today. Or touched me. And he's a bit too ... I'm not sure, but it's not comfortable.

The couple hardly spoke for the rest of the fifteen-minute journey until they were approaching the village. Gina had relaxed but suddenly she felt anxiety created by the uncertainty about what to expect. James checked his watch.

"I think we should go straight to the church, then I have to collect my mother and an aunt. They can't walk from home in the rain."

"Okay. Thank you."

That's good. I can handle that, but tea with Shirley ...... damn it, Sheila .... I think that could have been the hellish side of tough.

James parked the car around the corner from the church, still without mentioning the return trip to the station. He took an umbrella from the boot of car then linked arms with Gina to walk the hundred yards to the church.

Other guests had already arrived. To Gina's relief, James excused himself to talk to other guests then she watched as he left the church to collect his mother.

Gina had identified the best place where she could be anonymous, out of eye lines away from the central aisle. She perched on the bare, hard wooden pew, read the order of service without absorbing the content, then sat back to take in her surroundings.

Within a few minutes, I'd totally relaxed. Totally the opposite from how I felt when I arrived. The organ was hypnotically droning away breaking the silence and as a few people arrived, I could watch without any involvement. If I was religious – which I'm not – I would have said that some sort of spirit was with me – like enveloping me in a calmness. That lovely stillness that I've known a couple of times recently, since meeting Guy. Huh, since the first time was at a pub, I don't think it's anything religious. But it's lovely. I want this to last. I want to take this home with me.
Only then did it occur to me that a church service was a bit of an odd choice for Sheila as a practising druid, or spiritualist or whatever she must be. What do I care? Let's just get this over.

The small church was half-filled with people of all ages. Then Sheila arrived with another lady and James. Gina had forgotten that this moment would be testing so she casually turned to see another party of guests arrive before recognising that one was Sheila. For no more than a few seconds, they made eye contact.

Oh my god. It was like electric. I felt myself tense, but I had the presence not to quickly look away. I think Shirley was probably thinking the same. Oh my god – if looks could kill. I think she probably wished they could at that moment. Her expression was literally as black as you could imagine as soon as she saw me. We both stared for those few seconds then she looked away as she wobbled past down the aisle to the front row.

I calmed down and tried to get myself back to where I was just before she arrived, but that calmness was gone. And now the service was starting.

About half an hour into the order of service, the prospect of what would happen when it was over, began to fill Gina with considerable concern. The thought became so overwhelming that the idea occurred to her that she should leave before the wake that was due to be held at the same pub in the High Street where she had lunched with Guy and his mother on her last visit. That led to her considering her place with the others in the church. She had no relationship, no affinity and now she realised, no liking for anyone with whom she was sharing this most sensitive moment in her life. She felt totally disconnected.

As proceedings moved to the last page and the last hymn of the order of service, Gina picked up her shoulder bag, slipped out of the end of the pew, left the church and made good her escape.

43

Just when I thought things were as bad as they could get, the following couple of weeks had some nasty surprises. One in particular that would change my fortunes and my future, big time.

Through Watersource's channels, both Dizzy and Eric had heard about Gina's accident and the death of her boyfriend. Neither knew Guy's name but both conveyed the most sensitive thoughts in individual emails. That gave Gina some strength and reconnected her with her work for the charity. After those immediate exchanges of personal emails, the more routine aspects of running Watersource began to occupy Gina's time once again. She had thought to send press releases about the accident and Guy's death to drum up some fresh momentum on social media. Gina spent much of her working time inventing and relaying anything that would keep Watersource high on search engine listings and in the minds of potential sponsors. The importance of that momentum had been proven repeatedly during the last year so she had to get those activities back up to speed. But after typing three versions of the press release reporting her accident in too much detail, Gina couldn't bring herself to send the report that would share such a personal loss, even for her beloved cause. So she apologised for her absence online with only a brief explanation about being unwell following a car accident then she carried on with business as usual.

Filling her time was essential and never a problem, but it meant that Gina did little else other than sit at her computer writing press releases, articles for social media and responding to the never-ending flow of incoming emails.

She broke away to go shopping for food, but walked the shortest route to her nearest supermarket just off the High Road where she hardly spoke to the cashier before returning by the same route.

I knew I was feeling sorry for myself and that it was badly affecting my mojo, but I wasn't admitting it so I did nothing to stop the slide happening. I could disguise it in my emails and media releases but because I didn't see anyone, I wasn't doing anything to stop the process in my head. My efforts to find a flat in Camden slowed to a virtual standstill and my daily output followed the same slow down at a slightly slower pace.

The inevitable email arrived from James through the Watersource site enquiring about my departure from the church and suggesting we meet up. I wasn't in the mood to play games so I replied with a short message to tell him why I left and that I didn't want to meet. If he was sensitive, he would have realised that I was telling him politely, to fuck off. After a couple more emails pressing for a date, I think he got the message – or just gave up on his ex-brother's miserable ex-girlfriend. Whatever the reason, he soon became history.

But the email that really surprised me, came later that week.

Dearest Gina

How are you? You often come into my thoughts. I will be in London for a week starting 9th May so if you want to share your burden please use my email address to get in touch. I think my apartment is close to yours now so you are very welcome to come to visit, to talk or to pray with me if that would help.

My very best wishes

Chaz

Do you know what? My first reaction was that he was coming on to me. He's a pop star rapper so he's randy so he wants to entice me to his flat. I'll admit it - I'm ashamed of myself for that. I'm sure that's not the case – that's me pigeonholing someone. I did that when I first met Guy and look how that turned out. No, that's just a nice gesture. If I still feel like shit next month – or even if I don't, perhaps I'll go over and meet him.

Gina immediately responded to express her gratitude for Chaz's kind thoughts and invitation. The contact from such a celebrity helped her self-esteem more than she would admit. So by the end of that week, Gina felt that she was holding it together. In truth, she would not have recognised herself from a month earlier. Her spark and energy were those of another person; at the sort of levels that she would have expected when fighting a bad cold or suffering the effects of particularly heavy period, or both simultaneously.

The first indication that I had a problem with money came in a phone call from a woman early one evening.

"Hello – can I speak to Mr Tozer please?"

"No. Who are you?"

"When can I contact him? When will he be back?"

"You can't. He won't be. Who are you?"

There was a short silence while the woman thought about her next move.

"Look, I'm not trying to be difficult. I'm trying to avoid a problem, but I do need to speak to Mr Tozer - please."

"Why, who are you?"

Another short silence.

"Who am I speaking to – are you a friend or relative?"

Gina was cautious but admitted:

"Girlfriend, I live here. Who are you?"

"Right. I'm your landlady. My name is Freda McDonald. I'm trying to find out why his standing order payment for your rent has been stopped. Perhaps you can tell me."

Shit-it!

I'd forgotten everything about money for the flat. How stupid! I could tell you to the pound about Watersource and my own finances but I hadn't once thought about the flat expenses and all the direct debits and standing orders and things that were supposed to come out of Guy's account. How could I be so stupid? I just hadn't thought about it. His family must have frozen his account and anyway Holly Bush weren't paying anything into it. I'm so stupid not to think about that – what the hell was I thinking?

Anyway, I apologised to Ms Macdonald and told her about Guy's death. Well, I was panicking a bit so it was the quickest thing to do to get her off my back and buy some time to sort it out. Of course she was super-apologetic about chasing me under the circumstances and that made me super-apologetic about not sorting it out. So for the moment, problem averted, but only for the moment.

Next day I spent an age trying to work out what standing orders Guy had set up. I think I managed to get to the bottom of it eventually, but that worried me because when I added all the costs up it was so much money every month. I moved all the arrangements to my bank but my account was nearly empty because I hadn't needed cash because Guy was paying the bills – you get the picture. It was horrible. I jotted everything down on a pad as I made call after bloody phone call and listened to jingly-jangly bloody music for hours on end. When I got through it and added all the money up that I needed each month, it was just shy of three grand. Shit-it. Three bloody grand – all but. That's just the fixed costs, not food or clothes or anything. Okay, once I moved the few grand I had on deposit I had enough for the next couple of months but I needed the money that we had invested in the digital company shares. That would come good in a few weeks so it would be okay, just.

While I was in finances mode I decided to check on the Radyon shares that we'd bought. It then occurred to me of course that all Guy's money would go to his next of kin and I'm not one of them. Hundreds of thousands most likely.

I got the share certificates out for Guy's and my shares, then did a search for Radyon on-line. I remembered watching Guy use the abbreviation for the name. I typed the letters RADY into the search window on a financial shares website. Nothing happened. It couldn't find the abbreviation. No worries, I went back and used the full name Radyon.

The result that appeared on my screen could not have hurt more if it was a physical blow to my cracked ribs.

Recent news

21st March

Radyon in administration

Radyon (Assets) Ltd, the on-line digital technology company based in Boston, Massachusetts, is in administration after purchasing the assets of Radyon Digital Ltd in February due to a lack of working capital. All company activities have ceased as of Thursday while administrators work at the head office to assess the value of assets. Share dealing was halted on the news at the end of trading Friday.

I felt sick, literally. I didn't understand but I just knew this was very very bad. I was paralysed with my thoughts but not knowing about share dealing I had no idea if this situation could be saved. The lead from the drone had shown that the value would multiply over ten times in about a month from now. Perhaps this is what would happen. But if a company is in administration that means it doesn't have any value which means the shares don't have any value ...... doesn't it?

After worrying herself to almost physical sickness for a few hours, Gina realised that she had to find out more about the situation that she didn't understand. She assumed her bank could advise her, so after another series of identification-proving exercises, Gina eventually arrived at the headset of a lady with a Welsh accent who announced herself as 'Megan'. Gina explained the reason for her call and Megan confirmed that she should be able to help explain the workings of the world of stocks and shares. Gina provided a potted history of the purchase of shares that she read from her certificate. Megan apparently wrote notes at the other end of the line and started to make her own investigation on-line.

"That's Radyon, you say - is that correct?"

"Yes."

"Is that the digital technology company, based in Boston in the US?"

"That's right, I think so."

Megan spent too long with her investigations for the news to be good. Gina was getting very uncomfortable as she waited for what she assumed to be inevitable.

"I'm really sorry, but Radyon is...well, in effect, it's bankrupt. I'm really sorry but your shares are more than likely worthless. I'm sorry but I wouldn't expect you to get anything for them. Sorry. How many shares do you own?"

"Two million, six hundred thousand."

"Oh God…. I'm sorry, that was a shock."

Gina was speechless.

"Are you still there?"

"Yes."

"You are sure that your shares are in Radyon the technology company and not Radi-On the games developer, are you?"

"Yes, I think so, why?"

"Radi-On…." Megan spelled the name with the hyphen. "That's a games developer and there has been some movement recently - it seems to be created by a prospective take over…..I just hoped that was the…"

"A take-over, did you say?" Gina interrupted.

"Yes."

"Is the name Brand Lion…..no ….Brandylion, that's it. Is that mentioned?"

"Yes it is. How do you know?" Megan was excited by the prospect that they had made a mistake and Gina owned Radi-On shares.

"No, nothing."

"But you're right. That company you mentioned, Brandylion, has made the offer that's been declined but it pushed the value of the shares up a few pence…… in fact it more than doubled its value. Are you sure you have the right shares?"

"No. I have the wrong ones."

44

I couldn't get out of bed next day ... or the next or ... I don't know how many, to be honest. Except just to go to the loo occasionally. It wasn't because I was tired but I was frightened. Scared shitless. I wanted to pull the duvet over my head and shut out the world. It helped but it wasn't going to solve anything. I knew that but it was as if I'd been drugged. I knew what I should do but just couldn't. I should have faced my demons and got to grips with my problems, but I just couldn't.

On day two, or maybe it was three – I don't know to be honest - I was getting hungry and made my way to the kitchen to find something to eat. I couldn't get back to bed and found myself sitting on the floor under the kitchen table to eat slices of buttered toast. Like being in an air raid shelter sort of thing. I needed something to enclose me to make me safe.

I eventually made it back to bed and lay under the duvet until I couldn't breathe easily, then I'd duck out to gulp some fresh air like coming to the surface of water then duck back for shelter. I don't know how long that lasted ..... A few hours – a day maybe. I don't know, to be honest. At night I couldn't sleep properly because I wasn't tired. When I did doze off, I had the dreams again. I kept returning to Dartmoor in them, but I couldn't cycle – there was always something holding me back or blocking the road. Two, three times a night I would wake from variations of the same nightmare in a sweat.

I think I got beyond feeling sorry for myself ...... Maybe not ..... Maybe self-pity was exactly what was driving this.

I hadn't eaten or slept properly for days so I suppose that was messing with my head or I'd have realised earlier that I needed help. Of course I bloody did. There was a time when I could handle anything that came at me, but not now. I was fragile and ...... and sick in the head, basically. Maybe the accident had brought on the change to my head ..... I dunno ..... But I did know I had to break this cycle.

Gina eventually reasoned that the hospital could and should help her. She recalled some of the doctor's advice when she was discharged from St Thomas' Hospital. Gina had been warned that she could experience mood swings even before anyone could have anticipated her most recent setbacks. Gina called the direct line number that she had been given for contacting one of her doctors. When she described her mood and the state of her health, Dr Khan became very concerned and told Gina that he would arrange for a nurse to make a home visit at the earliest opportunity. He was treating Gina as an emergency.

During that conversation he said I was probably suffering post-traumatic stress, then in passing, he used the words 'clinically depressed'. I can't remember the context, but still the words hit home. What? Me, clinically depressed? I'd heard of it of course, but to be honest, I thought it just meant that someone was a bit like, under the weather. I used to think: 'well aren't we all from time to time – just buck up'. But now I know differently. It's like physical, not just a bit, you know. It's all-consuming and sort of paralysing.

Daisy Drew arrived in my flat and in my life the next morning. She was some sort of trouble-shooter agency nurse and she glided in like a roly-poly guardian angel.

231

She was epic. She was calm and sensible and said the right things in the right tone of voice – not simpering or bullying. She examined me and listened to my explanation of my symptoms then told me that she could administer a course of drugs to help, albeit with some side effects. She asked if I understood all that and asked if I wanted to go ahead. Of course I bloody did. Anything.

She gave me a pill right there and then while she continued to chat about my situation and how I'd got there. She knew about the car accident and Guy's death, but not in detail. She was so easy to talk to that...well, I just did. When I started to open up about my money problems, she was just wonderful. God, she was so wonderful – I can't tell you. She couldn't help financially of course, but she helped me put things into perspective. I can't imagine what her training was, but she was the best. What a wonderful lady.

By the time she left, I felt better than I had for ages. Maybe it was the pill – although that did make me nauseous as she'd warned, but that didn't last long. I really felt that I could cope. We devised a plan for me to get back slowly into a routine. When we'd looked closely at my finances, I realised that I might be able to cope as long as Watersource continued to function and attract donations.

Daisy Drew phoned or called in to see Gina every day for the next week.

That was such a great crutch. And the pills, I assume. I sometimes felt myself losing the fight when I hadn't seen or heard from Daisy for a day, then her call gave me the strength to move on. I still wasn't comfortable leaving the flat. Imagine me, not wanting to leave my flat. I was the lady that travelled the world for six months after uni – and went to Vietnam to sort her parents' deaths out and then I set up Watersource and I organise fund-raising...... Now I didn't have the confidence to walk to the shops without a potential panic attack. Shit-it. This is going to take a while.

And it did. Even though Gina's problems had been identified quickly and support was in place within days, progress was slow. From Gina's viewpoint, getting out of bed and getting dressed were the first challenges of each day. Her self-imposed objective was to be showered, dressed and to have finished breakfast by nine-o'clock. Even those simple tasks proved challenging on some mornings, but she maintained the routine, knowing this was a foundation on which to build a daily schedule that would eventually rebuild her confidence, one step at a time.

It just goes to show how out of it I was – my thirtieth birthday was somewhere in the middle of those black days. I only realised later because I'd lost track of the date. I loved my birthday and always did something to make it special. It was only when I eventually checked my mail box by the front door and there were five cards. And when I charged my phone, there were more messages. That was a horrible realisation. I'd missed my own birthday, for god's sake.

As the days and weeks passed, Gina's work had the most stabilising effect on her recovery. Every two days Daisy Drew telephoned or called in to ensure that Gina was maintaining her few routines and to replenish her supply of anti-depressants. And that regime worked, albeit slowly. Watersource absorbed the major portion of Gina's time even before the depression, but now she immersed herself in her online identity and activities.

That's true - and thank God for it. But I had to admit that my efforts weren't keeping pace with my financial needs. I was being super-responsible about where the funds went.

233

I could only take the barest minimum as a salary when I wasn't making much. The sponsors were great – both of them were great when I told them about my health problem. I made out that the car accident was responsible for my lower work rate, so neither changed their standing order payments so that was a great help. I kept up the PR activities online so that was okay. But I wasn't attracting as much money as I needed to send the next system to Kenya.

I never told Dizzy or Eric any more than they needed to know – about the same as my sponsors probably. I sensed that Eric knew I wasn't very efficient, but Dizzy sent a couple of pushy emails to both me and Eric almost demanding that we get funds to him. That was difficult.

Gina's interpretation was not entirely accurate. Her memory of how things had been prior to the accident was quite a distance from reality. She had now lowered her horizons and readjusted her work rate more than she recognised.

It was hardly surprising that I'd forgotten all about Chaz until his email arrived out of the blue.

Dearest Gina
How are you? Well I hope.
I will be in London for most of next week so if you would like to visit me at Chelsea Harbour you will be very welcome and I'd love to meet up. Perhaps on Wednesday morning if that's convenient.
My very best wishes
Chaz

Dear Chaz

Thank you very much for the invitation. I would love to come to meet you. Wednesday will be perfect. I will come at 10.00 if that's conveniant.

Thank you again,

Gina

PS   please tell me the address. Guy never told me.

45 Rigger Tower. See you at 10 on Wednesday.
CEJ

Dear Chaz

Thank you.

G

45

Gina's visit to Chaz E Jones was to be a big day. Her first trip further afield than to one of her local shops for several weeks; and the first meeting with anyone besides Daisy or supermarket check-out staff. The trip gave Gina an objective – to think about her clothes, her appearance, the route to and from Chelsea by public transport and how the meeting would go with such a big celebrity. In her state of mind, any and all these tasks looked like high hurdles.

But I knew that if I got through it I would have made progress – real progress. So that was it – I had to do it, no question.

Gina confided in Daisy who was mightily impressed that she knew Chaz E Jones; even more so that she was going to his apartment. Daisy's advice: *'Get everything sorted in advance so the journey can't go wrong because even arriving late might upset your confidence'*. Advice that reminded Gina of her manoeuvres to claim her winnings from the bookies across south London.

She was so right. By this stage, something as simple as a bus ride for a couple of miles was a big deal. I didn't even know if my Oyster card had any money on it, so Daisy topped that up for me, bless her. Then we planned the route and did everything in detail and wrote down notes for Wednesday morning.

- Alarm - 07.30
- Get dressed – Dina jeans, black shirt. Undiies on airer - brown slip-ons. Jadelle jacket
- Take – bag (packed) - Oyster - tissues - watch - address (note) - purse - money – brolly - phone - lippy
- DOOR KEYS
- Leave 09.15
- Bus on L Rich Rd 22
- Off opposite Antiques after bridge on New King Rd
- Lots Road to harbor
- 45 Rigger Tower on left after hotel

Gina arrived early and walked around the development, stopping to watch three ducks drifting between the boats moored in the tiny harbour. So far so good. Her plans had worked; she was here on time and feeling confident.

Gina pressed the buzzer at the entrance to Rigger Tower at ten-o'clock on the dot of her watch. She took the lift to the fourth floor where a young man opened the door to number forty-five.

"Hello – Gina?"

"Yes, I'm here to see Chaz."

"Yes, please come in."

Chaz appeared in a doorway wearing a baggy white shirt and light linen trousers. With the sun behind him, Gina's first impression was of him glowing. Chaz was taller and blacker than she imagined, but his infectious Hollywood smile was exactly as she recalled from the videos that she had watched with Guy.

"It's nice to meet you, Gina." Chaz spoke with a baritone resonance in a measured American accent.

"And you – thank you very much for inviting me over."

Chaz shook hands and gestured Gina into a large sitting room with doors onto a balcony with the River Thames beyond.

"What would you like to drink – tea, coffee?"

"Just some water please."

"Jimmy, would you mind? Thank you." Then back to Gina. "Please have a seat…. How are you?"

"Great."

Why did I say that?

"Really? That's good, so you may as well go then." And Chaz smiled broadly, changing the atmosphere in a moment which Gina later assumed to be the point of his frivolous remark.

"No, you're right. I'm not in great form at all. Sorry, I don't know why I said that."

"No worries. You can talk about it if you want – or about Guy – or not, if you don't want." Chaz was now watching Gina for a reaction. "No hurry. No pressure, but my offer to provide whatever support you think is appropriate for you is genuine. Whatever is best for you."

Jimmy returned with a glass of water which he placed on a coaster on a side table within Gina's reach.

"Excuse me, Chaz. I'll go and collect your laundry now, if that's okay."

"Thank you Jimmy, yes please."

"Nice to meet you briefly Gina."

"And you. Thank you for my water."

They watched Jimmy leave the apartment.

"I'm very lucky with the assistants that Holly gets for me here in London. Jimmy's a good lad, but not Guy. He was the best - but then, you know that, of course."

*It was all a bit surreal. The conversation was straight to
the point without the usual pleasantries about the weather
and journey, but it was easy and comforting and Chaz was
nothing like you'd expect from the image he created in his
videos. We chatted a bit about Guy and about the accident
– not in detail of course, but about where it was and about
the weekend we had planned before Guy got into Chaz's
big UK tour. We spoke about that for a while which led me
to make reference to one of the elephants in the room.*

"I have to ask, Chaz – about your image…"
Chaz instantly laughed aloud. Then abruptly changed his face to give Gina a theatrically quizzical look.
"Sorry, I don't know what you mean."
Gina's turn to laugh.
"I think you do. I've watched loads of your videos and Guy checked lots of your press coverage before he met you – when Brigitte first offered him the job – and, well you know what I mean about *that* image and this one." Gina gestured to the man sitting on the sofa opposite her.
"Yeah. Well that one paid for all this." He waved a hand casually around the room. "And my apartments in New York and on Tobago and so on and so forth. But I'm in the process of changing it - my image. That was me and I embraced it with no consideration for any effect it could have on my fans, but that's all in the process of changing now. My latest album starts the changes and this tour will preview more of the new me. Gone is the aggression – more thought-provoking lyrics now."
"When did the change start?"
"A year ago. May 15th to be exact. A very dear friend was knifed to death for no reason by a bum who was out of his head on amphetamines and my music. That bit came out in court along with a load of other evidence that my lyrics - not only mine, but some other aggressive rap stuff - was the route cause. The thing was, I was just playing that role. I knew what sold so that's what I gave the kids -

along with the image that you know from the media. It was like a mask - like a costume I put on for the shows and videos. I really hadn't given my lyrics and lifestyle any more consideration than that. I'm so ashamed to admit it. A wake up call of the first order. And some."

Gina felt that their roles had just reversed and she was the confident.

"Is it working?"

"Oh yes. I met someone who convinced me that the way for me to find salvation was to embrace Jesus Christ. *That's* what's working for me and it will for you."

"Maybe. I'm not religious. Well, I have beliefs about the spirit world and some of that sort of stuff, but they don't conform to any set religion; like a lot of people I think."

"Yeah, I think you're right."

I had to remind myself about the man I was talking to and his public image that was so aggressive and so chauvinistic, but he was like a priest sitting listening and sharing his life with me as if we'd known each other for years, not minutes. It was weird...but then, it wasn't. He was so easy to talk to. He never forced his beliefs on me but he referred to his born-againness several times as we talked.

The attention came back to me and it was my turn to open up. Well, I felt a duty after Chaz's admissions and I wanted to share some of the pain - and you know what? I found myself talking in the past. About how I had a severe bout of depression, not am having one.

Then Chaz moved the conversation on to talk about Watersource. That surprised me. He seemed to know quite a lot about it and asked sensible questions about how it worked, about our new experimental systems and whether they were working. He wanted to know how we spent the money we collected and what it had achieved. You know I don't need any prompting to spout forth (that's a line I've

*used before, by the way) about how it works so I went on
a bit I think.*

Chaz had listened to Gina's stories with an easy connection. Her explanation about Wateresource seemed to complete the picture of how her long-standing passion underpinned her recent life. As Gina started to think that she was perhaps over-detailing Watersource, Chaz stood and moved across the short distance to sit beside Gina on the opposite sofa. He took her hand.

Strangely, that didn't feel creepy or inappropriate.

"I have a confession…"

Shit!

"…..I've been following your activities with Watersource since Guy introduced me to it. And I think what you're doing is the most wonderful thing….."

Phew!

"….So I'd like to help. That's the main reason I invited you here because I wanted to meet you. And what you say about the way the charity works makes me very comfortable. So I'd like to be a benefactor … a sponsor."

"Well…that's very nice of you. I'm … I'm … a bit speechless. Thank you."

"Once upon a lot of generations ago, my ancestors were Swahili from the area that eventually became Kenya. I already do a bit to help fund a hospital in Nairobi, but I worry that that money doesn't get to the people I want to help. That's because I pay it to a big charity that doesn't monitor the way it's spent like you do. They've never told me how they use my money and that worries me, so I'm going to cancel that support and send the money to you – to Watersource. It's a modest amount, but I hope it will help."

"That's so nice of you – thank you." Gina's sincerity was unmistakeable. Chaz raised a finger as if to emphasise his next observation.

"But something has come to mind this morning as you were talking. I hope you don't mind me saying this, but I think you should go to Kenya to see the results of your work - to see where the money is spent; and I will pay for that trip separately."

What?!

"I'm sorry, I don't follow that. Why?"

"Two reasons. As you just said – all your PR and social network stuff is your most powerful selling tools. Well, that's how I interpret your words and I think it's true. But of all the pictures in your gallery, the end result doesn't figure as much as it should. If you went out there you would get a mass of pictures and personal stories – and you know what they say – a single picture is worth a thousand words. Not just the water stuff but everything that your systems brings to the communities they're serving. Believe me, Gina, I know a bit about PR and image. It's mega-powerful. So if you agree, I want to be a named sponsor 'cos that fits with my new image." Chaz seemed to realise how Gina may interpret that remark, so quickly added: "Not that that's why I'm doing it and if you don't want me to be named that's absolutely okay. If you do, I'll put a Watersource links on my website and regularly cover your activities on my social media output." Chaz looked awkward for the first time as he added: "Two point eight million followers."

Gina couldn't help reacting to that, but Chaz returned immediately to the point of his proposed trip.

"So you go over and document what you do at the end of the story that starts here in UK – show exactly where donors' money goes and what it achieves. That's what impressed me and it will do the same to others."

Chaz had hardly broken eye contact with Gina whose expression was not betraying her thoughts at that moment. Chaz added:

"And there's another equally important reason....I sense you need to break away from your life here in London. From the bad stuff that's hurting right now. Just a short break to get a new perspective. Your passion for Watersource is obvious so the more you get into that and the more it provides a distraction, the better and the quicker you'll mend up when you get back ..... Right?"

Gosh!

"Gosh!"

"It makes sense doesn't it?"

"Yeah."

"And I'll pay for that trip as my gift to you. If you prefer, you can think of it as my gift to Guy for being a good one – a good guy – if that helps your decision. And if that doesn't work, then do it for me, please. I don't only mean the PR commercial stuff. You see, I have a conscience about how much I have when I compare myself to so many people round the world. Clean water should be available to everyone in the twenty-first century. What you're doing is what I would like to do for my people in that part of the world that don't have that basic necessity. I wanted to help with the hospital but I think what you're doing and how you do it is so much better, so think of it as if you're doing work for me. And I want to pay for that service. As simple as that."

Chaz looked into Gina's eyes as if waiting for her response.

"What d'you say? You'll think about it, at least, won't you?"

"I am. Thank you – thank you so much. And not only for the money."

Gina threw her arms around Chaz's neck and hugged him. They both knew the meaning of Gina's last statement and Chaz smiled a broad pearly smile.

46

I couldn't wait to tell Daisy. I texted from the bus as we arranged and within an hour we were both sitting in my lounge drinking tea and listening to me blurting out the story of my adventure .... all the way to Chelsea. Well, it was a big deal a few hours ago. Now, already it looked like nothing. Daisy was as made up about it as me.

"Daisy, I went into that apartment a mess - as you know ...... and I came out with a bounce in my step. I was ..... whatever the opposite of *'a mess'* is, that was me."

"Did you touch the hem of his cloak?"

They both laughed. The first time Daisy had seen Gina laugh in the weeks that they had known one another.

"All right. Yeah, I know it must sound like that."

Daisy was about to speak when Gina tripped over another thought.

"Oh yeah – this goes to show how different my head was. When I stood at the bus stop waiting for a bus to come back here, I suddenly realised that if I crossed the road I could get a bus down the King's Road to get my hair cut again at Heady Daze down at Sloane Square."

"But you didn't."

"No, well, it costs a fortune – that'd be a total extravagance with my finances as they are – and I'm trying to get the last few grand to Eric for the new system to go to Kenya. But the fact that I even thought about going to get a haircut just goes to show how different my head was. It wouldn't have occurred to me on the way there."

"That's wonderful, dear. I'm thrilled for you. I couldn't be happier if our roles were reversed."

I love Daisy. In just a few weeks she has become my best friend, my crutch and now my confidante. There must be a twenty year difference in our ages but I think of her like my older sister, not my mother or an aunt. Then, as Daisy always does, after her obvious joy as she listened to me being excitable again, she always seems to be able to add her totally logical perspective to my situation.

"Gina, darling. Just a word of warning – and a very important one, so please don't think I'm lecturing. You have been very ill – you know that all too well - so please don't under-estimate that. In fact, sorry to say this, but you still are. This turnaround is wonderful but it's so instant that your head will take a while to mend properly." She looked at Gina for recognition that she was listening and heeding her advice.

"I understand, Daisy. Really, I do understand."

47

Of course I was going to Kenya.... I assume you realised that.

Planning for the trip became my total focus. It was so totally the right thing to do - I just needed Chaz to point it out – and to pay for it of course.

Just having that objective changed so much. Like the old days, it gave me a reason to get up in the mornings and not just for my recuperation.

I started by floating the idea with Eric and Dizzy which was more a case of me telling them that I was going. And I asked Dizzy about transport and some accommodation when I got there, but they both treated it as a request and said they'd have to make enquiries and that sort of thing. That really surprised me, to be honest, but I wasn't going to let them tell me I couldn't go so in my emails I told them what I was planning and let them sort out the arrangements at the other end.

Meanwhile here in London, I realised there were a lot of things I needed to sort out before I went. I was planning on a three-week trip to give me enough time to see a lot of stuff that I could record for PR. And going all that way for less time seemed silly.

It was during the planning that I started to realise quite how bad my finances had got. My personal account would not cover the flat costs during the three weeks away – that's how bad things were. A week ago that realisation would have set me back and probably sent me to bed for another week, but now it became a problem to solve. Not *the biggest. I moved some money from Watersource like an advance on next month's salary. I could pay it back over a couple of months when I got back. I worked that out like Daisy showed me before. And to be honest, you know what? I thought, fuck it – time for me to put myself first for a change. I'm going to Kenya come what may so I'll move every penny out of my accounts if needs be and worry about any problems when I get back. Right now this charity begins at home and it owes me big time, so there.*

I wanted to time my trip with the arrival of the next system that was already on its way by sea to Kenya so I could document the process of what is there before the system is installed and some of the installation works. Dizzy could send photos when it was completed so I'd have the whole story for the website.

Once Gina had completed her arrangements for the trip, she asked Daisy to drop by to check everything with her. She went through Gina's plans and notes in detail, made a few observations that did not amount to anything prohibitive, then gave Gina her blessing.

Daisy was already weening Gina off the course of anti-depressants, but she produced a new supply of pills and a sheet of printed instructions that she read through with Gina as she impressed on her the most important points about warning signs and possible symptoms and side effects. Whilst Daisy wasn't going to do anything to distract Gina from the mission that was transforming her mental state, she was professionally concerned that the change for the better was happening so fast that Gina could experience a relapse if the wrong things aligned to impact at the same time on Gina's confidence and moral.

Within a week, Gina had tied up all loose ends that she could identify at home and in her head, she was already in Kenya. Her health and stamina were continuing to improve and her confidence for the trip was nearly as high as in the days immediately following her meeting with Chaz.

When Gina had announced the trip in one of her regular blogs, Chaz had responded with his blessing and predictable reference to Jesus travelling with her on her journey.

I had been in regular email contact with Chaz to keep him up to speed with my plans, basically, so I realised that this public response online to my blog was to announce that he was supporting me and Watersource. What a great guy. As he would tell me, Christ operates in mysterious ways. This wouldn't be happening if we hadn't met Brigitte at a random event and Guy not taken the job with him ....

The logical conclusion to that train of thought was that Guy would also still be alive, so Gina immediately turned her thoughts away to check something about her journey. She needed any distraction from the series of events that had brought her to the lowest point in her life.

Daisy had arranged to drop by on the day before Gina's departure, just to say goodbye and make her final health check.

She arrived mid-morning and sat in her now-usual place at the end of Gina's sofa and checked Gina's pulse and blood pressure and temperature before declaring her patient physically fit for the journey. Then she checked her arrangements and plans and tested her on identifying her depressive symptoms. That was the problem that Daisy couldn't measure with a machine.

Then Daisy delved into the large bag that went everywhere with her and pulled out yet another piece of equipment – or so Gina thought until she announced:

"Here's something else I hope will be useful on your trip." Then handed over a cube wrapped in plain brown paper. Gina was confused as she took the package and ripped open the cover to reveal a box showing a photo of its contents - a camera.

"Daisy?! What have you done? You bought this for me?" Gina opened the box and removed the instruction booklet then a camera wrapped in plastic. "I don't believe it. Thank you so much."

"The man in the shop said this is perfect for what you want to do with photos and you can do interviews on video as well. He said that it will be much better than using your phone."
Gina slid along the sofa to give Daisy a hug.

"Daisy, you probably won't ever know how grateful I am to you. I don't know that I have the words to say how much I owe you for getting me here. I literally wouldn't have done it without you, so thank you so so very much."

"Oh I don't know about that, dear. But you're welcome." Daisy took both Gina's hands and squeezed them reassuringly as she had done so many times during recent weeks. Today the meaning was the same, only the situation could not have been more different.

48

The cheapest flights that Gina could find, took her via Amsterdam on a draining eleven hour schedule, arriving in Nairobi early in the morning. Dizzy had shocked Gina two days earlier when he announced that he couldn't meet her at the airport.

Cheeky sod - how rude. What could he be doing that's more important than meeting me after all I've done to help him get here? To be honest, I was pissed off with him, but my excitement at going to Kenya – my first trip to Africa after all these years of sending support – that was overwhelming. I'm still pissed with him though.

Dizzy had arranged for two people from Nantuni - Tambo and his wife Shani - to meet Gina at the airport and transport her on the three hour journey back to the village.

Gina was exhausted when she arrived at Jomo Kenyatta Airport. The excitement of the trip and her overly-firm aeroplane seat had combined to rob Gina of a night's sleep, but now with the sounds and smells and fresh sunny morning greeting her arrival in Africa for the first time, Gina was finding her energy for the day. She met Tambo and Shani who seemed a little nervous as Gina assumed to shake hands when they met at the arrival gate. Gina's full name was spelt incorrectly on their sign, so that provided a subject for some light exchanges along with the inevitable *'how was your flight?'* questions, but still Gina sensed the pair were not relaxed in her company as she kept the conversation moving on the walk to the car park.

The noise from the minibus's engine was already so extreme that conversation was difficult once Tambo started driving. Then when he opened the windows in an attempt to keep the interior cool, Gina gave up fighting the cacophony and sat watching the suburbs of Nairobi eventually become a parched savanna. After a tortuous two hours' drive into the rising sun, they turned off the pock-marked tarmac onto a red dust roadway where all manner of surface changes replaced the potholes.

Eventually, mid-morning, the minibus turned into the village. It was bigger than Gina had imagined, but the photos that Dizzy had sent showing his first installation were very familiar to her, so the variety of low huts and rickety houses were as she expected.

This was so exciting. Here I was at the very place I'd seen in so many photos that I felt I already knew it.

Tambo pulled up at a bungalow constructed from a patchwork of materials.

"This is our home, Miss Gina. You stay here."

"It's lovely. Thank you very much."

Gina knew that she was to be accommodated by a family in the village but this was the first time that Tambo or Shani had indicated that they were her hosts.

Their two teenage boys were in the house when they entered with Gina's wheelie suitcase that looked particularly out of place today. They were smiley and polite when they were introduced but, like their parents, they appeared uneasy. Gina assumed that they would relax in time.

"Would you like to sleep?" Shani asked.

"Well, if you don't mind, maybe for an hour. I am very tired from the journey. Thank you." Gina's instinct was to say 'no' but for the last hour she had been fighting exhaustion and thinking that a short nap might be what she needed to get over the flight.

Shani showed her to a small bedroom, which, judging from the posters of footballers who Gina didn't recognise and Daisy Ridley in her Star Wars costume who Gina did recognise, was usually occupied by one of the boys. Gina protested that she couldn't expect one of Shani's sons to move out of his room, but Shani was insistent that it was no problem. Insistent to the point that Gina decided that making more fuss could embarrass her hosts. Shani pointed to an outside wash area with a toilet and barely-private shower. That was the bathroom. But she showed some animation when she explained that the building materials stacked nearby were for Tambo to build a new bathroom with direct access from the house. Gina took that to be one of the results of having the new water system in the village.

It was quite a lot to take in, but it would be okay. I would be okay. At that moment I was only relieved that I didn't need to use the loo – 'basic' was a master understatement, but when in Africa .... It'll be fine. It did occur to me how odd this was. Here I am in the house of someone I've never met before today, in a village in the middle of nowhere in the middle of Africa with no-one I know, knowing where I am. But it'll be fine.

And with that thought, Gina fell into a deep sleep.

She woke to soft light picking out the features of the bedroom through thin muslin curtains. It took a few moments for Gina to readjust. She collected her thoughts and checked the time on her watch that still showed UK time. She tried to work out how 3.23 translated into Kenya time. After a few passes she gave up and ventured out of her bedroom still in a semi-comatose state.

"Hello Miss Gina." Shani greeted her as she tottered towards the living area of the bungalow. "Are you all right?"

"Yes, thank you. I think I've been asleep for a long time. What time is it please?"

"Nearly half past five."

"Gosh. I'm sorry."

"It's not a problem. You needed to sleep. Would you like juice?"

"Thank you. Yes please."

I had to start to think about what to eat and drink now. All part of the readjustment – juice will be fine.

And it was. Mango. Sweet and glutinous and delicious. As Gina started to wake up, she recalled her gift, excused herself and hurried back to the bedroom where she pulled a large box of shortbread from her hand luggage then returned to present it to Shani.

"I hope you like biscuits – they are traditional in the UK."
Shani looked a little awkward – again – averting her eyes as she thanked the floor more than her guest.

I didn't know what to make of that. Had I embarrassed her? Is it rude to give a gift here – shit, I hope not. Best to leave it and move on.

Gina had to tackle the outside sanitation sooner or later and this was as good a time as any. And desperation was now a spur. She took her toilet bag, which seemed rather ostentatious, but what else was she to do?

Yep, it was as basic as it looked. T'will be okay. I think those words will be my guiding principal for as long as I'm here, basically. Oops, still doing it.

When Gina returned to the kitchen after washing and changing, Tambo and both boys, Amani and Kito, were sitting at the dining table. Gina sensed the casual family chat changed when she entered.

"Hi guys. Whose bedroom am I in?"
Kito half raised his hand.

"Thank you. You're Kito aren't you?"
He nodded and almost managed a smile.

"I'm sorry that you had to move out for me."

"They used to share when they were smaller – it's no hardship," Shani insisted and the subject was not discussed again during Gina's stay.

I know it's early doors, but I hope this loosens up. The thought of egg shell walking for three weeks doesn't appeal.

Gina moved the subject on to what she wanted to do during her visit. Shani and Tambo appeared to be surprised by most of what Gina explained, even though she was only discussing precisely what she had arranged with Dizzy.

"Is that all okay?"

Shani looked to Tambo for confirmation.

"If you have arranged that with Mr Dizzy. Did he say it's all right?"

"Yes," Gina answered cautiously.

Blimey - I was only talking about taking some photos and doing some interviews. I sensed that the interviews were the sensitive bit. Maybe that's not what you do here. Maybe it's a privacy thing, or religious, or something. Dizzy didn't warn me. Bloody Dizzy – he should have sorted this.

"When will Dizzy be back – do you know?"

"Tuesday, he said."

Tomorrow could be a long day if they don't want me to do anything.

By the time Gina woke next morning, the house was quiet and the sun was already warming her room too much for comfort. Gina's senses immediately started to react to new smells and sounds. She checked her watch that she had now adjusted to local time. 10.22.

I felt bad that I had slept in, but is this sleeping in – I don't know. Or perhaps they would prefer me to be out of the way. No, hopefully not.

The previous evening had been a little awkward as the family were still not at ease in Gina's company. She excused herself and went to bed as soon as it seemed polite, blaming her journey and jet lag for her tiredness.

Gina now pulled on a loose dress and made her way through the house but found no-one. She was unsure what to do.

I s'pose it would be okay to have some juice.

Before Gina could open the fridge, she noticed Shani outside, bent over, apparently digging the dark soil in the small but verdant garden.

Gina strolled out to join her, but Shani didn't notice Gina until she spoke.

"Good morning Shani."

"Oh, Miss Gina." She immediately stiffened, continuing the mood of last evening.

"Thank you for letting me sleep on."

"Do you want some breakfast?"

"Oh, don't worry – I will just get some juice if you don't mind. But I should wash first."

Shani watched Gina turn back to the house before she continued tilling the soil with a rake.

As much to fill her time as to prepare for the photo and video shoots, Gina had thought that she should practise using her new camera. So she sat at the kitchen table working through the instruction booklet, familiarising herself with the baffling number of functions that it offered. As *the man in the shop* had promised, this seemed absolutely right for Gina's purposes.

She hadn't completed her instruction course when Shani arrived in the kitchen with a cardboard box from which an array of vegetable leaves protruded.

As pretty as a picture.

Without consideration, Gina stopped Shani to ask if she could take her photograph with the new camera. In fact, it was more of a demand.

"Shani - you look great. I must take your photo." Then she thought to ask: "Is that okay?"

If I'd thought what I was doing I may have been more cautious, but the sight of Shani in her bright colourful clothes with the box of veggies was so striking that I didn't consider if it was wrong to ask.

Perhaps because Gina was so forthright, Shani agreed – albeit with a moment's hesitation – but she followed Gina back out into the garden for the photo.

"Stand there – right in the middle of all the leaves." By which Gina meant, in the midst of a patch of very large cabbages and leeks. Gina thought about the angle of the sun and adjusted Shani then took several photos.

"Thank you – you look lovely. Thank you."

Once back in the shade of the kitchen, Gina started to review the pictures. At which point she sensed Shani hovering nearby, too polite to ask, but evidently wanting to see the photos.

"Here, look. Aren't they great? Don't you look a picture? My very first on this camera and my first for the trip. They will be great for the website."

Shani moved closer to see the pictures on the camera's screen. And for the first time, Gina saw a hint of a smile on Shani's smooth polished face.

"Is your garden so productive because of the new water system?" Gina asked.

"Yes."

"But not all the gardens have water yet, do they?"

"No."

"Why do you have water before anyone else?"

"We work for Mr Dizzy."

Gina assumed she meant that she worked *with* Dizzy so passed over the precise meaning of the remark, in part because she sensed a connection with Shani for the first time.

In for a penny.

"Shani, why do you think I'm here? What did Dizzy tell you?"

"You have to ask Tambo."

"Did Dizzy tell Tambo why I've come here?"

"Yes."

"And Tambo told you what exactly?"

Even with her back to Gina, Shani conveyed a tension.

"Shani, do you know that I provide the money for the water system here in the village."

Shani stopped washing the leeks but didn't turn to Gina.

"That's right. I run a charity in the UK that raises the money to buy the equipment that Dizzy helped you install when he first arrived – to build your well and pump to make pure water. Did you know that Dizzy worked with me in London to help me raise that money? Did you know any of that?"

Gina didn't need to see Shani's face to know that she was surprised by Gina's statement.

"Can I help you do that?" Gina stood to join Shani at the sink. "Here, let me do something."

"It's okay. There's nothing to do." Shani was visibly tense so Gina sat down and continued to play with the camera, realising that she could break the tenuous connection that she had just created.

"He say that you have bad spirit." Shani spoke quietly without turning. Gina didn't expect the remark or the information.

"Bad spirit?"

"He say you come to check what we do here to tell man in England, but you have bad spirit so you could make harm to our well and water."

"Why would I do harm to something I work very hard to buy for you?

There was no answer.

"But, then, you didn't know I bought the system because Dizzy never said anything about me paying for it?" She spoke as if thinking aloud.

"No Miss Gina."

Shani wiped her hands on a cloth as she turned to make eye contact with Gina at last.

"I'm here to do what I told you – and that's all, Shani. To take photographs and record what you tell me about how the water systems have changed your lives. I want to demonstrate... to explain to people back in England what we do with the money that they give me. And that's so I can get more money to buy more systems to send here. That's the only reason I'm here. Do you believe me?"

Shani appeared to assess the new situation.

"Yes, Miss Gina."

That exchange changed the atmosphere – well, between me and Shani at least. I had loads of questions and to be honest, the answers came easier during the day until the men arrived home, then Shani stiffened up a little bit, but I was glad that she was comfortable in my company when we were alone and that helped me relax in the house.

Mid-morning the next day, Gina was in for one of the shocks of her visit. A large white four-by-four car with dark windows pulled up outside Shani's bungalow. Most of the vehicles Gina had seen until then had been old and tired and worn-out by the poor local roads, so this gleaming monster blingmobile stood out even before the occupant emerged from the passenger door. A slim black man with a sprout of short dreadlocks, wearing very dark wraparound sunglasses and a bright orange batik shirt approached the house. Gina and Shani had noticed the car arriving from the kitchen window.

"It's Mr Dizzy," Shani announced.

Oh my god. I literally didn't recognise him.

He removed his sunglasses as he stepped across the threshold when Shani opened the door.

"Hi." Dizzy walked in without otherwise acknowledging Shani who immediately went back into the kitchen.

"Dizzy!" Gina exclaimed.

"Hi Gee – how are you?" He walked straight to her in the hallway and kissed her on both cheeks.

"I'm still in shock. Look at you. I literally didn't recognise you." Dizzy laughed.

"No? I imagine. There's been a few changes since we last saw each other in Camden. Oh yeah, sorry about your accident and all that bad shit. That was…." He ran out of words.

"Shit." Gina offered.

"Yeah, must have been. How are you after that?"

"Better, I think. But still fragile, to be honest. But getting stuck into Watersource stuff helps."

They wandered back into the kitchen as Shani placed a glass of orange squash and one of iced water on the table.

"Would you like a drink Miss Gina?"

Gina had assumed one of the glasses was for her.

"No, I'm fine thanks Shani."

Gina waited for Dizzy to thank Shani before she left the room, but he said nothing as he sat down at the table and took a long swig of water followed by a mouthful of the bright orange cordial. Gina watched him wipe his mouth with the back of his wrist before he spoke.

"Your hair's longer than when I last saw you. Suits you though."

259

"Thanks. Apart from where it's not grown out from my accident." She turned to show Dizzy the side of her head. "So's yours longer," Gina retorted, pointing at Dizzy's stubby dreads, which made him smile and tug at them for a brief moment. In that movement, Gina recognised the same Dizzy who she knew from London.

"One of quite a few changes since we last saw each other. For both of us, it seems," Gina added.

"Yeah" Dizzy nodded thoughtfully. "So, what you wanna do while you're here?"

"You know that I want to record everything I can about your work with the installation. Then to get stuff to show how our work changes the locals' lives for the better – so, any stories about what the water does to help people, like the garden here as an example." Dizzy seemed a little surprised that Gina knew about the irrigation system in Shani's garden.

"Right. This isn't pure – the gardens have unsterilized well water."

"Okay, but you know the sort of things that will impress people back home – anything that shows off the results of the charity's work."

"Right." Dizzy appeared to be thinking about that brief while Gina asked:

"But tell me about you. Where d'you live? What's with that monster car? How are things here?"

"They're good."

"Well I can see that. Come on, Dizzy, like how? Where are you living?"

That question threw Dizzy for a moment and he looked away before answering.

"I've got a bungalow on the outskirts of the village that's been loaned to me. It was empty so the owner lets me live there."

"A nice place, is it?"

"Yeah. You must come over for dinner one night."

"You cook?"

"No, but I have one… a cook and house-keeper"

"Blimey, Diz – get you."

"I don't have time. Too busy."

"And the car?" Gina was particularly puzzled by it.

"Yeah, that's good…. Don't worry, I haven't bought it with charity money," he added quickly.

"I should hope not. So where did that come from?"

"Oh, you know…."

"Err, no. Where on earth does a car like that come from round here?"

Gina saw uncertainty in Dizzy's body language for the first time. He tried to disguise a discomfort with a long noisy gulp of cordial.

"Dizzy…..Where's the car come from?"

"Someone wanted to help – cos I have to cover a helluva lot of miles now and we trashed an old Nissan van in three months - so he gave us the car."

"Us? Who's 'us'?"

"Us, the charity, of course."

"Right – lucky *us*, eh?"

Gina was none the wiser but sensed that she should drop the subject for the moment.

"Yeah. Anyway I ought to get going. The first load of kit for the new installation arrives tomorrow at a village about thirty clicks from here. I've just come from another job so I wanna get home for a shower then I need to get over there. I s'pose that's the sort of thing you want to photograph innit?"

"Absolutely. I'll come with you. It's not far is it? There and back today?" Gina asked enthusiastically.

"Yeah. But there's nothing to see now we've located the water source. Just the start of the well being dug and an open space waiting for the materials. You should come later this week when they're here."

"Sounds perfect already. I've only come to see you and the way this works, so anything to do with the work is great, Dizzy. I'll come with you….if that's okay with you?" Gina's sarcastic tone made it perfectly clear that the answer 'no' was not an option.

"Okay."

Dizzy started to finish the cordial when Gina remembered to ask:

"By the way…." She looked around to check that Shani was out of earshot then saw her in the garden. "Why did you tell Tambo and Shani that I have a bad spirit?"

Gina watched Dizzy closely for his reaction to the question. He took a little longer to finish his water than was necessary.

"I didn't… well, I was just saying what someone else told me." He thought for a moment. "Look, there's things what happen here you can't imagine from your life in London – I was the same when I first got here." Dizzy looked at his watch. "I gotta get moving. Let's talk about it later. I'll pick you up in half an hour."

"You can tell me in the car."

"Err, no, not in the car. Wait til later and I promise I'll tell you what I know."

I realised why he said that when he picked me up and I got in the car and there was another guy in it – a driver. A great big bloke who Dizzy introduced in passing as 'Duma'. Blimey, a big car with a driver! Dizzy was right about me not understanding how things work out here.

They arrived at the new building site soon after midday. The unseasonal heat was stifling when Gina opened the car door from the cosy air-conditioned, leather interior. It made her gasp then perspire within a few minutes. Dizzy and Duma seemed unfazed by the heat and went about their checks with no regard for Gina, so she walked about the site taking photos of the few activities that were underway.

That said, it was obvious that as soon as the car turned into the site from the main road, the handful of workers on site all became more active. I think they were all sitting in

*the shade before we arrived which I know I would have
been.*

"That's why I try to be around as much as possible, which is
why I need a good set of wheels," was Dizzy's response when Gina
mentioned it on the journey back to Nantuni. But no mention was
made of an encounter that Gina had witnessed from a distance at the
site. Perhaps 'confrontation' would be a more appropriate word.
Duma had stepped in between Dizzy and the two white men who
arrived soon after Dizzy's group. Gina was too far away to hear the
conversation but the aggravation between the two parties was easy to
recognise at a distance. Gina considered asking about it but thought
she would get a more honest response from Dizzy if she did so when
they were alone, so she logged it on her expanding *to be discussed*
list.

Getting Dizzy alone proved impossible over the coming days. On the
few occasions they were together, either Shani or Tambo or Duma
(who seldom left Dizzy's side) were in evidence and earshot.
Meanwhile, the number of questions on Gina's list that only Dizzy
could answer, was growing appreciably.

*I'd also started to worry about the way Dizzy treated
people, including some who were working for him – and
that meant they were working for the charity that
Watersource supported, so that meant he sort of
represented me. He was really abrupt - dismissive. Like he
didn't care about them or what they thought about him.
Maybe I was being too English, but he's English, so he
should be more considerate than he seemed to be.*

Gina had to miss some of the travel plans that she had arranged with
Dizzy when her digestive system took against the local food and
drink towards the end of her first week in Nantuni. But when she
could, Gina had travelled to the two sites that Dizzy was currently

managing. She had also started to record her first few interviews but they had proved tricky because adults were nervous and retiring as soon as Gina produced the video camera. Children, by comparison, were far more forthcoming if prone to over-excitement, but Gina loved their innocent openness.

When at the sites, Gina was in the habit of walking around doing her own thing while Dizzy checked progress in detail using plans and tape measures. If they arrived near the middle of the day, Gina would stay in the air-conditioned car or find the shade of a tree from where she could watch activities and plan what to photograph; then she would move into action, record progress with some still photos then dive back into shade and relative comfort. This routine resulted in her becoming almost invisible to the men on site who ignored her, enabling her to watch without being watched.

On one such visit to the new site, the same two men who had confronted Dizzy on Gina's first visit, returned. And the confrontation reran as previously. Duma had been sitting in the car when they arrived, but was out and at Dizzy's side by the time the men squared up to them. Gina watched for a while, too far away to hear their conversation, but she zoomed in with her camera lens and watched from her vantage point in the shadows. Moments later, as she still watched through the viewfinder, one of the men pulled a handgun from somewhere under his jacket. In an instant, Duma was holding a gun to the man's head in a stand-off. Gina pressed the 'start' button on her camera to record the scene as Dizzy tried to calm the man with the gun. That prompted him to swing across to level it at Dizzy's head. Dizzy raised his hands in submission which distracted both men for the split second that Duma needed to pistol-whip the man with the gun with a violent smack to his left temple. He fell to his knees and fired a shot into the ground. Duma was onto him with a second blow to the head and Dizzy put his foot on the handgun, trapping it into the red dusty ground. Duma raised his gun and pointed it at the second man who now had his hands held high and open to show that he was no threat.

I assumed we'd talk about this in the car on the way back to Nantuni. The atmosphere was tense in the car, but only because I was there. Dizzy and Duma seemed to take the incident like it was normal so they didn't talk about it. It was weird. That made me even more curious and worried …. Yes, seriously worried, in fact, about what was going on here in the name of my charity.

"Do you want to tell me about those two thugs who nearly shot you, or do you want to invite me back for dinner and we can talk about it then, Dizzy… because we are going to talk about it?"

Dizzy and Duma exchanged brief glances across the front seats of the car.

"Sorry about that, Gee."

"Sorry it happened or sorry I saw it?"

Dizzy thought about the question before answering.

"Both, I suppose."

"So…. I'm waiting for your explanation. What was it about?"

Dizzy thought about the question before answering.

"Come to dinner - not tonight - tomorrow. I have business in Nairobi tomorrow so I'm not going to site but I'll pick you up at seven tomorrow evening. Is that okay with you?"

"Yes, fine. Thanks."

The next morning, Gina was alone in the house with Shani but now the two women were more at ease in one another's company.

"Please don't cater for me tonight, Shani - I'm having dinner at Dizzy's house this evening."

"Yes, Miss Gina?"

Shani was preparing some bread and cheese for their lunch.

"Shani…" Gina was cautious but there was a subject that she needed to explore before tonight. "You said to me that Dizzy told you I have a bad spirit but he said he didn't say it. What more can you tell me?"

Shani appeared to know more than she was saying.

"Please Shani. I don't think it's polite to say that and not explain because I have been very worried... upset, about it since you said it." She watched Shani and was prepared to wait through a long silence if necessary, but it wasn't.

"I think he say it because one of the village elders say it."

"I don't understand. I don't know any of the village elders." Shani was obviously uncomfortable talking about the subject.

"Risala is a wise woman who sees things.... like spirits that tell her things. You don't have to see her."

"And you think this lady – Risala – has told Dizzy that I have a bad spirit – is that right?"

"Yes, Miss Gina. I'm sorry you have been worrying by my words. I'm very sorry I upset you."

That hurt. It took me back a month. I had moved on from all the shit in London and the spooky leads to money ...... Being so far away has let me forget all that bad karma shit. Now I felt a shiver when Shani told me about this elder woman. I still have a conscience about Guy's death and this brought it straight back. Like Shirley, when Guy and I went to her house. And as much as I've been telling myself that she was wrong – the truth is that she was probably right. I was bad for Guy. All this fucking way from London and here it is again. It travels with me. Why is this happening again? Shit-it!

Gina sat in her bedroom all afternoon after lunch with the excuse of reviewing her photos on her laptop. Alone with her thoughts and no distractions, Gina began to rerun too much of her life during the last year. It was a mistake because it made her maudlin and introspective – the very behaviour that had brought her down after Guy's death.

I knew it was happening. If I reasoned anything, it was that I should get closer to the black dog like Daisy showed me. But today it wasn't working. I was just upsetting myself.

Hopefully Dizzy can shed some light on my fears and I can get through this without having to take Daisy's pills again.

Gina washed, applied some of the few items of make-up that she had packed then changed into a loose cotton dress for her dinner with Dizzy.

His car pulled up at the house shortly after seven-o'clock. Dizzy met Gina at the front door and complimented her on her appearance. Gina thanked him with a smile that hid her anxiety and her suspicions that this evening could end badly. Gina had too many questions for something unpleasant not to be revealed at some point tonight – assuming Dizzy would tell her the truth.

Dizzy was driving because Duma was off duty, but Gina decided not to start a confrontation while they drove the short distance to his bungalow on the edge of the village. She talked about whatever they passed on the route, then thought to ask about the Internet.

"I do need to update the Watersource website and social media with some of the pics and interviews. Where can I do that?"

"The nearest place now is about half way to Nairobi for an Internet café. That's where I go. I'll get Duma to take you one day."

"Soon?"

"Yeah, sure."

"Thanks Dizzy – that's great. God knows how many emails I have to sort, so it could be for a couple of hours with everything I need to do. Will that be okay?"

"Sure it will."

I didn't want to start the evening on the wrong foot and I reasoned that I would get more out of Dizzy later if he was at ease at least to begin with. I think I've started to become very calculating lately.

Gina's first view of Dizzy's bungalow was confusing.

Outside was a bit of a building site, but once we drove past that, the house looked amazing. And smelled of paint. Shani had said that Tambo had been working on it. Then inside – wow. Really nice with some really nice African furniture and bits of nice sculpture.

"Wow Dizzy, this is really cool."

"Thanks. It's gettin' there." Dizzy opened the doors of a low cupboard to switch on some hi-fi equipment from which local African background music began to play.

While Gina was still looking around, a tall, slim girl, aged about fifteen was suddenly in the room with them.

"Can I get you a drink, miss?"

"Oh, hello…thank you."

Gina waited for Dizzy to introduce the girl, but nothing was forthcoming.

"I'll have my usual," he instructed in a tone that had become familiar to Gina during the last week with him.

"Hello, I'm Gina. Some fresh juice please."

"Nothing alcoholic?" Dizzy asked. Gina thought about that.

"Do you have vodka?"

"Yes miss."

"And tonic?"

"Certainly miss." And the girl turned to make the drinks.

"You didn't introduce me," Gina scolded Dizzy in a whisper. Dizzy looked genuinely surprised.

"Sorry. No."

"You know you've changed a lot since you've been here…but I suppose that's inevitable."

"Of course it is."

Dizzy gestured Gina to sit on a white leather sofa as he sat facing her from the other side of a coffee table. Gina had thought about this conversation and decided that there was no point in tip-toeing around the subjects on her list.

"Are you going to be honest with me now?"

"About what?"

"Everything on my list of questions – you must know there's loads of things I want to know – like that fight at the site yesterday – and where you get that car with a driver – or is Duma a bodyguard? And then there's this place."

"You know most of that. I've told you about the car – it's on loan from a bloke what wants to help us."

"A car, yes – but that one must have cost a fortune – and who's paying Duma? And why do you need him? Well, I suppose that episode at the site yesterday answers that, but why are you getting men threatening you with guns, Dizzy? You know the life and shit you wanted to get away from in London – from the little I've seen of you and your life here, I'd say that's what you're living now. Can't you see that? You've turned into 'the man' – the very people that drove you out of Town." Then an earlier thought occurred to her. "Are you dealing?"

"What, drugs?" Dizzy laughed with some relief.

"Are you?"

"No!" He was so adamant that Gina was confident that he was telling the truth on that point at least.

The girl entered the room backwards carrying a small tray with the drinks that she placed on the coffee table in their respective positions by Gina and Dizzy.

"This is Zahra."

"Hello Zara. Thank you very much."

Zahra smiled with perfect white teeth then left the room in silence.

"Is *she* your housekeeper and cook?" Gina whispered.

Dizzy swigged a long clear drink with ice clinking in a tall glass.

"Yeah."

"How old is she – fourteen, fifteen?"

"I dunno."

"Is that all she is to you – cook and house-keeper? Does she live here?"

"Yeah."

"Yes what - she lives here?"

"Yeah."

"Are you sleeping with her?" But Gina didn't need Dizzy to answer, his eyes did that.

"Dizzy - she's just a girl. For Christ sake, she's still school age. What's going on?"

Dizzy seemed to have tired of Gina's onslaught.

"I told you, Gee - things is different here. Okay, I may not be an angel, but everything I've done is for the charities to get water to the people here. And to do that, I've played it the way I discovered people what get things done here, do it. Just waiting for stuff to happen doesn't do nothing. I learned that fast. They all thought I was some sort of expert organiser and expected me to run the show when I arrived so that's what I've been doing and it gets results."

"Okay, okay. I see that – well, to a point, but what's with the aggro at the site – who were those two guys?"

Dizzy was considering his answer, but before he could speak, Gina added:

"Dizzy – I'm no threat to you here. I can keep supplying funds to help to buy the kit you need and that's exactly what I will do when I get back to London – as long as I know it's getting to the people that we want to help. There was a time when you convinced me that you shared that passion."

"And I do. I do, I do, Gee. It's just that to get things to happen here, I found a quicker way and that seems to upset some people – occasionally."

"All I'm asking is that you're up front with me. Totally honest. What have you got to lose? Nothing. I'm no threat to you or your empire-building….right? Unless I stop sending funds to Eric, that is."

Those words registered with Dizzy. Another sip of his drink while he contemplated his next move, then stated:

"Okay – total truth, okay?"

Gina stared at him.

"Cuttin' to the chase – fresh water is currency here. There, that's it?"

"What?"

"It didn't take long for me to realise the value of fresh water here – and not only drinkable – they call that *potable* water in the village – but any fresh water has serious value. And I know how to find it with our equipment and get it outta the ground. Look, Gee, when I got here it was a bloody shambles – you know the site at Kastrena where you came on Monday? That had been being built for nearly a year when I arrived. Some of the fucking instructions were still in German. They didn't have a fucking clue. It wouldn't be nearly finished now if I hadn't gone over there a couple of months ago and found most of the parts still in crates – after a year. That's how bad it was. Eric was collecting the money – including all yours from Watersource – and sending the kit but never took any notice of what was happening when it arrived. So I've run the installations on a sort of industrial basis for the first time. It's not difficult but no-one was helping the poor buggers out here til I arrived. And the results of that's what you see here." He gestured around the room. "I've found ways to make that knowledge make me a nice income while I do your work as well."

"That doesn't explain your *'water's currency'* statement."

"Yeah, right. Well if you can get a reliable source of water here you can do everything else. For domestic stuff of course, but for irrigating crops and for sanitation – everything we take for granted in the UK. Having fresh water makes people happy and content – and happy, content people don't cause aggro and they vote you back in power, so lots of people have reasons to want fresh water....and they're prepared to pay for that.

"Take the Land Cruiser – my car, what interests you so much. The guy who's loaned it to me has a big nursery outfit just this side of Nairobi. Seriously big, but he had a crap irrigation system provided by the local council what was totally unreliable and mega-expensive. I used our kit to find a water source on his land – not very deep, as it happens - then we dug a well, capped it off and installed a simple pump system - which he paid every penny for - and now he has his own system what costs him the electricity to run the pumps. That's worth a fortune to him every year - so he paid me with the Land Cruiser. He has what he needs for his business and I get a reliable set of wheels - everyone's happy. And that's how it works."

Gina's turn to take a long swig of her vodka and tonic while she thought about that explanation.

You know what? It was a relief - a big relief because at the end of the day, he's probably right. He adapted to what he found here and has made it work. That's okay .... isn't it?

"What about those two guys at the site?"

Dizzy raised his eyebrows emphasising the inevitability in his answer.

"Where there's money, there's heavies like that, what want some of the action. I've done a deal with the guy what sent them - their boss - so they're out of the picture now. That was a bit of my business in Nairobi earlier. You do have to cover your back here, but I learned those lessons quickly enough when the local hoods started to clock what I was doing and turned up with shooters and their hands out for payment."

Gina was about to ask about Duma when Zahra came in to announce that dinner was ready. Dizzy downed the remains of his drink and gestured for Gina to follow Zahra into a dining room where a table was set for two. Zahra turned back to the kitchen.

"Where will Zara eat?" Gina whispered.

"In the kitchen tonight – she's fine – really."

She returned with two plates, each with an avocado starter that she placed and immediately returned from whence she had emerged. Dizzy poured crystal clear iced water from a jug into two stout glasses.

"Wine?" Dizzy gestured to a perspiring bottle of white wine in a clear cooler.

"Thanks......Are you happy here?" Gina had considered that a break from her barrage of questions would be better than another onslaught – there would be plenty of time for the remainder on her list. Dizzy smiled, as much at the relief of an easy question as its directness.

"What d'you think?" He smiled broadly as he poured the wine.

"I think you look like someone who's found his niche – at least for the moment."

"For the moment?"

"Longer?"

"Well, they say, never say never, don't they? But right now, the idea of returning from this to what you know was my life - my existence - in London, is a no-brainer .... Well, innit?"

"Yes." Gina smiled as she raised her glass. "To the future." They chinked glasses.

"The future.........No, right now I'm building what I think will be my future and London ain't any part of that. For once in my short life I can see a future worth building and right now I think I'll be here, or hereabouts, for the rest of my natural born days."

"I'm really happy for you Dizzy."

"Thanks Gee. And you?"

"Me what?"

"Are you happy with your life in London? It's been a bit shitty lately. You're not interested in throwing in your lot and moving out, are you?"

"To where?" Clearly the thought hadn't occurred to her.

"Here?"

"Kenya?"

"Well, you could do worse?"

"No thanks." Gina laughed for the first time that evening with the thought about her living in Kenya.

"Shame. It'd be great to have you here. I'd like you to stay here."

Is he flirting with me?

273

"Are you flirting with me?"

Dizzy smiled flirtatiously.

"Yeah, a bit."

"Dizzy - your girlfriend is in the kitchen preparing our dinner and you're propositioning me...."

"So?" He seemed oblivious to the connection. Gina shook her head as she finished her avocado and placed her knife and fork on the plate.

You know what? To be honest with you, just for a moment I felt a pang at the thought of shagging Dizzy ... or being shagged by him – yes that was the thought that flashed through my mind. Huh – I got this sudden image in my mind. God knows why. Is it something to do with bad boys? He's very attractive, but for God's sake – I didn't come here for that. Cheeky sod, propositioning me.

"Another question – she said, moving on rapidly..."

"That's a shame – I think the last subject was more interesting."

Gina ignored his obvious meaning and his cheeky smile.

"What's with the bad karma that I bring? You promised to explain it. Something to do with a village elder, you said."

Dizzy's response was interrupted by Zahra returning to collect the plates.

"That was delicious, thank you, Zara."

Zahra was pleasantly surprised by the praise.

"Thank you miss."

Gina waited for Zahra to leave the room.

"My bad karma...?"

"Yeah. It might be because I upset some people when I first got here. If so, I'm sorry but you shouldn't worry about it."

"I am worried. How are you responsible?"

"When I got here and they all expected I was here to sort out their water system, that's what I did – as you know from my emails and the photos. No-one else knew how to do it or would have, so I just got on an' done it. Well that upset the elders 'cos I was suddenly the brown-eyed boy who'd brought potable water into the village and the elders hadn't, so they sort of took against me. If I had known better I'd have been more sensitive, but I didn't care about those things at the time and just got on and done it as best I could. So they still hate me and keep doing things to try to mess me about. It's jealousy, that's all. Don't worry about it."

"But that doesn't have anything to do with *my* bad karma, does it? It's not *my* fault."

"No, perhaps you're right. I wouldn't worry about it though – it's all bollocks, if you ask me."

"You named the woman who said I was bad news…"

"Yeah, Risala, she's one of the village elders. She's a sort of wise-one who they think has some sort of second sight and is in touch with spirits what can put bad juju on people. It's all bollocks of course but that's one of the downsides of being here. Someone said to me that a joke with the ex-pats out here is that when BA planes land at Nairobi they announce that *we're about to arrive in Nairobi – put your watches back three hundred years.*"

On cue, Zahra returned holding a tray with two dishes containing a stew and a basket of bread.

"Thank you Zara - that smells delicious."

Zahra smiled her wide pretty grin, then withdrew. Gina waited for the door to click shut behind her.

"What you don't know, Dizzy, is that I was in a bad way when Guy died. You know my boyfriend was called Guy?"

Dizzy shook his head as he ate.

"It was a big relationship. My biggest. I was head-over-heels, to be honest, so I was in a seriously bad way when he died. I got depressed and blamed myself for bringing it on him….Yes, stupid I know, but depression isn't logical. So, when Shani told me that someone I've never met from half way across the world, had warned that I have bad juju, as you call it, before I even arrived, it upset me again. It's really unnerving."

275

"Sorry Gee."

Yeah, what more do I expect him to say. It doesn't make too much sense to me, so without a full-on half hour explanation, why would it mean anything to Dizzy. Move on.

"Yeah .... thanks."
As much to relieve herself of the burden of further interrogation, Gina had a story behind her ear for use at some point during the evening and now seemed to be a good time.
"You know Chaz E Jones, the rapper ..."
"Not personally, why?"
"I do." Gina waited for a reaction. Dizzy obliged with a sideways quizzical expression. So Gina related the story about Guy being employed by him and Gina's meeting with him at his apartment in Chelsea. Dizzy was transfixed and admitted that he is a very big fan.
"I think I have a couple of albums on my MP3."
Gina's story had scored a direct hit.
"You wouldn't get that sort of thing happening if you moved out here." Dizzy stated with just a touch of regret. "No world celebs here. But who needs it? That meeting only happened 'cos of your grief, so it's sort of a sad story as well as a feel-good one innit?"
Zahra had cleared the plates and brought a bowl of colourful, plump fresh fruit.
"But we do get this sort of thing," Dizzy remarked as he gestured for Gina to take some fruit. "Are you sure I can't persuade you to stay on – or think about coming back more often at least?"
"Maybe the latter."
That animated Dizzy into a wide-eyed expression suggesting that there could be a chance of something happening between them.
"And stay here next time, yeah?"
"Dizzy, you're incorrigible."
"But in a nice way, yeah?"

Gina shook her head as she finished eating a mango and wiped her hands and mouth on her white cotton napkin.

"You could be nicer."

"To you?" Dizzy was puzzled.

"Not me, everyone. You're very blunt and don't seem to notice people. I'm sure you weren't like it in London... were you?"

"Dunno. But if I correct that, will you come back to stay - here - with me?"

"Enough."

"Coffee?" Dizzy asked.

"Thank you."

"Let's go through."

Zahra heard the movement and was immediately in the sitting room to take an order.

"Oh Zahra – will you kindly prepare some coffee for our guest and I? Thank you so much."

Gina watched Zahra puzzle over the manner of Dizzy's request before she turned back to the kitchen.

"That's better.....but taking the piss isn't polite," Gina whispered before adding: "Okay, so the story of this place. Who owns this?"

"I think it's the village's but no-one seems to know cos it was empty for years after the last owner died and no-one claimed it. So the village elders let me have it soon after I arrived - before we fell out. I've asked if I can buy it but they're dragging their heels now that I'm – how do you say it? Persona something..."

"Non grata."

"Yeah.

"But how's it worth doing all the work when it's not yours?"

"What's it matter? No-one will take it off me – I could live here for ages and no-one will do nothing – that's just not how it works here so meanwhile I have rather nice free accommodation." He shrugged as if to emphasise the inevitability of his statement.

"And the walls and gates - what's that about?"

"Defence."

"De-fence? I thought it was de-wall..." Gina was pleased with her response and pulled her own theatrical face.

"Ha - that's funny. De-fence - very good."

"So?"

"Yeah, my first line of defence when it's finished. Tambo and some mates is building it for me. I'm afraid it's what you need here if you have something someone else might want."

"Or enemies?"

"Yeah, right."

I must admit that I left Dizzy's house in a better mood than when I arrived. And not because of the vodka and wine. As he drove me back, I realised that I felt better now I had some answers and an idea of what was really going on. Like a weight had been lifted. I think Dizzy had been honest – he didn't seem to be trying to keep anything from me. And then it occurred to me how much I was enjoying the evening. Too much?

"I spent the afternoon sorting all the photos and the interviews that I've been getting so I'd like to get to the Internet Café whenever it's convenient please?" Gina spoke as she watched the ghostly shapes of houses pass along the unlit streets.

"Sure." Dizzy thought for a few hundred yards as he drove. "In fact, you could do it in the morning. If Duma drops me at the site first, he could pick you up by ten. How's that sound?"

"Are you sure you won't need him?"

"No, it'll be fine."

"Thanks....where does Duma live?"

"His house backs on to mine."

"And who pays him?"

"Same man what gives me the car. Really.... he don't cost the charity nothing."

"Good."

At which point they were back at Gina's accommodation. Dizzy pulled up and expected her to get out of the car but Gina turned to him as she gathered her shoulder bag.

"Thanks for tonight, Dizzy. For everything, but mainly for being honest and clearing up all my questions and things that were worrying me...lots." She thought for a moment before adding: "And for being such good company. I've really enjoyed it." Gina leaned across to peck Dizzy on the cheek, but he turned his face and kissed her full on her lips. Gina didn't resist but melted into his soft, tender kiss that became more passionate than either could have expected or planned.

Wow.........

"Good night, Dizzy." Gina stepped down from the car and went into the house without looking back.

49

The morning dawned as every other had during Gina's visit, but she woke with a sense of a burden having been lifted. More than she might have imagined because she had become tense and agitated about so much that she had witnessed, but after last night and Dizzy's apparently honest explanations, she now felt that she had a grip on how the systems worked; or the parts that had been a mystery to her. In essence, things were different here on the ground and Dizzy was making them work to his and Watersource's benefit. The elders and simmering problems were a side show that Gina convinced herself not to worry about.

I also admit that I lay in bed contemplating that kiss ...... along with Dizzy's flirting. I couldn't and shouldn't let it go any further – not while he's got his schoolgirlfriend in tow. Zara – what a sweet child. That's crap of Dizzy, but that's what happens here. No Gina – get real – don't be stupid. You'll be home this time next week and this'll look like an adventure holiday a long way from home .... but what happens on adventure holidays a long way from home, stays .... enough Ginapops.

Gina's mood was noticeably upbeat this morning. Even Shani mentioned it after asking about her evening at Dizzy's house.

"Well it seems to have made you happy, Miss Gina."

"Yes Shani. We talked about lots of things that I didn't understand about the water installations and you know that I wanted to know how my money is being spent and now I have answers, I feel much better."

Just in case she thinks something else happened last night to put that bounce in my step.

The drive to the small town with Internet was a quiet affair. Duma wasn't a great communicator which suited Gina not to have to keep a conversation alive for the duration of the journey. She asked a few questions about his family and working with Dizzy which received few-word responses, so eventually Gina gave up and they both watched the red dust road in silence.

Duma knew the precise location of the Internet facility, pulled up outside then went in with Gina to ensure she got good treatment from the manager who knew Duma and Dizzy well. Once she was set up, Duma returned to the car leaving Gina to open her inbox to the inevitable cascade of mail that had accumulated during the last two weeks away.

Dizzy was having a familiar morning on site which placed few demands on his concentration, allowing him time to reflect on the previous evening. He was happy to do just that as he watched his team at work. One day he may admit to Gina how much she means to him. Spending time alone – easy, relaxed time in her company – had stirred up emotions that he hadn't experienced for too long to recall. Perhaps never like these. Now, in this still-unfamiliar environment where he knew so much about so little that every day was a journey of discovery, now he was feeling a tug that put some of his principles to the test. He knew last night, as he lay beside Zahra in bed, that their relationship was over. He had slipped into it with so little consideration and so much lust for her beautiful young body that only after being with Gina for a few hours, he realised how much more he should expect to share with a partner. And while he was in future-building-mode, Zahra shouldn't be part of that. She should return to school and make her own future as a chef, which was her passion. He could help her to achieve that.

One of the workers wandered over to Dizzy with a roll of paper plans for some advice, breaking Dizzy's daydreaming for the moment.

At the Internet café, Gina was back in a familiar routine of deleting volumes of mail that had crept past her defences and junk diversion. Responding with short polite notes where necessary with a promise of a fuller response when she was home after next week. She was making good progress through the 582 unopened mails when she thought to glance through her junk mailbox. Sometimes important incoming mail ended there by mistake, but today it was all very obviously scams and circulars .... until:

Subject: **A fond farewell from Hilary Flik**
From: **hilaryflik33@hotmail.com**

Oh my God ! I wasn't expecting that. I hadn't thought about her for ages. It was like a piece of history coming to life.

Gina immediately opened it without a second thought about what she would find.

Dear Ms Melina,
I hope you are well. Unfortunately my health is not good and I am concerned that you and I have some unfinished business. If you feel the same, please send me an email to let me know if you would like to meet, but if not, I apologise for any inconvenience or distress I have caused since we met on Dartmoor last year. I know that you have experienced both for which I am grievously apologetic.
I send you my sincere best wishes for your future,
Hilary

Jesus.

Dear Ms Flik

Thank you for your email I have only just read because I am in Kenya with my charity. I will be back in the UK next week and would like to meet but I don't know where you live now.

Gina

Gina sent the email then immediately returned to her other business.

But for sure that had distracted me. I felt so far away from her and the whole mess that started with her on Dartmoor. But I knew that I should get to the bottom of any explanation because, even though she feels so far away and out of my life now, as soon as I got home I would wish I had sorted this unfinished business, as she calls it.

Dizzy was back with his contemplations as he sat under the makeshift awning looking at the sun-bleached scene ahead of him but not registering anything of consequence. He was now considering Gina's scolding about his attitude to other people around him. As he reflected on his relationship with Zahra, he realised that Gina was right. He had started to take people for granted and not taking their feelings into account. He excused himself on the grounds that this is a harsh environment that would have beat him up if he had been too soft. But as he reflected, he realised that he was wrong and that was just an excuse for bad behaviour. And that brought him back to the thoughts that gave him the warmest feeling today – he wanted to be with Gina. He wanted her and would make the sacrifices to be with her. As soon as the notion had crossed his mind and he found himself mouthing the words *'the problem is, you're falling in love with her'*, he knew it to be the truth. He had never met anyone like her and now he wanted to be with her, perhaps for always. He wanted her to be with him to guide him and scold him and make love to him. And he would look after her and they would have a wonderful life here and he would change and be a nicer person and she would be proud of him and love him and make love to him.

What were the chances? Could it happen? Not if he wanted to be here in Kenya, which he did, but Gina wanted to be in London, which she did.

"That's somethin' to work on – a challenge, no more, no less – you can 'andle that Dizzy-boy."

After an hour of waiting in the air-conditioned car, Duma thought he should check on Gina. He was in no hurry, he was used to waiting so he was good at it, but as a politeness, he wandered in to see Gina working diligently at her terminal.

"Is everything all right Miss Gina?"

"Oh, hi Duma, yes thank you. Are you okay for time?"

"Yes miss. No problem – take as long as you need." As he spoke he recognised some of the photos that Gina was posting on the Watersource website and was immediately engaged. He had seldom seen the Internet or websites so to see someone creating one, immediately drew his attention. Gina was amused by his fascination and was happy to explain what she was doing and gave a potted demonstration. Duma pulled up a chair and watched her every move without taking his eyes off the images and Gina's sorcery.

At the building site, Dizzy had lost track of time in his thoughts. His warm cosy feeling was nothing to do with the outside temperature nearing forty degrees, it was entirely due to his reflections on last evening and his plans that might well be shot to pieces soon, but for the moment, they fell together in his mind like a well-ordered site plan. When he looked at his watch and realised that the time had passed midday and the team were still working, he stood and called them in. That confused them for a moment and they looked one to another expecting that someone had annoyed Dizzy so was in for a dressing down, or worse.

"Guys," he shouted across to them. "Come into the shade. It's too hot. Come and get some water."

Really? That confused them further. Dizzy seldom, if ever, offered them shade and a drink when the temperature got too high, but they were glad to accept. They downed their tools, climbed out of the pit and made their way to sit under the awning watching Dizzy pour water into plastic cups until the bottle ran dry.

"Thank you Mr Dizzy," one man volunteered and the rest joined him to concur.

"Joe – do you have the keys for the Hi-Lux?"

"Yes sir."

"Let me have them and I'll go and get some more drinks."

Joe robotically handed the keys to Dizzy then watched with the others, almost disbelieving as Dizzy departed in the truck with:

"Back soon."

Gina had lost track of time. She was amused by Duma's fascination with her website and her dexterity with the keyboard and mouse. He sat, swelling over the edges of the small folding seat, staring intently at the screen with a fixed smile across his polished conker face.

I was fascinated by his fascination with something that I took so much for granted. But oddly, even though he didn't know about the of mechanics of the Internet, he would make really interesting observations about things like the balance of pictures to text and the colours I'd used.

"Why you use so much blue, Miss Gina?"

"It's the connection with water, but you think it's too much?"

"It's a cold colour and you want to be warm with people."

"Right....but I have used yellow here, look." Gina pointed to a panel on her blog page.

"Yes but yellow is known as aggressive colour."

"Is it? How do you know that?"

"I think someone tell me. I know it's right."

See what I mean? I so enjoyed that morning with Duma, like seeing things through the eyes of a very clever child. And when I let him use the mouse – well, that was like I'd given him the best toy ever. It was lovely. But I had to get some tasks sorted so eventually, when I suddenly realised how long we'd been there, I suggested that Duma go back to the car so I could skip through some things I needed to do – the rest could wait til I get home.

Gina was about to shut down when she remembered to check her email.

Even in that time I had ten new mails in my inbox but none was the one I wanted from hilaryflik33, so I tapped out a quick second response to her mail to me.

Dear Ms Flik
I have to leave this internet café now and it may be for the last time until I get back to London. Please give me your address and I will make plans to visit you when I am home.
Gina

Dizzy couldn't see the workers under the awning where he had left them, as he pulled the old Toyota Hi-lux into the site. The flatbed truck bounced across the potholed surface, shaking the water bottles and cartons of juice until some fell from the bench seat into the passenger foot well. Dizzy watched them to see that none had burst open. Then as the truck cruised into the parking space, he reached down to pull the largest bottle back onto the seat.

As he looked up, there was a man standing where he was about to park in front of a wall. The moment Dizzy bobbed into sight, the man levelled a hand gun directly at his head. BANG – BANG. The shots pierced the windscreen and lodged in the back of the cabin above Dizzy's body where he was now prone across the seat.

Dizzy had instinctively braked hard. The truck slid on the loose surface, sending the remaining drinks cascading from the plastic seats.

Dizzy crashed the Hi-lux into reverse gear. Crunch. And accelerated. The vehicle found grip and started to power backwards. But unseen by Dizzy, a military drab green Land Rover had raced to pull across behind the Toyota to prevent its escape. CRASH! The Hi-Lux smashed into it, moving the Land Rover sideways, but halting the truck.

Back into first gear. Crunch. Dizzy slammed his foot on the accelerator. He was driving blind from below the steering wheel. He didn't know where the gunman was but he was aware of the wall ahead of him. As soon as his truck found grip, Dizzy wrenched the steering wheel right. Two more fast shots smashed through the windscreen. BANG-smash BANG-smash.

Outside, the gunman jumped aside to avoid the flatbed truck that was powering at him. He dived into the sand, turned and fired a burst of rounds as fast as the semi-automatic Beretta would allow. The shells ripped through the thin skin of the van's passenger door with clangs as loud as the report from the handgun. Clang clang clang clang clang.

The Land Rover reversed at speed to cut off Dizzy's escape.

But it wasn't needed. The Hi-lux was slowing, its engine barely driving it forward, until it nudged the wall obliquely and stopped with a final jerk.

In the truck, Dizzy's neck was pumping blood from an artery ripped open by one of the bullets. Another had lodged in his skull. Their combined impact had ended Dizzy's fight and were soon to end his life. Blood poured from his body, slumped on the bench seat, to mix with the water and juice from fractured containers on the floor of the car.

The gunman brushed red sand from his clothes as he walked cautiously towards the Toyota, then raised the gun for the last few steps before tentatively reaching for the passenger door handle and wrenching it open. Water, juice and blood poured out onto the sand.

BANG-BANG. The gunman was being paid to be certain that the job was completed. He turned, climbed into the Land Rover and it sped away towards Nairobi.

Within a mile, less than a minute later, it passed the white Land Cruiser heading in the opposite direction.

50

---

*I couldn't get out of bed next morning. It was a rerun of
the darkest days in Putney. My black dogs had returned
with a vengeance. And my dreams – lots, all night – every
time I woke. But I had to make the effort for Shani's sake.
It then occurred to me that they could blame me. That
elder woman, Rayana or whatever her name is,
prophesied me being a bad omen, how was that going to
pan out? Fortunately, when I emerged from my room, the
atmosphere in the house was sad, but not threatening. We
were all in the same boat ...... And the same mood.*

Two plain clothed policemen had arrived in Nantuni earlier that
morning and made their way directly to Dizzy's house to interview
Zahra who knew next to nothing about Dizzy's business affairs, but
she could explain a little about Watersource and reveal that, by
chance, its UK representative was currently visiting the village. So it
was that mid-morning, the police arrived at Tambo and Shani's
house looking for a 'Ms Milner'.

The elder of the two men introduced himself and his colleague to
Gina with names that she didn't remember, but she registered that the
elder of the two was a detective inspector. She corrected his version
of her name then sat across the kitchen table answering his questions
about Watersource and its connection with Nantuni and Dizzy as
both officers made notes in small ring-bound notebooks. Gina
explained about coming to Nantuni to document the processes that
she funds from the UK and how her intention was to get evidence to
increase awareness of Watersource's good work that she hoped
would help her to raise more money to buy more water systems.

That led to the site visits and the stories about the heavies turning up at the building site when I was there and me literally witnessing the aggro, but it just goes to show how out of it I was because it wasn't til one of the officers used the word 'video' that I suddenly remembered that I'd filmed them. How can I have forgotten? How could I be so stupid?

Gina covered her oversight by explaining that she was planning to find the sequences that she had shot, but wasn't expecting the police to arrive so soon. She scurried away to her bedroom to retrieve the camera and the cards on which the evidence was recorded. The police watched intently when Gina returned and began to scroll through the videos in fast speed.

I didn't want them to see everything I'd shot, especially the bit where Duma pistol whipped one of the bad guys, so I moved the screen away until I'd found the first sequence where the two heavies had turned up and had a bit of a row before they got violent. I froze the image where both men were quite recognisable.

Both policemen reacted immediately Gina turned the screen for them to see the still image. There was no doubt that they recognised one or both men, but they were measured in their response to Gina.

"I need to take that with me," the elder policeman announced.

Shit.

"Of course. Or can I copy this onto a memory stick for you. I'm sure I have some other bits on another card so I can copy anything else that's useful."
The D.I. considered that idea for a moment then agreed.

"Can you do that now?"

"Yes, right now."

"We have to interview..." He flicked the page of his notebook."...a Duma Florial and some of Mr Gillespie's neighbours. We will come back later and collect the video. Do you know Duma Florial?" The policeman threw the question into the room to involve Tambo and Shani who were hovering within earshot. Tambo and Gina exchanged glances then answered together.

"Yes."

Tambo added:

"He work with Mr Dizzy. He lives in house behind Dizzy's."

As soon as the officers left the house, Gina hurried back to her bedroom to get a memory stick then began searching through the video cards to find sequences in which the two thugs were recognisable. Gina hadn't spent much time editing so was slow and cumbersome but she soon managed to find, then isolate, some sequences in which neither Dizzy nor Duma were being aggressive.

The police returned to the house at lunchtime and took the memory stick without viewing its contents. They thanked Gina, but gave nothing away about their conclusions from their various interviews during the morning. In reality, they were already piecing together enough clues to know the course that this case was likely to take. Both officers had instantly recognised one of the two thugs in Gina's freeze frame. He was a lieutenant in the leading crime gang in Nairobi. Ya Chama was run by the Duale family, now headed by the founder's son, Axmed, known universally as 'Tusk' – a brutal administrator, too clever to ever get caught with the blood of his many victims on his own hands. And this case would be the same. The second man in the frame was almost certainly a paid assassin hired to do Tusk's dirty work. Probably from South Africa or Zimbabwe, judging by his appearance, so would have been driven straight to Nairobi Airport after the killing and booked on the next plane home before Dizzy's body was cold.

291

Why? The officers had also pieced together their answer to that question.

Ya Chama ran every known illegal racket from prostitution to Internet fraud; the oldest to the newest. That included protection, which Tusk 'offered' to anybody with a means to pay his extortionate extortion fees, including the local Nairobi government. When Dizzy helped the nursery near Nairobi to bypass the council-run water supply, he unwittingly removed the nursery from Ya Chama's income stream. That put him on Tusk's radar and sealed his eventual demise. Dizzy had tried to pay off his problem at a meeting with Tusk in Nairobi on the day that he had dinner with Gina. Even offering to split some of his income with Ya Chama. When Gina quizzed him about the sources of his apparent income that evening, Dizzy hadn't been totally honest with her. He was sailing closer to the wind than he admitted by taking dirty money from some dangerous people. Tusk recognised Dizzy's confidence and drive and realised that anyone who could make as much money and as many business contacts in a few months as Dizzy had, would not be content to live out his days in a bungalow in Nantuni. It was only a matter of time before he became a serious threat to Ya Chama's business interests and Tusk knew precisely how to eliminate such potential danger. He had done it numerous times in the past so a familiar procedure was activated. The police knew all this, but could never find the evidence to prove Tusk's involvement in any of the resulting murders.

Neighbours began dropping by the house to talk about the shooting. They all knew Dizzy of course and all wanted me to know how much they respected him. I can't remember anyone using the word 'like' but then I have problems recalling what happened that day after I'd sorted the video for the police. Now, without that focus for my thoughts, my mind started wandering off to places I didn't want it to go. I had Daisy's pills so I followed her instructions to the letter to make certain that I did what she would have done if she'd been there. They started to ease the pressure as they had done too few weeks ago. Daisy's warning that I could relapse now seemed to ring in my ear – and that was before she could possibly have guessed at what would trigger my depression.

I went through the afternoon in a daze. I wanted to be alone with my thoughts and memories of Dizzy but when I was in my room, the blackest of black dogs were fighting the anti-depressants with memories of the blood bath and Dizzy's body in the car and the constant tormenting thoughts about how I was responsible...the warning from the village elder lady who prophesied it happening before I even arrived....and the worst bit - that I'd kept Duma away from the site for all that time - and that Dizzy would be here now if we had left the Internet cafe five minutes earlier.

The horrendous strain of those thoughts was crushing the spirit out of me. I had to fight them so I went to find Shani to talk about anything else, but there was nothing else. She tried to be understanding and reassuring, but it was an impossible task for someone who knew next-to-nothing about what had brought me to Nantuni in the first place. Or about my life over the last year. When Tambo wandered back into the kitchen, our conversation ended abruptly.

Gina was told that Dizzy's body would not to be sent back to London, but would be buried in Nantuni on the day before Gina was due to fly home. She wanted to get away as fast as possible now, to distance herself from everything Kenya had come to represent, but she owed it to Dizzy to be at his funeral.

Gina tried to be occupied during every waking hour so offered to sort out his personal possessions and arrange for them to be sent back to his mother in London.

His mother in London. Fucking hell – I've got that to look forward to when I get home. I must go and see her.

There was no relief from the unremitting darkness.

Tambo took me to the bungalow at a time when he knew Zara would be there. I had to see her and do what I could to support her. That meant I had to be strong and have my story worked out to let her down as lightly as possible. I was planning to talk about her schooling and plans for her future, but I found someone apparently in full command of the situation. She was calm where I expected hysterics. Maybe she didn't love Dizzy – was she just using him? Her attitude threw me, but I was relieved that this was one worry off my list ..... that is until:

"I think I might be pregnant."

Shit!

"You *might be*?"
"I am."
"What will you do?"
"My mother will help. It will be all right?"
"Will you have the baby?"
"Maybe."

I .... I couldn't believe it. Fifteen, pregnant by a dead boyfriend and she only thought to tell me as an afterthought. I can't believe these people. They're extraordinary.

I realised when I got back to Shani and Tambo's house that Zara had given me the energy to pull myself together at least for the last few days of my stay and for the funeral. What right had I got to make their lives more difficult by being a miserable, demanding guest? None.

And so Gina coped. With the rest of the week; the investigation by the police who interviewed her twice; with sorting Dizzy's few personal possessions destined for London; and eventually with the funeral.

That was a crazy affair with colour and noise and some dancing at one point. I've heard people say they want a certain funeral to be a celebration of someone's life but I've never seen it work – well, not like it does here. They make it feel like the dead person mattered and they want to shout about the person's life. Of course it could look like they're partying because he's gone, but I know that wasn't the case. Enough people said nice things before and during the service that I know they loved Dizzy in their own ways.

Dizzy's grave was positioned a respectable distance from the water installation that he had helped to build when he arrived in Nantuni. The location of his first project in the country that he adopted, became his final resting place.

51

Gina felt her systems adapting back to London as soon as the plane touched down at Heathrow early on a cool, misty morning to emphasise the distance that Gina had travelled from the balmy heat of Nairobi.

Her flat was stuffy with three-week old stale air but was reassuringly calm and comfortable when she opened it up and made a cup of herbal tea to welcome herself home. Despite the distance, Gina had brought the burden of her mood all the way from Kenya. She knew that the anti-depressants were probably providing the only barrier between her present fragile mood and a painful relapse. And that thought brought Daisy to mind.

My second line of defence........or perhaps Daisy is my first.

Later that afternoon, Gina texted Daisy to tell her that she was home and invited her to call by sometime when she was passing. She made no mention of her depression or the reasons for it. Those stories could wait until Gina could relate them in person. And she wanted to see Daisy to give her the gift that she had bought at the airport – a small intricately carved wooden box for trinkets. Gina loved it at first glance so assumed that Daisy would also.

Gina's next shock occurred later that evening when she casually checked her phone and found a text from Daisy - except it wasn't. The name on the screen gave Gina an instant lift when she assumed that Daisy was responding to her earlier text, until she read: '*wrong number I dont know daisy.*'

That threw Gina for a moment so she checked Daisy's number in her addresses that confirmed she had sent the text to the number that she had used for the last few weeks. Without more consideration, Gina dialled the same number. After a few rings, a man answered.

"Hello."

"Oh, hello. I have this number for Mrs Drew – do you know her?"

"No. You sent me a text about Daisy somebody didn't you?"

"Yes."

"Sorry I can't help. You obviously have the wrong number."

"Seems so…. How long have you had this number?"

"Years. It's the only mobile number I've ever had."

"Okay. Sorry to trouble you."

Gina thought about the oddity of the situation, but whilst she assumed that there would be a perfectly plausible reason, she couldn't figure it out now. She would have to go back to the original contact with Dr Khan at St Thomas's Hospital. She couldn't do anything tonight so she would phone St Thomas's in the morning and trace Daisy through her agency.

Gina eventually switched on her computer the next morning. She tensed when she anticipated the volume of emails that would need responses. This was back to work. Only as she scrolled through them did she think about Hilary Flik, but there was still no reply to Gina's last email.

That seemed odd, but her last subject title – something about 'fond farewell' – could have been because she's ill or worse. Perhaps she can't respond.

That sort of cheered me up. Sorry to say that, but it did. Could that be the end of this year of horrendous teribilus or whatever the Latin expression is?

Then I remembered her last email had arrived in my junk so I opened that and lo and behold there she was - I wonder why that keeps happening.

Dear Ms Melina,
I am located at:-
Rosebury House, 16 Rathmore Crescent, Torquay TQ2 6NN
Please advise me when you would like to visit. Any weekdays
are ideal (best to avoid lunchtimes).
Sincerely,
Hilary

Gina randomly chose Tuesday and responded accordingly in the hope that she could contact Daisy and arrange a meeting for Monday. But she hadn't contacted Daisy yet, so it was time to do some detective work. Gina found the phone number that Dr Khan had provided for support at St Thomas's Hospital and called it. After the familiar button-pressing instructions, she was through to a lady who took Gina's case reference number and looked up her file.

"Dr Khan. Is that right?"

"Yes."

"And you got home visits from the nurse you want to contact, yes?"

"That's right. Mrs Drew."

"Okay, she would have been from Wessex Nursing Support. Do you want their number or do you want me to contact them for you?"

"I'll do it if you give me the number."

The voice chanted a phone number then gave a new case reference that would help the agency to identify Gina.

"Thank you - that's really helpful - bye."

That felt like progress. Great. At this stage I assumed
there would be a logical answer. One that Daisy would
wave away in her usual casual manner. But then ....
fucking hell!

Gina spoke to a helpful man at the agency who promised:

"That's no problem – do you have a case reference number for yourself?"

"WNS / 121899 / Q"

"Thank you.............. Yes, I've got that. Are you Ms Melina?"

"Yes."

"How can I help you?"

"I've lost the phone number of my nurse - Mrs Drew - Daisy Drew. Can you give me her new mobile number please?"

"Certainly. I just need to ask you a couple of security questions... Sorry, did you say her name is Drew?"

"Yes, Daisy Drew."

"We don't have anyone with that name. Your nurse has been a Miss Umogo."

"No she wasn't. I should know – it was Daisy Drew."

"Sorry Ms Melina but we don't have anyone on our books with that name."

That threw me. I didn't know what to ask. Now I even thought that the hospital had made a mistake with the wrong agency but the man told me he was looking at my case file and knew all about my depression and that I'd been in Kenya.

"So tell me this – if Daisy hasn't been visiting me, how can your notes be up to date. That information is all correct, so who provided it?"

"I assume it was Miss Umogo..... Yes, the file was last updated on the 26th May by Claire Umogo. Are you telling me that you have never met Ms Umogo?"

"Yes – absolutely that's what I'm telling you. Maybe Daisy was reporting to her."

"But your Mrs Drew isn't one of our nurses - never has been, so that couldn't happen. Sorry, Ms Melina, but your Daisy Drew doesn't exist..... Well, not here, anyway."

No! No! Those words – 'Daisy Drew doesn't exist' hit me with a bang! I started to feel frightened. And very anxious. I'm sure there were other questions I could have asked about the other nurse and, presumably, the other Gina Melina with depression - for God's sake - it was doing my head in. My ears started to hiss with anxiety now, so I needed to get off the phone.

Gina hung up without another word. She moved from her dining table to the sofa where she began some breathing exercises that Daisy had shown her.

Haven't you been listening? Daisy doesn't fucking exist – never did !

She began to sob. Then she cried out loud.
"Aaaaah!"

52

Rosebury House was a large Victorian pile at the end of a short drive, located conveniently close to the rail station, so Gina walked the route that she had memorised from an online map.

Gina announced herself at the reception desk.

"Oh yes, Mrs Flik has told us to expect you, Miss Melina. Let me get someone to take you to her room."

The receptionist called to a passing nurse wearing a crisp uniform and broad smile who offered Gina refreshments as they walked down freshly decorated corridors to one of the identical white panelled doors. Gina waited as the nurse knocked and checked that Ms Flik was ready for her guest. Gina could feel anxiety coursing through her senses.

"You can go in."

"Thank you."

But Gina's optimism was abruptly dashed when she saw the occupant.

No! She's the wrong lady. No .... How can this happen?

A very elderly, very fragile lady was sitting awkwardly in a high-backed armchair. She seemed to expect Gina's reaction.

"Good morning Miss Melina. Yes, you are in the right room. I'm Hilary Flik."

Good grief ! I had no idea she was that ill. She's unrecognisable.

"Please have a seat. Would you like some tea or coffee?"

"I've been offered one already, thanks."

"Good. They're very nice here. Please sit down; we have much to discuss....Well, I have much to explain. Thank you so much for coming all this way."

"I hope it will be worth it."

"Yes, I hope so too." She rearranged herself in the chair, trying to find a position to ease her apparent discomfort. Gina stood to help her but Ms Flik raised a hand to suggest that she could do it alone. She continued as she relaxed in her chair.

"I have thought about this meeting so often since we met last summer. I thought it was probably inevitable, but that doesn't make it easier. I have to confide in you that....well, frankly, the story is....is..." She just ran out of words. At about the same time, there was a light knock on the door and Ms Flik called for the nurse to enter which she did, carrying a cup of clear tea that she placed on a small side table within Gina's reach.

"Is there anything else I can get you, Hilary?"

"No, thank you Jane."

Jane left a void as she departed. Gina stirred her tea to break the awkward silence.

"I've come a long way for this and to be honest, I need an explanation to preserve what sanity I have left, so I'm in no hurry, but I've only come here for that explanation, Ms Flik, so if you have one – as you say you do – I think I deserve that."

"Of course you do. I'm not as prepared as I thought." She sighed. "The thing is that it doesn't make much sense to me - it never did - so when I thought about how I would explain it, I realised that there are still as many questions as there are answers.

"You see, what happened to you last year on Dartmoor, had happened to me in April 1989 in Brittany in France. I had gone on an adventure-type holiday without my husband and was hot air ballooning with some others in the party when a wind - more of a gale, really - blew up from nowhere and the pilot lost control of the balloon. There were four others in the basket and we were terrified. Absolutely terrified. So was the pilot, I suspect, but he managed to bring the balloon down quite low when another gust drove us into trees and upturned the basket. I fell out but a tree or something broke my fall and I was knocked unconscious. When I woke, I was recovering in a house, not hospital. It was owned by Michel Lacombe, a middle-aged Frenchman who spoke a little broken English. He was charming and totally plausible. As was his little farmhouse and his story about saving me from the tempest. I did think it odd that I wasn't taken to hospital but he explained that he saw me fall and thought it best that he get me into the warm. That sounds familiar doesn't it?

"Well, I made what seemed to be a full recovery over the next two days and returned home none the worse for the experience. Or so I assumed. But then my life took the most amazing twists and turns, reminiscent of yours since we last met, I suspect. From that day in Brittany, I started to experience a succession of incredible situations. Some were unbelievable turns of fate. When I gave up nursing, my husband and I started our own shipping and import-export company - very small and not very profitable - but from the time of the accident, I started to get phone numbers from nowhere. I'd find them on my pager - they were before mobile phones - or hand-written on a napkin in a restaurant. One time I recall receiving a cryptic note with clues that led to one of the royal palaces that needed antiques shipped to and from America. Extraordinary. Whenever I called those phone numbers I got work - lots of it, We couldn't do anything wrong for a short time, probably six months, perhaps a bit more. That's when we bought Coombridge to start breeding horses that was my husband's passion. Then, as fast as it began, it all stopped. Within a year, everything fell apart. Destroyed. My wonderful husband, Douglas, died in a freak riding accident when he was exercising one of our horses. Then all the good luck turned to the worst of bad fortune imaginable for the company. I lost almost everything, including Coombridge that was destroyed by fire. So just when I thought things couldn't get any worse, I was homeless. I was okay, but I didn't have the energy or will to rebuild it - too many bad memories - so I took the insurance money to create a very modest lifestyle from the ashes, of my life and of Coombridge.

"That was when I started my hunt for Monsieur Lacombe. I just sensed that he would have the answers to my questions. His rescue and his cottage and – well, lots of things about the accident that started it all, pointed to Michel Lacombe. But like my trail, he had left nothing in Brittany. Well, the house was there, but had been empty for several years. That was before emails and the Internet, so it took a lot of work to find him, but I eventually tracked him down to his goat farm in the Dordogne and he explained what I am explaining to you now. It was just as difficult for me to comprehend as I'm sure you are finding this right now. That meeting was less than two years after my balloon accident but Monsieur Lacombe had aged by some thirty years. He told me he was eighty-six until the day he got the calling to come to my aid and that day his body clock turned back so I met a man in his fifties, two hundred miles from his real home in a house that should have been unoccupied." Ms Flik knew that this statement would be difficult for Gina to comprehend.

"I don't understand. Is that what happened to you last year?"

"Exactly."

"How old are you now?"

"Ninety-three..... I told you it's difficult to explain. I have no idea why we change in age let alone how something so bizarre happens, but it always does, apparently. Always the same pattern with a lot of time and some distance involved. Perhaps we aren't meant to find our saviour after that one meeting." Then came another pause that Gina didn't attempt to fill.

"It seems that we - Michel Lacombe, me and now you - have all been chosen - or maybe fate has randomly chosen us because we were where fate needed someone - anyone - for the most complex process to run its course."

"Process?"

"Yes, some sort of process that will one day put you where I was last June when you needed me. I've just passed you the baton precisely as Monsieur Lacombe passed it to me all those years ago.

You are now a sleeper. In thirty or more years from now you will get the same call and you will redirect the fortunes of someone who may not yet be born."

"For exceptional good, then total disaster?" Gina offered.

"Apparently so."

"Why? What's the point of this mad *process*?"

"That, I don't know - not for certain. Of course that was my question for Michel Lacombe. He had asked the same of his saviour and the best that he had been told, or so he recalled, was that something has gone wrong with the process that every human-being undergoes during their lifetime. You see, Miss Melina, we are all being tested all the time. That's virtually the sole purpose of our lives here on earth - this lifetime. And it has nothing to do with good or bad fortune. How someone handles being born into wealth with a silver spoon in their mouth is just as telling as an orphan in the third world. It's what we do with our good or bad fortune upon which we are judged, by all accounts. Why are we being judged - tested - and for what? There is no definitive answer - or if there once was, it didn't make it as far as Michel Lacombe. I've had the benefit of time to make a study of the subject, as best anyone can. I've spoken to mediums and clairvoyants and some self-appointed experts with frankly quite questionable theories on this subject. I think I became quite obsessive a few years ago as I hunted for answers that were slow in coming. But I now believe that most (perhaps all) of the events in our lives are pre-programmed. How else could anyone tell your fortune, sometimes years ahead of events? That programme is to determine how we are set up in some sort of afterlife that will be our *true* life. So throughout this lifetime on this earth, we are tested to decide what happens next. I'm talking here about the normal good, bad and tragic things that happen to all of us at some time during our lives. Things we think are random - sometimes coincidences - a meeting, a relationship, an event, a person who does something to change our direction of travel. We all have them through our lives and assume they are coincidences, but they are part of the process happening at normal speed. To be frank, dear, I have come to doubt that few things in our lives happen as a *coincidence*."

Ms Flik stopped to take a rest from her monologue. Gina was content to wait in silence knowing that there was more explanation to come.

"Anyway, when it's all over - when we die - then we're assessed on merit, or otherwise, on how we handled the tests. But for us - you and me and Michel Lacombe - something's gone wrong and part of the test at least is condensed into the course of one year. With good and bad extremes. Great good fortune followed by tragedy, seems to be the common format. How we behave, what we do during that testing period, determines our destiny. Or so I have come to believe."

Ms Flik stopped and stared at Gina but wasn't surprised by her stunned expression. The silence continued until Ms Flik asked:

"How's your diet? Has it changed?"

Diet?

"My diet?"

"Or anything else that suddenly changed. Your health maybe, or language or sleep patt..."

"Language?" Gina interrupted abruptly.

"Has your language changed?" Ms Flik asked.

"Yes. Why's that?"

"Probably because a period of our natural lives has been condensed, so other bits of our character that would have changed over several years as we matured, change in a matter of a few months. My diet changed abruptly. I recall how I always hated melons, then suddenly during that summer I found that I loved them and couldn't get enough of them. And I've loved them ever since." She thought for a moment. "Oh yes, and I suddenly took a dislike to my lovely long hair for no obvious reason and got it cut short."

Gina tried to recall any other abrupt changes. Her diction had already come to mind, but then she recalled her sudden interest in her appearance; and her attraction to men, especially Guy. Was this the explanation? Years of maturing condensed to a few months? Gina considered the possibility for a full minute, until she became aware of the silence.

"What happens now?" she asked to move the conversation on.

"Oh, well, you make the best of the hand you've been dealt. You're young and healthy and resourceful. This part of your test is over - it only lasts for a year - so now you have time to rebuild your life, wiser and better prepared for what the rest of it holds for you."

"You make it sound all too easy."

"Isn't it?"

"Not from how I see it. I believe I lost any control of my own destiny in that thunderstorm on Dartmoor last year. Some other power has been... I dunno... like pulling the strings that control everything about my life. The good bits and bad bits, the people I meet, the decisions I make, the places I go - everything. And now you tell me there's every likelihood that one day I'll do the same to some other poor soul. Right now that prospect frightens me beyond belief - more than I can describe. The very idea that I could be complicit in creating the distress I've suffered during recent months that will result in people dying because of some horrific *process*, that's literally unimaginable. I can't do that....... I won't do that."

"Oh, you think that now but believe me, you won't have a choice. I used to think exactly that many times over the years but when the day came, I didn't question it. I think that's part of the control that you lose. I couldn't fight my instinct to help you."

You're wrong. No bloody way ..... I think.

But Gina knew that there was no way she could be certain and the thought brought a wave of depression crashing over her, enveloping all her other feelings.

"And what if I hadn't reacted to the opportunities?" Gina asked. "What if *you* hadn't, and just let them pass you by and got back to your normal life, what then?"

"That wasn't going to happen for either of us was it? Nor for Monsieur Lacombe. Perhaps that's why we were chosen because we

307

each have our reasons to follow the path of destiny that's presented to us. I wanted to build our company and wasn't going to say 'no' to all the new opportunities that were offered - any more than you were because of your desire to help people through your charity...."

Gina filled the space.

"Watersource."

"Yes, of course, sorry. I've watched its fortunes for a year now, so I don't know why I forgot the name."

Guy's analysis of the selection process came into Gina's thoughts. He had suggested that Gina was chosen because of her passion for Watersource. The thought upset her. She fought back the memory of sitting in the Camden flat in the midst of all the optimism of the good times and their early loving relationship. That took her over the edge and she reached into her coat pockets until she found a tissue to dry her tears that had become uncontrollable.

"I'm sorry dear." Mr Flik showed genuine concern for her guest. "I don't want to upset you, but I know it's inevitable. I'm so very sorry."

Gina brought her tears under control.

"Is that it?" she asked.

"Yes, I think so," Ms Flik responded.

"As you said, more questions than answers. But thank you for that."

Gina took one mouthful of tea to further calm her emotions then composed herself and stood to leave. Ms Flik watched her, sympathising with the impact that her explanation will have made on someone who she had come to like and respect from the shadowy distance afforded by the Internet. She made no effort to stop Gina. For her part, Gina felt the empathy and knew that she didn't need to draw out their farewells.

"Oh, have you had dreams?" Ms Flik remembered this as an afterthought. The words stopped Gina as she picked up her shoulder bag and made ready to leave.

"Yes, I've had some dreams. More than normal. Why, are they part of the story?"

"Maybe. I had recurring dreams after my accident that made no sense until Michel Lacombe asked the same question. He maintained that he'd been told by his saviour that the trigger for his involvement was in the dreams. His had something to do with acquiring a boat as I recall.... Yes, that was it, a small boat. After much consideration, I realised the constant factor in mine was a foal – a young gelding that I'd bought as a birthday present for my husband a month or so before my balloon accident, before there was any possibility that we could start a stud farm. It was probably the prettiest horse we ever owned. Rushou, that was its name. Gina took the briefest moment to react.

"Did you say Rushou?" The question arrived abruptly.

"Yes. The name of an ancient Chinese messenger god, I think someone once told me. Does that mean something to you?"
Gina shook her head.

I couldn't be bothered to explain. Just when I thought the surprises were over, there was one more nail banged into my subconscious for good measure.

Ms Flik didn't believe Gina's denial, but she wasn't about to press her for an explanation.

"If Michel was right, then that was the route for the demon to come into my life – the sort of carrier of bad luck. But if you can't think of anything, I don't suppose it means much."
Gina walked to Ms Flik's seat, leant forward and kissed her very lightly on her right cheek then spoke in an almost reverent whisper.

"Thank you. Goodbye."

"Goodbye, dear."
They both knew that they would never meet again. And they both knew that for one of them, the rest of her life would never be the same.

53

Gina sat on a bench in a small park midway back to the station, overlooking a bowling green that overlooked the sea. Some men and women in whites were playing a game of bowls in slow motion. Tap....Tap... It suited Gina's melancholy mood ..... Tap.

By the time I arrived there, I'd solved part of the riddle that had jumped to the top of my thoughts since Ms Flik's question about dreams and that mention of the name Rushou. Fucking hell, that was a shock. So now I was puzzling about the dreams that I hadn't thought about before. Nothing was obvious to start with, but as I walked away from Rosebury House I began to rewind my memories of the various dreams I'd had over the months. Then it came to me. Every dream had a bike of some shape or form connected with it in some way. If Hilary's theory's right, that old £10 racing bike I bought for the charity ride, that's still in the lock-up in Camden, that must be the bearer of the bad karma she was talking about.

The thought that she had solved this tiny part of the whole ghastly puzzle gave Gina the smallest satisfaction. But that didn't compensate for the enormity of Ms Flik's explanation that confirmed much of what Gina had suspected. And served to convince her that the drama that she had witnessed was being orchestrated by a power far beyond her control. The final confirmation, if it were needed in Gina's considerations, was provided by the link through the disappearing jewellers and Ms Flik's horse, both named Rushou.

You bastards! You took total control of everything - including my fucking dreams. You even controlled me when I was asleep – fuck you! Like the ultimate fucking mind game.

Another thought then occurred to Gina.

I'll bet the Frenchman's boat was called 'Rushou'.

"Aaaagh!" Gina looked at the sky and wailed, briefly attracting the attention of some of the bowls-players. Gina slumped on the bench and supressed her sobs before returning to her private memories of the incidents and people and events of the last thirteen months. Was anything beyond the control of *the process*? Was everyone she met placed there to advance *the process*? Hilary Flik had been, of course, but what about the taxi driver with the Evening Standard, Sid the blackmailer, Eric, Chaz E Jones, the staff at Holly Bush, Daisy Drew, Tambo, Shani and Duma in Nantuni – each had played his or her part in Gina's drama. And of course, Guy and Dizzy. Were they all being controlled by *the process?*

If Hilary's right, this part's finished now, but how do I know if it really is? How will I ever know? How the hell am I supposed to go back to London and pretend none of this happened? Lead a normal life, start new relationships, perhaps get married and have children one day?

Gina had to fight back her tears again. She sat motionless with her thoughts for a long time. The bowls-players had changed ends twice and the tide was in, lapping the concrete steps that flank the beach, when Gina eventually drew herself out of her sustained melancholy slump.

I'm sorry, but I have a confession to make. You've been such a good companion and listened to me and my

311

thoughts for all this time, but I didn't tell you something quite important. You know when I returned to Putney from hospital after Guy's death and then discovered I'd lost all my money – you know how depressed I was? Well I was close to suicide then. I never told you but I worked out how I would kill myself and, if I had enough pills in my flat, I think I would have done it. It would have been easy, bloodless, and .... whatever the opposite of messy is, that's how it would have been. And painless, I think. Then Daisy arrived in a nick of time .... Huh, Daisy fucking Drew, or whoever she was. Coincidence? Of course not. Now, reliving that blackest time and recalling those thoughts of suicide, I suddenly knew right there and then on that bench, beyond any doubt, that I didn't want to continue my life. That was the one way I could take back some control. That realisation suddenly filled me with a calm comfort. Just like the first time Guy and I went out to Trappers in Camden on a balmy night last summer. I've had that feeling a few times since, as you know, and I love it. It's.... it's wonderful, actually. Such relief. I can't tell you.

Think about it - I have nowhere to go, no prospects, no money and no-one who needs me, so no-one to miss me.

Gina thought about the statement and how it summed up her position quite accurately. If this was to be the end of her life...

I think I will be leaving the world - well, a tiny little bit of it at least - in a better state than if I hadn't been born. A few thousand people in a few places in Africa will be glad I existed, so that's quite good. But there's no way I will be the cause of the misery I've known since Guy died ... And Dizzy. God! I'm not going to do that, nor will I live my life waiting for that day when I'm going to be part of destroying someone else's life. They will never know it but that person would have thanked me for not letting that happen.

Gina contemplated her decision and the relief that it was bringing from her crushing anxiety.

"Thank you, Mrs Flik," she murmured to herself.

Her explanation - Mrs Flik's - now felt like a prognosis. Like she had just told me I have a cancer that will eat me away for the duration of the rest of my life. A slow grinding death. Well, tough, I'm not going to let you do that.

Gina looked up again as if addressing someone in the sky watching and controlling her destiny.

"Fuck you!"

She imagined a face with a wry, knowing smile appearing amongst the cumulus cloud formations. It brought the hint of a smile to her pained expression. Then back to the expansive scene in front of her. The bowlers were packing up and beyond them in the bay, the waves were beginning to recede. Rising and falling in a gentle, inevitable rhythm that now exposed fresh, clean sand. If only she could feel as cleansed. For a moment she felt a little optimism with the thought that her fortunes should turn, according to Hilary Flik, but that glimmer was quickly extinguished. No, her mind was made up. She was content that she had made the right decision.

She stood and walked away with the railway station behind her.

Buildings sprouting from the hills overlooking the sea suggested the direction of the town centre where there would be no shortage of hotels.

In her new state of melancholy, Gina strolled casually, taking in views of the sea from the promenade with a smattering of people apparently enjoying the out-of-season atmosphere of this fresh early summer day.

Firstly at a petrol station, then twice more at a chemist and a chain store, she bought packets of the strongest branded pain-killers on sale. A total of sixty pills. Then to a mini supermarket to buy a bottle of vodka before she continued her walk away from the seafront until she found a small anonymous hotel that appeared to be open for business.

The receptionist took Gina's details and asked if she had any bags, but wasn't apparently surprised when she told him she had none.

In a bedroom that suited the exterior of this dreary place, Gina hung her coat over the only chair, laid out the pills and the bottle of vodka on the bedside table then fidgeted in her bag for a pen and some paper, but only found a pack of tissues which she removed, then methodically pulled out a single handkerchief and stretched it across the small desk under the window.

She thought for the first time about what to write, if anything, then after some consideration she wrote the single word 'SORRY' in capital letters, carefully trying not to tear the fragile paper.

She centred it on the desk and systematically emptied her pockets of the little cash she was carrying, her phone, more tissues, lip balm, her return train ticket to London and her wallet which she flicked open to check its contents for no good purpose. A modest collection of possessions but her bank card would make it easy for her body to be identified. A neat and tidy death without drama or mess or blood.

Gina turned to the bathroom where she removed a plastic cup with a cellophane wrapper that she screwed up and dropped into the small bin by the desk.

She cracked the seal on the top of the vodka bottle and poured a cupful of clear alcohol, then piled the pillows before sitting on the bed to compose herself.

She removed every pill from its plastic blister sheet onto her lap.

I'm genuinely sorry to end it like this. Really sorry.
Thank you for your company on my journey and sorry to leave you like this. I hope you don't think this is a coward's way out ...... I know I'm doing the right thing for

*the right reasons. It'll be better this way .... Better for
everyone ..... Really.*

She looked around the dreary, loveless room decorated in a palette of
beige browns that seemed appropriate for her spiritless mood; her
subterranean self-esteem; and her imminent departure from a world
that had broken her will and crushed her spirit. As she reached for
the plastic cup of vodka and picked up the first few pills from her
lap, Gina became aware of the temperature in the room cooling.
Slowly, almost imperceptibly to start, then it suddenly dropped
dramatically. So abruptly that Gina tensed against it with a shiver.
She stopped to check the room, the door, the window. It was as if a
chill breeze had blown into the room, but nothing had changed.
Nothing but the air. Gina sniffed, her senses suddenly aroused.

Is that.....?

A familiar aroma became overpowering. White Charm eau de
Cologne.
"Mummy?"

J R LANDON

Also author of

NEVER 2 RETURN

Available at Amazon

Printed in Poland
by Amazon Fulfillment
Poland Sp. z o.o., Wrocław